Once
Removed

Also by Mako Yoshikawa

One Hundred and One Ways

Once Removed

Mako Yoshikawa

Bantam Books

ONCE REMOVED
A Bantam Book / June 2003

Published by Bantam Dell
A Division of Random House, Inc.
New York, New York

Library of Congress Cataloging in Publication Data is on file with
the publisher.

ISBN: 0-553-80155-4

Manufactured in the United States of America
Published simultaneously in Canada

BVG   10   9   8   7   6   5   4   3   2   1

To my sisters, Yoko and Aiko,
For climbing in to dig me out of more
holes than I could possibly count

Once
Removed

Chapter One

Claudia
Boston, 1999

IT HAS BECOME A RITUAL: AFTER WE MAKE LOVE, VIKRUM sings to me. He has an easy, supple voice, deep with a dusting of gravel to it. His sense of pitch is flawed at best, but that does not bother him nor, it seems, those of us who are his listeners. He takes requests—lately, with me, it has been Beatles songs. Does he sing lullabies to his children and odes to his wife? I love to hear him at all times, but especially when he sings only for me.

As a child, my stepsister, Rei, used to sing as Vikrum does: without care for who might be listening, and with scant regard for the exact words or tune. Perhaps, today, I will find out if she still does.

HIS RENDITION OF "Yesterday" over, Vikrum rolls over onto his back and watches me as I hunt for my clothes.

"Where are you going, why the rush? Stay awhile," he says, coaxing. "Take a minute, or thirty, to let your lover tell you how much he adores you. We can even debate the benefits of a twentieth-century human being born with a tail, if you like. Because there are some, you know."

"Tempting," I say. "But not today. I have to go meet Rei."

"Who? Oh, of course, your long-lost stepsister." Vikrum whistles softly. "So the big reunion is set for this afternoon."

The dress I was wearing is a little wrinkled, but it will have to do.

"So let me see if I'm getting this story straight. She calls you out of the blue, after an absence of who knows how many—"

"Seventeen—"

"—years, and you're going to abandon your lover, who wants nothing more than to hold you and lavish you with compliments and sweet nothings, and to stimulate your mind with intellectual arguments of far-ranging scientific consequences, to go have coffee with her?"

I tilt my head, considering. "In a word, yes."

"Fair enough. But given that she made you wait seventeen years for this coffee date, couldn't you make her wait a paltry seventeen minutes while we come up with a reason for another song?"

"No," I say, turning to face him with a smile. "After all this time, seventeen extra seconds would be too long for me to wait to see her."

"In that case," he says, conceding defeat with grace, "I hope I also get to meet her someday soon." He smiles back at me, which is to say that his whole face brightens and grows soft, and his eyes—large and deep-set, darker even than Rei's, and framed by long lashes—crinkle up at the corners. At the age of thirty-two, Vikrum has deep creases around his eyes. Even though Rei is probably already on her way to meet me, I cannot resist: I lean forward and kiss his eyes, first his left and then his right. Then I kiss him down the length of his nose, three times. For a grand total of five, just as

I always do. For a moment we gaze at each other, nose to nose, and then I pull away.

There was a time, not so long ago, when I would suddenly find that I was tilting toward Vikrum. If we were walking, I would be tipped over sideways at a thirty-degree angle, head inclined and one shoulder way higher than the other; if we were sitting across from each other in a restaurant, I would be leaning forward so far that my bangs were in danger of trailing in the food. My posture is better these days, but only because I am mindful of the years still ahead of me and the need I will have of my back.

I turn away and recommence getting dressed. "Could this actually be," I ask, amused, "the first time that I'm leaving you in bed rather than the other way around?"

It's the wrong thing to say.

Vikrum is quiet for so long that, busy with my hairbrush, I have almost forgotten what I said by the time he responds. "The scary thing is that that actually might be right." A strained quality in his voice makes me turn. He lies on my bed with an arm covering his eyes. "I'm spoiled, aren't I?" he says. "I should be spoiling you the same way. You deserve it, no one more."

What does it mean to have a married lover? A question that Hana, my former stepmother, could now throw at me if she were spiteful. Since she never was that, she could pose that question instead, perhaps with a sigh and a quarter-smile and a thoughtful shake of the head—the conversation starter to end all conversation starters, guaranteed to break the ice so thoroughly it would usher in a whole new era, the age of the hairless dinosaur and the end of the woolly mammoth's. Hana and I never did have much of substance to say to each other.

Having a married lover means: major holidays spent alone. Not getting to meet most of his friends or any of his relatives. Not being able to call him whenever I want to. Having the extraordinarily sweet but also sweetly ordinary experience of waking up next to your beloved turn into a privilege rather than a prerogative, enjoyed but one night out of a hundred. Knowing that no matter how fervently and how often he assures me that his marriage is a sham, the rest of the world views him as one half of a couple that is not me and him. Being haunted by the thought of his wife and his— their, a pronoun rendered vicious—children. But of course, I would cry out to Hana (and, guessing what I am about to say, she would raise an amused eyebrow in anticipatory agreement), there are compensations.

Not least, the knowledge that I truly love Vikrum and that he perhaps even more truly loves me. Because why else, really, would we continue to suffer in this hellhole of a situation?

TAKING HIS ARM AWAY from his eyes, Vikrum looks at me. Then he beckons me close with a finger. "You buttoned your dress wrong," he says gently. "Come here, I'll do it up for you."

I look down. I might as well be one of the children in my class, my dress hangs so obviously askew.

"I must be tired. I couldn't even sleep last night," I confess, lifting up my chin as he redoes my buttons. "That's how much I've been looking forward to seeing Rei again."

The dress fixed, he draws me close, and for a few moments I allow myself to sink into the yielding warmth of his torso. Vikrum likes to play baseball and basketball; sometimes he goes for long runs. His limbs are muscled, and he is tall and well built and anything but fat. Yet the first time I slept with him I was surprised to find that I had beneath me (and over and behind and across me— our first time together was gymnastic, or what would perhaps more accurately be described as acrobatic, the sense of soaring through the air to a partner who was always there to catch me) a man whose belly was deeply soft. A few heady weeks later, I could assert with confidence what I had only guessed at then: Vikrum is that rare person, at peace both with himself and with the world. For proof, I thought, I need only point to his slack stomach. Witness here a man who not only has never done a sit-up in his life, but who has probably never tensed up his stomach muscles with dread or with fear.

It has always seemed mysterious to me that a man with such a soft belly could have worry lines around his eyes and on his forehead.

"Do you know," he says, in my ear, "it gets harder to say good-bye to you every time. I wish—you know what I wish."

Enfolded in his arms, I can hear his heartbeat. As if to belie what seems to be the excitability of his temperament (the waves of enthusiasm he is given to, powerful enough to lift me and, I imagine, everyone else who comes into contact with him—his wife? of course his children and his audiences—onto a high tide of comparable exuberance), his is the steadiest, slowest pulse I have ever heard, and it is rapidly becoming the rhythm by which I measure my life. Even with the knowledge that I am going to see Rei within the hour—within minutes! I could count them, or even sing them out loud and I never sing—it takes real effort to remove myself from the circle of his arms.

While I have been listening to his heartbeat, he has been listening to mine. "Your pulse is racing," he says, sitting up. "You really are looking forward to seeing her again, aren't you?"

"Well, she is the only sister I've ever had."

"Is *that* why you're so happy she's here? Because she's family?"

He is laughing, but his incredulity is only half feigned. If enough pressure is applied, Vikrum will admit a fondness for his sprawling, taxonomical challenge of a family: parents, grandparents, sisters, aunts and uncles (great-, great-great-, and garden-variety), and cousins of various stripes (first all the way up to fourth, as well as too-many-times-to-be-counted removed). But it takes no pressure at all to make him proclaim with glee that, glory be, they almost all live far away, many of them still back in India. And, once this proclamation has been made, it is only with pressure that he can be stopped from going on at great, albeit amusing, length about the burdens of having to buy and send wedding presents to people he barely knows, of needing to send money to bail his younger sisters and cousins out of scrapes, and of having to fend off yet another phone call from one of his well-meaning but overly curious grandmothers.

I have tried to explain to him what it is like, having a family that consists of me and two parents. He listens, nods sympathetically, worries with me about my father's health, and echoes my oft-stated wish that he and my mother did not live quite so far away. But there are limits to the power of the imagination. He cannot really know what it is like to worry about having to spend Christmas alone someday, any more than I can imagine what it is like to have the luxury, or is that the burden, of having so many cousins that you despair of ever remembering all of their names.

"Family's a good thing, of course," I say. "But with Rei..." I shrug. "It's more than that."

Since we are meeting at the café around the corner from my apartment, I need to leave a scant ten minutes before the designated hour of four. There is still half an hour to go, but I open the closet and begin rummaging for my favorite shoes; they are nowhere in sight. Are Rei's feet also still too large for her height? Could she and I still share shoes; have the size of our feet as well as our taste in clothes kept pace throughout the years?

I glance in the mirror—clothed, hair brushed, old pair of shoes in hand—then I go and sit on the edge of the bed. Vikrum places an arm around my hip, wedging me in.

"When I met her," I say, "we were both nine."

Where was Rei's sister, Kei, when she and I first met? Where was her mother—an already vivid presence in my life, sweet-scented and as pale and lovely as the moon? All I can remember is scuffing my toe (encased in my best patent leather) in the dirt, my head bent studiously down. Then my father's whisper—"Say hi to your new stepsister"—and the feel of his broad hand between my shoulder blades, nudging me forward.

For years to come Rei and I would talk of this first meeting. *It was like looking in a mirror.* Did either of us even notice the difference in our skin color and the shape of our eyes? Same age, same height, same length hair; stomachs thrust forward at an identical angle, legs equally skinny and scabbed, two pairs of pigeon-toed, unusually large feet. Later, when we took to wearing the exact same outrageous outfits, shirts in bold stripes of orange and black or dresses with large matching purple flowers, it would seem a minor miracle that people could tell us apart.

"And?" Vikrum says, prompting me.

I look down at him, this man my lover, lying naked on my bed. I sometimes think I fell in love with Vikrum for the way that he watches me. Has anyone ever looked at me so intently before?

I turn away. "Rei and I looked alike," I say. "It sounds silly, but we did. I thought of her as an actual sister. As my twin, even."

"You looked alike," he repeats, suppressed laughter in his voice. "Even though she's Japanese and you're blond and Jewish-Catholic?"

I nod.

He squints at me and holds up his hands to frame a shot around my face. "Of course," he says, deadpan. "How could I have missed it before? I can see it now: the East Asian girl in you."

Then, propping himself up to reach me, he kisses me on my forehead, my earlobe, and the shivery part of my neck. Vikrum has magic in his lips.

"I've got to go," I manage to say. It is never easy to part with him, but it is, at least, less excruciating than usual this afternoon. "It's time to go see her. You can just pull the door shut behind you."

I leave to the accompaniment of him singing Verdi in the shower. I have never been a fast walker, but as I walk down the block to the café where Rei awaits, it feels like I am flying.

Chapter Two

Rei
Boston, 1999

IS THAT CLAUDIA IN THE MATCHING SKIRT AND JACKET,
her hair, now russet rather than dark gold, combed flat
to shiny perfection? Or is that my stepsister with the
nose ring and sleek leather pants, a well-preserved
thirty-four-year-old indeed? Why would that gray-
haired, rather overweight woman wearing glasses on
the end of her nose be casting so many glances in my
direction, unless it's to verify that I'm the one she's
here to meet?

It's not until I find myself searching for traces of
Claudia in every white woman aged twenty to fifty
who walks into the café that it even occurs to me that
I might not recognize her. From there, it's a small step
to the far more disquieting thought that I might just
have erred in my assumption (the assumption, worse
luck, that I had to gamble on in asking her here today,

after so many years apart) that people don't ever really change. Physically, sure, but not deep down.

The key to Claudia's character, at least when she was young? Best gleaned from an analysis of her relationship with small fruit. She was partial to fruit of all kinds, but in particular those that came in small sizes, not grape-small but small enough that a child's hand could grip it with ease. Clementines, kiwis, figs, plums, miniature apples and, most of all, a special kind of tiny pear. She said she thought that small fruit were sweeter, since their taste ended up being concentrated, but she preferred the way they looked too. ("You'd like Japan," I told her. "All the fruit there, and the vegetables too, are smaller than in New Jersey." "Aha," she said, biting into an apple, crunching and swallowing. "I knew there was a reason I loved hearing stories about it.")

Absorbed in her mathematical research though she was, Rosie was Claudia's mother—while we're on the subject of fruit—to the core, just spoiling for a chance to spoil her only daughter. So their house was always just spilling over with fruit of that size. Every day I went to their house to play, and every day before I left, Claudia would give me fruit to take home. What she gave me varied, depending on whatever she thought looked good. But no matter what kind of fruit it was, she always gave me two of them.

One day, though—we were probably about eleven—there were only two plums left in the bowl. While there was a lot of different fruit she could have chosen, she knew I liked plums and she handed the two of them over to me.

"I'll just take one," I said. "You have the other. I'll think of you eating yours when I eat mine."

Claudia shook her head and folded her arms—a sign, I knew well, that she was not going to budge, no matter what I said or did. "You have to take them both."

Rosie, who was just entering the kitchen, smiled at her. "Are you forcing fruit on poor defenseless souls again?" She looked at me and exaggeratedly sighed. "She's just out of control. She keeps pelting people with them—the postman, the milkman, my graduate students, everyone who comes within two feet of the house . . ."

I laughed; Claudia ignored her mother, as she so often did. "Take them," she said to me. "You'll enjoy them, won't you?"

"Why is it," I said, countering her question with one of my own, "that you always give me two of everything? Two apples, two pears, two peaches? Why do I have to have two plums today?"

She looked at me levelly. "So the plum won't feel lonely," she said, sounding matter-of-fact.

I glanced at Rosie, who shrugged and then winked: that's Claudia for you; what can any of us do about it?

She was right, of course; there's no arguing with Claudia, so I pocketed both the plums and went home. It was a ruse, I was sure of it. Claudia wanted me to eat more. She was worried that I was too thin.

Then, a few weeks later, I was on my way to meet her when I saw her on the street, crouching next to a storm drain. As I came closer, I saw her reach into her jacket pocket, take out one of the tiny pears that she loved, and roll it into the drain.

"What are you doing?"

She jumped, or at least as much as one can while crouching.

"Sorry," I said, lowering my voice. "I didn't mean to scare you."

Shielding her eyes with her hand, she looked up at me; the sunshine was strong that day. I crouched down next to her, so she wouldn't have to squint.

"I saw you throw that pear in there," I said, whispering.

She looked away. "I dropped one in there," she said sheepishly. Her voice was lowered too. "By accident. I tripped."

Why were we whispering? Out of respect for the pears, or was it because the way we were positioned, our heads close together as we crouched and peered into the drain, suggested secrecy? Whatever the reason, neither of us seemed to be able to stop.

"But I saw you," I said. "You threw that one in."

"I threw the second one in," she corrected me. "The first one, I dropped."

"Oh."

Together we looked down into the drain. Faintly visible through the bars were two round shapes resting side by side. It was too dark to see their colors well, which was a shame, as they were beautiful pears, dusky red and yellow, Cezanne fruit. Once when I brought a couple of them home, my mother painted them for me; I have the picture still.

"You threw the second so the first wouldn't feel lonely?"

She nodded.

"But now you don't have dessert," I said, "and you love those pears. Couldn't you have rolled a pretty pebble into the drain instead, called it a day?"

"It's not the same," she said, flushing a little. "There needs to be two of a kind. Think how alone it would feel otherwise. Like it was abandoned."

"You're probably right," I said.

We looked into the drain for a few moments longer. Then we stood up, stretched, and walked arm in arm to her house.

NO, CLAUDIA CAN'T have changed much, at least not fundamentally. Even if she does turn out to be that dark-haired woman who just made a grand entrance—that one, there, sporting too much makeup, the low-cut shirt, and what is almost certainly a fake pair of breasts.

Chapter Three

Claudia
Boston, 1999

WE STILL LOOK ALIKE. IT MAKES NO SENSE, GIVEN OUR different blood and our lack of any kind of genetic family tie, let alone the fact that we have not seen each other for more than seventeen years, but there it is, and I feel guilty remembering that I had sometimes wondered over our long sojourn apart whether there was a statute of limitations on stepsisterhood. She wears her hair unfashionably long and loose, as I do; she is dressed in an ankle-length dress, black with a striking design of small red stars, which could be a distant cousin of the blue one that I am wearing. Her head is bent studiously, even devoutly, over a tattered copy of a fat novel—could it be *War and Peace?*—but as I watch through the window, she crosses and recrosses her legs, and then bends down to scratch an ankle, and then picks up her coffee cup and puts it down without drinking. Rei never could sit still while waiting.

I tap lightly on the glass. She turns so quickly she knocks over the small vase of flowers at her elbow, daisies and water spilling over her left arm and her book. She glances down at the table, looks over at me, throws her head back, and bursts out laughing. Although the glass is too thick for me to hear her, I know the glad bark of her laugh so well I can play the soundtrack to this silent movie in my head. She drops a napkin over the mess, shakes the drops off her arm and her book, and in one careless motion sweeps the flowers back into the vase. She jumps to her feet (her unusually long feet, her bare feet—her shoes are discarded, kicked under the table) and, picking up the ends of her skirt, she leaps the three paces over to where I am standing, skinny legs whirring in a blur of motion and hair pouring out in a black stream behind her; with smiles on their faces, a number of café customers look up to watch the madcap Asian woman fly by.

Arriving at the other side of the glass from me, she is suddenly motionless, brought up short, perhaps, as I am, by the fact that we are thirty-four years old, an age we once did not believe we would ever reach. Rei has changed little, her face still narrow and dark, her eyes bright, and her features sharp. Her hair is slightly unkempt; it almost certainly still falls over her face to cover her eyes. She is almost unbearably thin, the dress hanging on her like a sack.

Smilingly she examines me from tousled head to too-large feet, and for a second I study my reflection in the glass, an image superimposed over her: dark blond hair, gray eyes, a face that's weathered, a nose that's hopelessly snub, and a body, ungainly and too tall, that has seen better days. Does Rei notice how messy my hair is, and how flushed my cheeks? Can she tell how recently I have been loved; does she suspect that that is why I was almost late for this, our first encounter, so eagerly anticipated, in what has been far too many years?

My hands are resting, palms flat, against the glass. With care she places her thin brown hands against where mine are, lining up our fingers so they match, and for a moment I think I feel the warmth of her palms through the thick pane.

When I woke up this morning, I was so heavy with questions that I thought they would tumble out of me, six hours too early. Did you accomplish your ambitions; are you a dancer and a singer and a world-traveler, and do you have five cats that you take with you wherever you go? Did you meet the man of your dreams; was there a prince waiting for you, just as there was for your mother? Do you like to wear hats; are all of your earrings long, and do they come in bright colors? Do you remember how, after a trip to Jamaica with Hana and Henry, we decided we had to have dreadlocks—how we, per the instructions of a kind hippie we met there, didn't wash our hair for as long as we could stand it? I caved in first, done in by the unfortunate smell of the project, while you, motivated by the possibility of being the only dreadlocked Asian-American in New Jersey, went for almost a month longer, practically the whole summer.

Then, in a darker vein: why did you write so few letters; how could you have let so many years pass by without a visit? Do you know how much I have missed you?

I press my hands harder against the glass, wishing I could grip on to hers. As girls we used to walk hand in hand, arms swinging in tandem. Her fingers used to be longer and thinner than mine; still far thinner, now they are shorter by a hair. Are her hands clammy like mine with excitement? (Do you still make fun of yourself for worrying about clammy hands—do you still say with mock solemnity, wiping your hands against the sides of your pants and making yet another song out of the rhyme, "Don't forget: Asians aren't supposed to sweat"?). Although I want to look down to see if there is anything on her palm to mark where her recent illness began, I force myself to keep my eyes on her face.

The questions had seemed uncontainable this morning. But as I face her now, with our hands pressed together through the window, there is only one phrase in my head.

Rei grins. Her lips still stretch cartoonishly wide when she does so, an expression altogether different from her smile. She leans into the glass, one inky strand of hair falling over her left eye, and mouths the very words that I have been thinking.

It's like looking in a mirror.

Chapter Four

"THE ONE AND ONLY TIME MY MOTHER MET THE PRINCE of Japan," Rei would say, drawling, holding on to the line and savoring it, like the pro that she was, "she had paint on her face." A dramatic slash of blue-green—cobalt, to use the name on the tube—that started at the tip of her nose, cut across her left cheek, and managed to wend its way almost to the corner of her eye.

The year was 1954; the setting, a train bound from Nagoya to Tokyo. The heroine, a girl whose paint-splattered face was the least of it. There was also a dab of yellow on her ear, a streak of black that ran from her sleeve to her forearm, and orange splattered on her shoe, and it would be no mean feat to catalog all the colors that could be found on her hands and beneath her fingernails. Hana herself was well aware of the colors that adorned her: her shoe and her forearm were impossible to miss; she had been admiring the interplay of shades on her fingers, and she had seen her face and her ear reflected in the window when the train passed through a tunnel. No wonder a few of the other passengers had been staring as she walked down the aisle, searching for a seat; that the conductor had been smiling as he punched her ticket now seemed perfectly understandable.

Still, what could she do? She had wet her fingers with her tongue and tried to rub the cobalt—such a satisfying color, so cool and serene—off her face, but she could not remember with accuracy where the slash started on her nose, and no other tunnels seemed to be forthcoming; she could see only through the window now, to rice paddies that were themselves a beautiful color, emerald green, perhaps, or Windsor, vivid and deep. So, with a shrug, she left the cobalt to glow dramatically—but also with serenity and coolness—on her nose and cheek.

An artist, but one only in the making. Hana was twenty-one, and she looked younger that day, dressed as she was in what she considered to be a nightmare of a school uniform and what a pedophile would see as a wet dream: a white sailor's suit blouse with a square collar and a scarf that knotted in front; a knee-length, maroon pleated skirt; and bobby socks and canvas shoes, the whiteness of which was sullied only by the aforementioned orange splatter. Hana loved her school, which was tiny and select, attended by girls only; her teachers were smart but easygoing, and they encouraged her in her artwork. But the uniform they made their students wear! While Hana's fit her poorly—its sleeves were too long, the skirt too short—the reasons she hated it all had to do with its girlishness. As her mother never tired of reminding her, she always slouched when she wore it.

It was early September, and hot outside, but Hana munched on warm chestnuts, spitting out the bits of shell into their bag (an unladylike habit that her mother despaired of ever curing her of) to pass the time until she reached Tokyo. Once or twice she dozed off, and when she did so she dreamed, as usual, of colors, vivid swirls of reds and oranges that she would later try with only limited success to replicate on canvas. Unlike her friends, girls who also wore sailor's suits but hated it less, Hana never dreamed about boys.

The whistle blew, the conductor called out Tokyo station, and with a screech and a shudder the train came to a halt. Waking up with a start, Hana shook herself, trying to remember where she was. She rubbed her eyes, stood, and bent down to pull at the bottom of her skirt, wishing it were long enough to cover her knees. She gathered up her bags, which were light since she and her aunt Sachiko were traveling together just for the weekend, and then she walked down the aisle and out the door. The hazy Tokyo sunshine made her feel as if she were still dreaming.

THE DAY THEY FIRST MET, Rei told Claudia the story of her mother and the prince. The two girls met in New Jersey, in Hana's house, on a sunny day in May of 1974; both of them were nine.

Over the next eight years Claudia would drink in all of Rei's stories, yarns and nonyarns alike, tales of children found in peaches and bamboo shoots, chickens who wander through modern Tokyo, and cranes who pluck out their own feathers to weave a kimono. She would listen, enthralled, to descriptions of a far-off land where everyone is born with hair in shades of black, dinner is eaten while sitting on the floor, and figs and clementines are served daily to the dead.

The stories that Rei most liked to tell were those involving journeys—rides taken on the backs of turtles, in rice bowls with a chopstick used for steering, in trains that shoot off steam, in airplanes and boats across strange seas. But the tales Claudia most liked to hear, the ones that left her spellbound and breathless even after the hundredth retelling, were about Hana, the girl who came so close to living out a fairy tale.

IN 1954 THERE WERE still many in Japan (Hana's mother notably fervent among them) who worshiped the Emperor. Nine years had passed since he had come on the radio and revealed—through his high-pitched, almost falsetto voice as much as through his admission that America had won the war—that he was all too human. Still, many continued to believe that he and his kin were the direct descendants of Amaterasu, the sun god. And why not? His family had ruled Japan for two thousand years. They had triumphed over political turmoil, pretenders to the throne, and wars of both the civil and international variety; in spite of revolutions and barren wives and a long bout of obscurity during the Shogun era, they had managed to stay in power and to produce more or less viable candidates for the throne for generations upon generations.

Hana herself had been trained since childhood to bow to a large picture of the Emperor every day in her classroom at school. So what if she was young and therefore perhaps inevitably skeptical about the system of values of her parents and teachers—a system that taught her that a squeaky-voiced man who led her country into a doomed and terrible war was kin to a god? So what if the aftereffects of the war could be felt all around them still—just look at Aunt Sachiko!—so what if the prime minister was the real ruler of Japan now, the Emperor but a figurehead? When Hana walked out onto the train platform and overheard the conductor telling another passenger that the Emperor's oldest son was to pass through this very station, she felt a very small twinge of curiosity.

MOST ALTHOUGH BY NO MEANS ALL of the stories that Rei told Claudia had their source in Rei's mother. Hana herself was singularly unthrilled by this business of the Emperor's son. She had told her daughters that story just once, and only because they had heard about it from an old friend of hers, a woman who had also worn a sailor-suited uniform (but who had kept it free of paint) and who had shared her dreams about boys with Hana as they walked, whispering and giggling, to class.

Hana did not understand her daughters' wide-eyed interest in the prince. "Why do you care about him?" she asked, with real curiosity (or, at least, more than a very small twinge of it). "He didn't do anything. He was just lucky with his parents."

Hana had not wanted to tell her daughters about the chance encounter between her younger self and the prince in the Tokyo train station because (as Rei explained to Claudia) she had been worried that it would disappoint them. She even apologized to them before she began her account: "It's not really a story." Which, of course, it wasn't, at least in the sense that it did not stand on its own, only making sense as one tile of the almost-fairy-tale mosaic that was Hana's life.

THE PLATFORM HAD BEEN freshly swept and scrubbed. It was the fact that the station had been emptied of people, though, that reminded Hana of the disdain she felt for the hidebound institution that was Japan's royal family and made any curiosity she felt in the prince (a young man, just her age, who was, she recalled her friends saying, more than a little good-looking and was interested enough in fish to study them scientifically; what would he be able to teach her about the fish that swam about in her mother's pond?) vanish.

As if he belonged to another, higher form of life, as if he were too valuable to breathe the air that the rest of Japan took in, the prince led a sheltered life. His principal home, a grand palace surrounded by acres of gardens, occupied multiple precious blocks right in the center of the city. Its privacy was so closely protected that even

Tokyo's dense and elaborate subway system, one of the great wonders of the modern world, was forced to bend, quite literally, to its will: because the subway was not allowed to go underneath the Emperor's palace, a few of its lines had to contort themselves in ways that were ridiculously inefficient. Hana was all for efficiency; she believed strongly in taking the quickest route between two points. The thought that the subway, which was streamlined and gratifyingly fast, which responsibly transported who knew how many millions of people every day, had been compromised for the sake of one little family's residence always riled her up.

Hana herself lived with her parents and her younger sister and brother in a tiny, run-down house with a Japanese garden that was her mother's pride and joy. Along with a stone pagoda and maple as well as pine trees, the garden had a pond inhabited by large, slow-moving carp, or *koi*, which came in breathtaking colors, red and gold and dappled white, and which would live for more than a hundred years (or, as her grandmother had once told her, forever, but surely that wasn't true; that was one thing she would like to ask the prince) if only the neighborhood cats gave them the chance.

Why were her friends suddenly so interested in boys; why would she ever want to meet someone like the prince? What would she have to say to him, and he to her—although she did, of course, have other questions to ask about fish, and thoughts of her own about them; she had been trying to capture their sheen on canvas for a long time—what did young men such as the prince have to offer her that the infinite possibilities of her paints did not?

Thinking these thoughts, Hana walked swiftly through the station and then ran up the stairs to platform #2, where she would catch a connecting train to Nakano. She had a few minutes before the train arrived, and it was not as though she had anything particular to do on the platform; while she believed in efficiency, she didn't necessarily practice it herself, preferring to sit and daydream rather than, say, start on her school reading. Still, she ran up the stairs; Hana ran everywhere. (In the years to come, she would not change in this regard, just as she would continue to be indifferent to the presence of paint streaks on her face. When her daughters, who got tired of running to keep up with her, asked her with exasperation why she had to speed through the parking lot and race down the grocery aisles, she would say, pursing her lips to contemplate the question—and without slowing her pace by even a beat to do so—"I guess I hate to walk.") It was a long flight of stairs so she was a little out of breath, her face lightly flushed from the September heat, as she approached the platform.

The prince was dressed in a dark-blue business suit, well-cut and elegant, and he was the first thing Hana saw when she arrived at the platform. She was in fact so close to him, and her ascent to the top of the stairs had been so swift, that he started a little and pulled back. There was a murmur of concern from behind him, and Hana saw that he had a retinue—a group of four men, two young and two middle-aged, who stood perhaps two meters behind him. It was when she also saw that, despite their concern, these men made no move to bridge the gap between them and the prince that Hana began to feel sorry for Prince Akihito.

Two meters was, after all, a good distance. (Years later, when she told this story to her American-born daughters, she would interrupt herself at this point, anticipating their question. "It's about six feet," she would say, used to not being understood by them; it was when she could not keep up with them, when she could not even figure out what they were talking about, that she minded.) She herself—a commoner, someone who took and even liked the subway—was probably breaching some rule by standing so close to him. She and Akihito were no more than a meter and a half apart, close enough that she could see that even though he was very short, perhaps even as small as she was, he was every bit as attractive as her girlfriends promised. Who would have thought that his skin would be so smooth and pale; who would have guessed that he'd be beautiful, with that noble nose and the delicate features more like a girl's than a man's?

And, as she thought a moment later, they were close enough too that he could see the paint on her face.

Hana covered her nose with her hand, but it was too late; in a moment a grin transformed the face of the young man in front of her, and then just as suddenly it was gone. Sorry for him no longer, Hana felt her own face grow warm.

How dare he laugh at her; who does this boy think he is?

A god, perhaps, or an emperor's son.

Hana bowed deeply. Then she lowered her hand from her face, lifted her head high and, walking rather than running for once, swept past him.

IN THE SUMMER and in most of the spring and fall, Rei and Claudia usually sat outside, cross-legged on the lawn, for their storytelling hour. In the winter and on rainy days, they found private spaces inside the house: under the bed; in Hana's closet, beneath her silk shirts, textured pants, and skirts in myriad hues; behind the sofa in the seldom-used formal living room.

Giving in to Claudia's pleas, Rei told and retold the stories about Hana with only a little reluctance, but it was hard for her not to think sometimes that Claudia's reverence for this almost-mythic figure was peculiar. Still (she told herself), she should not be surprised. Her mother, whose name meant *flower* in Japanese and who often seemed as fragile as one, was, after all, Claudia's stepmother—a spiteful, witchy figure in the Western counterpart to the myths Rei grew up on about tongueless sparrows and beautiful women who turn into cranes. Maybe, Rei thought, it was because Claudia took those stories as well as Rei's to heart that she regarded the adult incarnation of the almost-princess with more than a touch of suspicion.

No words were exchanged in the encounter between Hana and the prince, and they did not touch—a nonstory indeed, although it did not quite end there. That night, Hana, lying on a futon not far from Sachiko's at the inn, found herself in the unusual position of being unable to sleep. She thrashed about, scratching at nonexistent itches, kicking the covers off and then pulling them back over her, wishing that she could stop thinking about the prince and how for one fraction of a second he had stood there and looked at her, grinning widely at the paint on her nose.

A couple of months later, Hana learned from her mother (who was almost tearful in her pride; Hana had never seen her like this, not when she came home with top grades, nor when she won the local award for best young artist) that she was being considered as a possible bride for the crown prince. There were many other candidates, but only from families far better than theirs; her mother speculated (with only a small furrow, the most delicate wrinkle, on her forehead betraying the doubt that she felt about her own words) that it was because Hana was so accomplished that she had been singled out.

Hana was not used to having her mother fawn over her; she found it a pleasant albeit slightly odd experience. She also knew how cranky her mother could be when crossed. Still, she did not shrink from saying that she was not interested in marrying the prince, and no matter how her mother pleaded and argued and yelled, she never wavered from that stance.

Because of her mother, everyone soon knew that Hana had been mentioned as a possible bride for the prince. But her encounter with Akihito on a Tokyo train platform during a hazy September afternoon Hana kept to herself: not her friends, not even her favorite aunt, Sachiko-san, and certainly not her mother ever found out about it. She would also keep to herself her suspicion that she had been traced through her school uniform, with its collar and skirt in distinctive maroon rather than in the standard navy, until years later, when her two daughters begged her for the story of the prince who wanted to marry her.

When Hana finished telling them her story, there was a short pause, and then Kei and Rei, acting as one, raised their voices.

"But you thought he was beautiful. You wanted to talk to him about fish; you couldn't sleep afterward," they said, bewildered. "You liked him."

"I liked him," said Hana, coloring a little. "I just didn't want to marry him."

"Why not?" they clamored, yet press though they did, she refused to give an answer.

WHILE THERE WERE OTHER stories Claudia enjoyed more, the one about the prince intrigued her the most. In later years, she would wonder whether she asked her stepsister to recount that story so often because she was trying to understand, even then (at an age when she lacked the necessary skills even to formulate the question) what kind of woman would decide to break up another woman's home.

But if the tale of the prince held the answer to this question—if it contained even a morsel of a clue about who Hana was—Claudia couldn't find it. In terms of resolving the ever-baffling mystery of what made Hana tick, all that that narrative seemed to yield was the unsatisfying (because already known) nugget that she was a person who did what she wanted to do, regardless of the opinions of others.

That this story further seemed to suggest that Hana did what she wanted to do even when it ran against the grain of her own desires was too confusing to take into account, and so was dropped from Claudia's musings on her stepmother.

But long before Claudia came to question her own fascination with the narrative of Hana and the prince, she and Rei would analyze the story together. Their understanding of it would change as they grew older, so that their initial wonder at a life that seemed at once strange and wholly familiar (the boy with a retinue; the girl with colors on her brain; the father, worshiped as a god, who almost destroyed a country; and the fleeting encounter that led to the possibility of marriage) turned into amazement at the befuddled, lurching path that fate could take—the coincidences and excruciating near misses that brought Rei and her sister into being. Then, in high school, during their first enthusiastic embrace of feminism, the stepsisters would feel outrage at the way in which this girl's picture had been studied, her medical records pored over, so that her fitness as a prince's wife, the mother of future human gods, could be appraised.

Later still, after their own initiation into the push and pull of sexual attraction, they would marvel at how a passing whim, an idle moment of lust, could shape and mold the very contours of a life.

Chapter Five

Rei

Boston, 1999

IT'S LIKE LOOKING IN A MIRROR. THE PHRASE IS OUR PRIVATE joke, of course. How could we look alike, after all? We never did and never will, despite how we used to wear the exact same outfits, despite the way in which we used to pretend we could pass for each other, despite the fact that even after all these years apart—who would have guessed it, other than the two of us?—we still dress alike.

Claudia's in trouble. It's what I first think, even before I come to a standstill in front of her, even before I start to take in what about her has changed, and what has not. Still, it's been seventeen years, so almost certainly, or probably or at least maybe, my judgment is off.

Seventeen years. A lifetime, albeit an incomplete one.

She's changed more than I thought, enough that I wouldn't have known her if we had passed on the street, although my fears of not recognizing her today were clearly groundless. She's considerably taller now, and stockier too, yet her hair hasn't changed at all. The braces worked: the gap in Claudia's front teeth is gone, and I'm almost sorry to see it. Her smile, flanked by those two soft dimples, is the same old gentle sunshine, but it is, perhaps, a little more wistful than it used to be—those lines around her mouth, and a hint of sadness lingering in her eyes—and underneath it she looks worn out. Tense, as if she's not sleeping well. Maybe it's just that her patients are wearing her down—or is that her students? Probably not clients, although I would bet sums of money too vast for the likes of me to hang on to that the woman standing in front of me works with people.

She wears no ring, which must mean that she has not yet started on the brood of children that she used to want so badly, and it's a surprise to me that that fact doesn't surprise me.

There is just the barest whisper of her father about her, one that only someone who is longing for it could pick up. Like Henry, she moves slowly, as if unsure of how to manage the unwieldy length of her limbs. Still, muted though that whisper is, it's enough to bring him back to me for a spate: one summer day coming in from outside. Dirt stains on the knees of his pants, a leaf stuck in his hair, loot from the garden in his hand, and him muttering, almost to himself, "People don't give onions enough credit. They're a beautiful vegetable." I wanted to laugh, but at the same time I looked again at the onion, covered with specks of dark earth; beneath the dirt, the bulb was translucent, with rich green stalks that shot away from it like a rocket's flare.

The night he came to take me out to dinner one last time. He in shock still, at a loss as to what had happened. Me struggling not to cry into my soup, and he politely pretending not to notice, even as he engaged in the same struggle with only marginally more success.

No, there is little of Henry in Claudia. She looks more than ever like Rosie now. Blonder, much taller, and dressed in far brighter colors, but her mother nevertheless. The same build, the same softly sloping face, and although Rosie's are hazel while Claudia's are gray, the same watchful eyes peering out from under sharply angled brows. I won't tell Claudia how much she resembles her mother now, even though she doubtlessly knows it. She always wanted to take after her dad.

As I did too, with, go figure, even less success.

It's an odd thing, when you come right down to it. While step-sisterhood seems to be an enduring condition, it turns out that stepdaughter and stepfather are more impermanent states. As soon as Hana left Henry, he became a-man-my-mother-was-once-married-to. Not even *the*-man-my-mother-etc., a designation that would have conferred upon him a certain dignity, not to mention a distinct status. Never mind that for eight years he used to make me scrambled eggs in the morning, drive me to school (his fingers on the wheel so bony, so unbelievably long), go over my homework with me at nights. Never mind, even, that once or twice I slipped up and called him "Dad" just as Claudia did; never mind that he didn't blink when I did, just answered in his normal courteous fashion.

He was nice to me in part because he missed Claudia, I think; seeing her on weekends and the occasional Wednesday didn't come close to cutting it. And because—even though she and I looked nothing alike, since, after all, how could we—I reminded him of her. But even if she and I hadn't been the same age, even if I'd been a boy, Henry would have been nice to me, simply because it was the right thing to do.

That's another way, come to think of it, also not immediately perceptible, in which he and Claudia resemble each other—their desire to figure out what is right and then do it. I've always wondered, given this desire, how much he struggled to make the decision to leave his wife and children.

I point with my chin toward the right, gesturing toward the

door. Claudia nods, and we take our hands off the glass. I turn and begin to walk toward the entrance, but she doesn't; out of the corner of my eye I see that she's using the end of her scarf to wipe her prints carefully off the glass.

I stifle a laugh. You see? It's the same old Claudia.

IT'S AN AWFUL LOT TO ASK, of course. Even if she weren't in trouble, it would be. The nerve of me, showing up at her doorstep after so many years, and hoping that once again she will take me in. Will it help if I tell her how when Hana and I moved to Paris, a scant two months after we moved out of the house we'd lived in with Henry, I wanted desperately to write her but felt too afraid? Too much had happened between our parents, and too little said by her and me about it. Will Claudia accept my apologies for the fact that it wasn't until two years after that, when I moved to California for college, that I called her; will she forgive me for the way that I made vague plans to come visit but never followed up?

Perhaps what I need to do is go back even further in time. Perhaps what I should explain is how much my relationship with my mother changed when I was fourteen, and my sister left home. Yes, maybe what Claudia needs to know is how Kei took me aside the day she flew out to Ann Arbor. *Take care of her,* she'd said, nodding at Hana. *I'm leaving her in your hands.* I nodded back, blithely unaware of what I was committing myself to, and woke up within the next few weeks to a world of new worries. I watched Hana, noticing for the first time how guarded she was with herself, reserving the few words she spoke for the lightest of conversational topics—the weather, food, and the like. I saw how when she was alone, her face looked pinched, and her eyes forlorn.

But telling Claudia about what turned out to be a misbegotten desire to protect my mother is unnecessary, and probably not all that helpful besides.

There is, in fact, probably very little that I can say to make these past seventeen years right. So why, then, don't I feel anxious or even guilty; why this sense of untrammeled joy?

There's an unexpected crush of people at the doorway. Caught behind the small crowd, forced to wait her turn to step forward, Claudia smiles ruefully at me. I want to jump up and down, but I remind myself that we are in Boston, a city of demurely dressed, demurely behaved people, and hold myself to rocking back and forth on my heels.

At last she's at the door. She pushes it open with both hands, then walks through it. My arms are out; have been for some time now. Claudia's body is warm and so soft I feel as if I'm being enveloped. She holds me very tightly, and for a long time.

"I'm sorry," I say, into her shoulder.

She shakes her head quickly. "It's okay," she says. And so it is, at least for now. In spite of my best intentions, I find that I'm jumping up and down after all.

How strange, that here I am showing up at her doorstep, and I feel as if I have finally come back to my own.

Chapter Six

Rosie
New Jersey, 1974–82

SHE NEVER MEANT TO LOVE HER. OF THAT MUCH ROSIE
was sure. She already had a daughter of her own. Not
to mention mathematics, her lectures, and a full load
of teaching. Why, she had a veritable posse of graduate students, shy but eager youngsters with dark rings
under their eyes who _needed_ her, for Pete's sake—
students who took her girth for motherliness, her
diminutive stature for approachability, and the prema-
ture gray in her hair for wisdom and ended up taking
more of her time than her own (admittedly very
grown-up, almost surprisingly undemanding) child.

What was Rei to her, after all? Not a daughter, not
even a stepdaughter (that clunky term invoking the
drop of bitterness in the honeymoon of a new marriage, just as _stepmother_ calls forth a self-dramatizing
nightmare of a lonely childhood spent in soot), not a
niece or godchild or daughter of a friend. The English

language, with its uncountable myriad of words, doesn't include a term to represent what Rei was to her, and Rosie took that as proof positive that the two of them shouldn't even have known each other, let alone be close. Theirs was a relationship that defied logic. Hell, if they went by the English language, theirs was a relationship that did not even exist.

Rei was the stepdaughter of her ex-husband, a relationship so convoluted that when Rosie thought about her, she felt obliged to resort to a descriptive title connected by hyphens, as if the child were Native American rather than Japanese: Rei the-child-of-the-woman-who-slept-on-what-used-to-be-my-side-of-the-bed Watanabe.

She was the olive-skinned girl who helped her mother dress in white on a picture-perfect Saturday in June one year, a day during which Rosie wished for the first time in her life that she drank. She was the black-haired, slant-eyed, alien upstart who received the fatherly attention for which her own daughter seemed to be slowly but surely starving. In short (a phrase that Rosie savored delivering in her lectures, giving a dramatic pause to invite the laugh), Rei was the enemy.

ROSIE HAD GONE into her marriage believing firmly that having children was the whole point of it. She loved Henry, of course. Yet even though one might consider that a reason for marriage in itself, for her that was only the story behind the scenes: although it was because she was so in love with him that their having and raising children together became an imperative, the imperative was still the children.

How incredible was it that together they could produce tangible proof of their love—breathing, teething, laughing and peeing and crying proofs that they could throw up in the air and dandle on their laps?

The answer was very. It was a miracle; it was fantastic and weird and too good to be true. But because it was possible it became necessary as well.

And then, too, there was the fact that Henry wanted children. Indeed, he had wanted them long before she did; whereas he had always been sure he would have a family, she had reached that state of clarity only after meeting him.

The problem was that becoming pregnant turned out to be a long-term project, and an all-consuming one at that. For the first time in her life, she found that she did not want only to wrestle with numbers during the day.

In those early years, Rosie thought that she wanted above all to make her husband happy. And perhaps she did. Still, when Henry, after the second year of trying, ever so gently suggested that perhaps they weren't meant to have children—being with her was enough, and would be for the rest of his life—Rosie told him that it wouldn't be enough for her. And that sweet as he was being, he couldn't fool her: she knew when he was lying.

Even she could tell, though, that when sex becomes a means to an end and not an end in itself, and then a means that doesn't get you to that desired end, it takes the joy out of the act, to say the least.

The day that Henry came home and said, white-faced and stammering but more resolute than she had ever seen him before, that he was in love with another woman and wanted a divorce, Rosie had gone into shock, overwhelmed at how quickly the life she had loved could change. But she would later come to see that it had been stupid of her not to see what was coming. Even though it had seemed as if her life had been turned upside down in the time that it took the asparagus on the stove to overboil, that particular half-revolution must have actually taken far longer, which also and even more unpleasantly meant that perhaps it could have been prevented. A more clever woman than she would have noted the signs long ago; a shrewder wife would not have neglected the marriage as she had. She was still furious at Henry, of course, and deeply hurt by him too, yet now she was able to accept that she had made his decision to leave her for another woman far less agonizing than it might have been.

Was it the schedule of their sexual activity that she mapped for them and taped on their bedroom wall in their third year of trying that did it; was that when she lost him? Since she had been pretty much oblivious at the time to everything except for what her fertility books were saying (although she was of course doing it for him, for *them*; after all, he had wanted children long before she did), she couldn't be sure.

So chances were she had lost him long before then.

ROSIE BECAME PREGNANT after seven long years of trying, when even she was just about ready to give up. She was intermittently euphoric for the next thirty-eight weeks, and unremittingly nauseous. Her research into imaginary numbers suffered, not because she was too excited to think about numbers, not because she had to stay in bed—prone was how she solved problems, in the best of times—but because the nausea made her mind too blurry. She missed her work more than she would have thought possible.

So on November 9th, a cold and blustery day, she was feeling more than ready for the baby to come out. And while the labor hurt terribly, much, much worse than anything she had ever felt, it was mercifully short, a mere four hours of pushing and pain—for an overweight woman such as herself, not at all in shape, Rosie knew she'd gotten off easy. It was also mercifully hard to recall; that was the effect of the drugs, no doubt, or of the pain.

What Rosie did remember about that day was what one of the nurses had told her afterward: that after three hours and fifty minutes of labor, a tiny, chubby fist had reached out from the womb, and then was withdrawn. After that, everything happened astonishingly quickly, with the top of Claudia's round head and then the rest of her almost slipping out.

She was probably stretching, the nurse said. It looked very graceful too—maybe your daughter will be a ballerina.

Your daughter. No one had ever used that term to Rosie before. Exhausted, overwhelmed with the responsibility of holding the minute, squirming red *thing* that had just come out of her body, Rosie had burst into tears. It was a mistake; she realized now that she wasn't quite ready yet for a daughter, or for any child for that matter; couldn't she just take it—her—back inside her body for a while? The nurse clucked, brought her a box of tissues, and soon took away the baby, saying Rosie needed to sleep.

So consuming of both time and energy were the responsibilities of early motherhood that Rosie did not bother for a long time, even years, to think through what the nurse had said. Perhaps Claudia had been stretching. But Rosie thought it more likely that her daughter (a term that rolled off her tongue now, as smoothly as butter) had been testing the temperature of the room, if not of the world, in which she was about to emerge. Rosie knew her child's character, her watchfulness and her caution, how slow she was to take action but how, once she'd made up her mind, how decisive she was, and how efficient. She had seen how Claudia, on even the hottest days, dipped her foot into a pool to test the water, while her stepsister, who ran into the water as soon as she could rip off her clothes, splashed about, calling for Claudia to hurry.

Slow but steady, and reliable as not just a rock but a mountain, that was her daughter. In that respect, at least, she took after her father.

The day that Rosie was first introduced to Henry, outside the door of their advanced-chemistry class in their senior year of college, she had made a wish that all of their children would grow up tall like him. He was such a skinny young man! With his shirt-sleeves and his pants a little too short, so that the knobs on his ankles and wrists were all too noticeable, as if, at the ripe old age of twenty-two, he was still outgrowing his clothes. Toweringly tall, he seemed to her, even more than most people did. Funny-looking, maybe, but if you really looked, beautiful too (she thought then, and thought so now, despite everything that had happened), with his dark hair and grave eyes, the brows like accents over them.

The wishes Rosie made the day that she met Henry, implicit and otherwise, all came true. He came to love her, they married, and all of their children grew to be tall. The problem was that she had not been specific enough in her wishes that day. She should have stipulated that she wanted three or four children, and not just one; she should have said that they should take after Henry in many ways, and not just in terms of his height. She should have specified—of all the stupid oversights to make!—that she did not want him to leave her for another woman.

Still, her fairy godmother or whoever it was who'd heard her did come through on the issue of height. It's Rosie's good fortune that she has to crane her neck far back to talk to her only daughter.

Claudia has Rosie's rounded face, her slightly wavy hair, and her eyes, large and deep-set. While her height guarantees that she is not as thickset as her mother is, she, too, is solidly built (somehow, ballerina is not what springs to mind), with nary a trace of Henry's lankiness in her frame.

Sometimes, even now, Rosie wonders whether Claudia, always her daddy's girl, regrets that she looks like her mother.

OF COURSE, not everything about Claudia can be traced back to either her father or mother. Take, for example, her childhood habit of bringing home all manner of orphans and strays—a practice that was indisputably her own. When creeping in to check on Claudia as she slept at night, Rosie knew from experience to tread with caution, as who knew where on the floor was the box holding the latest her daughter had brought in from the cold: the turtle with the cracked shell; the crow, perhaps stunned, who kept turning in counterclockwise circles; a whole nest of baby sparrows, featherless and squawking increasingly feebly for food; a large variety of terrified rodents that Claudia had managed to wrest from the mouths of their cats.

What puzzled Rosie about this endless stream of feathered/furred/scaled, whiskered/beaked/gilled, four-legged/two-clawed/finned but always, always ailing visitors was that Claudia didn't really love animals. She liked them well enough, but even though Rosie urged, she showed no desire for a healthy poodle or guinea pig bought at the local pet store; while she was always polite and kind to the cats, petting or feeding them whenever they beseeched her to do so, it was clear that she regarded them as her mother's pets and furthermore that she was content to let that remain the case.

Although it seemed odd and almost inconceivable to Rosie, she had to accept the evidence in front of her: it was the fact that these animals were in trouble (and not their furriness or fetching ways or bright, darting eyes) that drew her daughter to them. Claudia took the orphans and strays in not because she wanted to keep them but because she wanted to nurse and nudge them back to health. No matter what her intentions were, though, through a combination of bad luck and forgetfulness, she had a bad run of it.

While Mr. Jones, the tiny robin she brought up on minced earthworm and water from an eyedropper, grew big enough eventually to fly away on his own, after a mild storm a mere day later he was found dead outside the house, killed by the same winds that had swept him out of his nest in the first place. The baby rabbit that Jezebel had been torturing, and that Claudia insisted on keeping even though Rosie and even Henry advised her to let it go, refused to eat or drink, sat frozen with shock and fear in the shoebox that Claudia kept it in, and died within two days.

Then there was the time Claudia found Jezebel sick and half starved in the park. She took her home, fed her, and then went out to play football with a group of neighborhood kids until sundown. It was only by sheer chance that Rosie went into the garage in the morning and found Jezebel tucked away in a corner, too weak even to meow.

How could she have been so hard on Claudia that day? While it had been an almost fatal oversight—Jezebel had been very close to death; only because she was so tough had she managed to survive and, eventually, thrive, becoming the sleekest and most loved of all their cats—Rosie should not have raised her voice at Claudia.

Dear Lord, she had only been nine at the time. And while Rosie was not certain how much Claudia understood at that point about her parents' relationship, that had happened during a difficult time for her, to say the least: her father had just decamped to go live with a Japanese woman he had met at a hardware store.

But what made Rosie's scolding of Claudia really unforgivable was that after any one of those animals died, Claudia cried in a way that frightened Rosie, so violent were her sobs, and so long-lasting. Where did all those tears come from, and what had happened to her self-contained little girl? And was Rosie frightened by the sobs merely because up until this point she had had it so easy in the parenting gig, with a child who had been an exceptionally healthy, easygoing baby, or was what she feared true—was this kind of intense crying, followed by weeks of silence and depression, a symptom of an unbalanced temperament? Sitting next to her and stroking her head, murmuring words that she knew Claudia was not hearing, Rosie would without knowing it bite her upper lip, chewing on it until it shredded and bled.

To yell at her daughter for forgetting about a sick cat, when she had that kind of reaction when the sparrow that a truck had hit died at her feet—well, Rosie could hardly blame Claudia for loving her father more.

After all, Rosie knew that Claudia had acted with the purest and shiniest of intentions. If her memory did have a tendency to fall short, it was only because her heart overcrowded it by taking up so much room in her body.

IT HAD BEEN TEMPTING but almost too easy to blame the separation for Claudia's nearly obsessive attachment to these orphaned animals. There had also been a number of reasons that inclined Rosie to think that (much as she'd like it to be; how simple and also, she had to admit, how satisfying it would be to blame Henry for their daughter's unhappiness) the separation could not really be considered the true source of this problem.

For one, the parents of many of Claudia's classmates had separated and moved on to different people seemingly without any disastrous consequences at all, stepparents and stepsiblings and stepcousins apparently a satisfactory, standard way of life. Then, too, there was the fact that whenever Rosie asked Claudia how her life was going, and whether she missed her father or their old way of life, she would just shake her head. "The only problem with me, Mom, is that I don't have a best friend." And she didn't. There had been friends she brought home, but no one who ever took, and while she played regularly with the other children who lived on her block, those her age were all boys.

So maybe Claudia's desperate need to help the helpless grew out of her loneliness (if only she had a sister, as Rei herself had, or even a brother—if only, for that matter, having just one child had not been a heartbreakingly long, possibly marriage-busting struggle for Rosie). That theory seemed to receive confirmation when Claudia became friends—best friends, and even something like sisters—with Rei.

Was it possible that out of all the dozens of almost-lost causes Claudia picked up and took home, her stepsister Rei was the only one she successfully managed to rescue? Perhaps—Rosie couldn't quite remember, but she thought there may have been a squirrel who finally managed to scamper its way back up a tree. But what she could state with confidence was that Rei was in fact one of those orphans Claudia took home with her. When Claudia brought home Rei, a girl merely five months younger, after her first day at Claudia's school (a day that had not, apparently, gone well), Rosie thought she didn't speak English, so quiet was she, and so remote, barely noticing when Rosie spoke to her. The girl seemed to be very, very shy. But after a few weeks passed and the shyness showed no sign of wearing off, Rosie began to wonder whether she was in shock of some kind.

Claudia took this strangely unresponsive girl in. She fed her, mostly fruit and cookies she'd baked herself; she listened so attentively to her that Rei eventually began prattling away with confidence. She watched over her in school and, if she did not exactly keep her stepsister in a box on her bedroom floor at night, she certainly had her over to stay in a sleeping bag on numerous occasions.

Maybe Rei would have snapped out of whatever traumatized state she was in by herself, but Claudia (Rosie thought with pride) almost certainly speeded up the process. The real question, though, was who rescued whom. After she became friends with Rei, Claudia continued to bring home the occasional stray, and they continued not to do well in her care—there were a couple of badly wounded country mice, yanked out of the jaws of the cats just before they became lunch, who may have turned over on their backs and given up their animal ghost at least in part because they were left out by Claudia in the garage (which was, in her defense, the one place in the house that was guaranteed to be cat-free) on a December night that rapidly turned bitterly cold.

Yet when these animals died, Claudia cried less, without that edge of uncontrollable sadness that had made Rosie shred her own lip with her teeth.

CERTAINLY THERE WAS EVIDENCE enough to support the theory that a desire for a friend was at the root of Claudia's fixation with taking in the wounded feathered and furred. But Rosie nevertheless thought it odd that she never admitted to missing her father. Yes, Henry and Claudia saw each other three nights a week—yes, a standard way of life divorce might be. Still, Rosie thought it possible and even likely that somewhere inside, Claudia had to be scared that she would be replaced, as her mother had been, in her father's affections and life. It was all too neat. Henry had found himself a new wife, a new house, a new cat, and not just one but two new daughters.

About herself Rosie was clear. Although she had yet to begin dating again, she was fine with what Henry had done. So what if he, in a time frame that gave a new meaning to the term whirlwind romance (many years later, she would hear Rei, using a meteorological metaphor apparently of her own devising, call it a lightning romance), moved in to his new love's house on the other side of town within a month, and then, a scant five days after the divorce became final, married her?

Rosie shrugged. So what, indeed. Love, or at any rate infatuation, can be like that.

She, too, would start dating, as soon as she finished the imaginary-numbers project she was now at work on. In the first year and a half after Henry's departure from their house, she told herself (or rather *promised* herself, the proper term to use with a special treat) that often: she, too, would start dating soon. The only question was who with? Okay, maybe just one more question, at the most two: why should she? What could dating offer her, when her life was just as she liked it, and chock full to bursting with her daughter and her work and her lectures and, of course, it was important not to forget those graduate students, shy, but once they got over that, so eager too. Wouldn't it be too unbearably messy to go through it all again, the dating and the mating and the intrusion into someone else's life?

No, no, she just wasn't ready. Someday soon she would be interested in love and maybe even sex again; she would meet someone who would make the inevitable messiness of it all seem just like— like what? Fun, maybe, like the fog in her mind before she figured out a problem, before the equation came to her in fantastically beautiful forms that were as close as she could come to (and so much more than she, lapsed Catholic that she was, deserved) a religious experience.

She had spent the last sixteen years of her life loving Henry. She could not have guessed it then, but she would spend the next eight trying to let him go.

THE DAUGHTER-OF-THE-WOMAN-who-took-my-husband-away would change through the years. Rosie would watch her gradually come out of whatever shell she had been in and blossom into a thin, lively child, a quicksilver sliver of a girl. Bright and curious and with a glad shout of a laugh, her daughter's stepsister would have long, straight hair that seemed to be horizontal more often than it was vertical— always flying after her or whirling about her in a circle, doomed to be always two beats behind the rest of her.

In that first year, though, the girl seemed but a wisp of black hair. She was the patter of footsteps moving away from Rosie when she turned, a pair of black eyes watching her from behind the door or in the shadow of the bookshelf. When Claudia started bringing her stepsister home with her every day, it turned out that what Rei most liked to do was to sit with Rosie as she worked. Rei usually had a book with her, and sometimes she braided her hair or even dozed for a minute or two, but she always kept at least half an eye on Rosie.

It was weeks and possibly even months before Rosie caught on. She tended to get absorbed in her work, but the real reason she didn't figure it out was that Rei was very quiet, sitting still, as Rosie later learned, for almost half an hour at a time—a long time for a girl of nine, even if she did have a book, to sit with a middle-aged woman pondering numbers.

Rosie usually worked on the couch in her study, her head and her feet propped up by cushions, papers spread out on her stomach and in a three-foot-radius fan around her on the floor. The couch had been so scratched up by the cats that its stuffing seemed in danger of escaping in more than one place, but Rosie more or less successfully managed not to notice. When the stuffing did escape, setting off her allergies, she worked on her bed, stomach down, her skirt falling about her thighs and her pale stubby calves swaying back and forth like palm trees in the wind.

She first caught sight of Rei in the window next to the couch, her thin young face reflected darkly behind her own. She turned around quickly but Rei was already gone, ducking her head out of sight. Rosie turned around and went back to work yet began to notice that if she raised her head and listened carefully she could sometimes hear the sound of someone else's breathing, far more rapid and shallow than her own.

She would never find out how Claudia felt about her stepsister's curiosity about her mother. Rosie suspected that Claudia was bored by it—how fun could it have been for her that Rei came over

and spent the afternoons sitting alone in a room rather than playing with her?—but also mystified and maybe even intrigued by all
the attention lavished on her all-too-frumpy mother, the woman
her father had stopped loving. Rosie sometimes caught Claudia
watching her too, at dinner or at bedtime, with curiosity, as well as
what might have been a newfound respect.

Then one day while Rosie was in the kitchen refilling her coffee,
she looked out the window and saw Rei and Claudia playing out in
the yard. Rei seemed to be giving a speech of some sort to Claudia,
or perhaps telling a story, and there was something familiar about
the way she was moving, a trick that she had of using the entire
length of her arms as she spoke and of jerking her chin almost as a
punctuation to her words. Rosie watched her for a while, frowning,
racking her brain to figure out where she had seen those gestures
before. She was just about to finish her coffee when it came to her.

"I'll be darned," she said out loud.

That movement of Rei's arms, that jerk of her chin—they were
her own. Though Rei's arms were shorter, the sweep of them pro-
portionately smaller, Rosie could have been looking in a mirror as
she watched that tiny Japanese-American girl talking with her
daughter. Rei had stolen her gestures.

Rei must have been studying her as she spoke with Claudia. She
must have been spying on her not just as she worked in her study
but also as she talked over the phone or met with graduate students
over coffee in the den.

The question was why, of course. By all accounts, Rei had a perfectly serviceable mother of her own. Rosie had met Hana by then
and thought she seemed fine. She was pretty, certainly, and small,
though not as short as Rosie, not much of a talker but what's wrong
with that? It was worse when she spoke; her accent and her obvious
struggle to find the correct words made Rosie cringe a little.
Claudia, who spent as much time at their house as Rei spent at

Rosie's, did not seem to like Hana much either, but she would eventually, no doubt (Rosie could not help sighing), come around.

One afternoon Rosie decided that things had gone far enough. She lay in wait and then, when she heard the sound of that quick breathing behind her, she turned and ran for the child. There was a second in which Rosie saw Rei freeze, her eyes glazed with terror and her mouth an O of surprise, and then she spun around and ran. Rosie chased her down the hall, down the steps, and around the bend toward the back door. She may have been heavyset, but at that time she could still outrun a nine-year-old girl. Rosie caught up just as Rei was making her escape outdoors. She grabbed her, both of them breathless, and tickled her until she screamed with laughter.

SHE NEVER MEANT TO LOVE HER, and for a long time—years, even—she didn't. Sometimes she flinched when she looked at Rei in a certain light, because the girl looked like her mother. And even when Rei was not in that light, there were times Rosie flinched from the sight of her anyway. But over the years she flinched less, and when Hana left Henry, taking Rei with her, Rosie missed her as if she had been a second daughter.

She was the child who the man Rosie loved had taken as his own. She was her daughter's best friend, and perhaps a sister to her too. She was the girl who remained fascinated through her childhood and beyond with Rosie's deep absorption in numbers.

In later years she still had hair that was horizontal more often than it was vertical, and when she became a teenager, her chatter and her antics made everyone around her smile. But for Rosie she would always also be a pair of black eyes that watched her in silence from behind the door; for her she was a face in the window, reflected darkly behind her own.

Chapter Seven

Claudia
Boston, 1999

A FEW MOMENTS OF AWKWARDNESS, EVEN OF SHYNESS, at the start of the conversation, and maybe even beyond. Or so I told myself this morning to expect. But this I could not have anticipated. Formality, who would have guessed it? My oh my, have we changed.

We are sitting at the table, facing each other and smiling, a large blueberry muffin by her elbow ("It's not fat-free, right?" Rei anxiously confirmed with the woman behind the counter), two steaming cups of coffee in front of us. Yes, we are grown-ups; the last time I saw her we only drank Diet Cokes and—feeling extremely proud when we did so, self-consciously nonchalant and cool—beer.

Our conversation follows a gentle rhythm of questions and answers. I say I teach elementary-school students, and that I love it; Rei says that she is an art historian, specializing in conservation, a job that allows her to travel a lot and to work with and be around art. I say that sounds exciting, but she tells me no, that stripping old paintings of the accumulated dust and dirt and smoke of history has lost its appeal, that although she once loved her job, she is tired of working with art and she feels more than a little restless these days. She'll probably consider a change in the next couple of years.

(Has she been restless, or unwell and unable to travel as she once did? Not a peep about what she mentioned over the phone—the sickness that started in the palm of her hand. That's okay, there is time yet. I have waited so long to see her; a little more patience is not difficult to muster.)

Yup, she'll be in Boston for the next six months, at least—isn't it wonderful? Think of all that we can do together. As if to punctuate these words, Rei jumps up and down again, as she did when we hugged, but this time in her seat. Although this seems in the abstract as if it might be difficult, she makes it look completely natural, even easy.

No, not five—funny that you remembered, it's true I always wanted five—just three cats, for now. Heidi, Mr. Bellafonte or, as he sometimes prefers, B, and little Worm. Will I come over to meet them soon? Like, say, Wednesday? Or better yet, what the hell, tomorrow, if I can overlook the unpacked boxes that still crowd the new apartment?

Yes, Mom's good. Living in England, where she got a cushy job teaching math at a small college. I take a breath and open my mouth—and then I shut it, so abruptly that it makes a snap audible even over the hum of the café. I am not going to tell her about my parents' remarriage yet, not today; I do not have to spoil the sweetness of my reunion with Rei after so many years. I allow another moment to lapse, long enough—surely, hopefully that was long enough—to signal the oral equivalent of period, enter, and then tab, the end of one subject and the beginning of another. Dad's retired. He had a stroke a few years ago—no, don't look like that, he's fine now. Really. He can talk, walk, garden, think, make bad puns, and everything else besides; it's just that he does everything slower. It is hard to believe, isn't it? Defies all of our mortal powers of comprehension. Henry, even slower than he was.

Another pause. Rei bends her head down and fingers the corner of her napkin, and I know that she is mentally shuffling through a list of questions about my father, the thought of any of which makes me flinch: where does he live now, who's taking care of him, and—the biggest flinch-draw of all—did he ever remarry?

As a child, she loved him, of course, and doubtlessly still does: the only father she can remember.

Rei taps a finger on the table, and then with a swift, decisive motion lifts her head up from her absorbed contemplation of the napkin.

Well, Kei's fine (she says). Married to a nice guy, a Jordanian—so nice you almost have to pity him; you remember how bossy she always was. . . .

My breath comes out suddenly: I had not even known I had been holding it in. And with that, the scene that I have been fearing is over.

She was always such a typical older sister (continues Rei), and in that sense she hasn't changed at all—still likes to tell me what to do. But you know what? We're not at all alike, and we'd never be friends if we weren't related—it's not like you and me—but Kei and I are sisters, after all, with the same mother and father, and it turns out that that means something. She has a baby daughter, Naomi, and she's pregnant now with her second child. Hana continues to produce art, and to sell it too. She's back in the States, living out in California.

The full rundown on her sister and the brief sentences on her mother a perhaps intentional contrast. If I were made of more finely tempered steel, I would ask one of the countless questions about Hana that I have milling about in my mind. An innocuous one, easily answered—about how her work is progressing, say, and whatever happened to her quest to produce an image of the perfect mushroom? Yet Rei has finished this family summary in a way that closes off further comment, and I am more than a little relieved.

I tell her I have a boyfriend, Vikrum. Uh-huh, from India; he moved here when he was two. A magician and a post-doc in neurobiology. In answer to her next question, I shake my head quickly. No, no, never taken a walk down *that* aisle.

Rei tells me she has been single now for half a year—an unusually long time for her, she says with a quick smile. No, she hasn't been married either. The last guy she was with—Max—she kind of hoped for a while, but it didn't happen. Thank God, she adds with a droll look that may or may not be hiding more emotion, that sure would have been a darn short marriage.

I want to ask her more about her last relationship, but there is something about the lightness of her tone—or is it the way she looked away from me as she spoke, her usually friendly profile, with its bunny-slope nose and sharp chin, suddenly alpine cool and remote?—that makes me think twice. Taboo subjects have opened up all around us like craters on the moon. But there is time enough for heavy questions—yes, even those about my father—later. God knows that the heaviest topic of all (grand-piano heavy, hernia-alert heavy), her health, has not even been broached.

Again the thought occurs to me, this time with a sigh: we are grown-ups, for this is what I would have once labeled an adult conversation, politely and lightly skimming the surface of our lives, careful not to create even a ripple.

It's hypocritical of me to feel this way, of course. How can I be relieved and grateful that she put off asking difficult questions about my father on one hand and saddened by the shallowness of the conversation on the other? Not to mention stupid: I had expected so much of this meeting. I was bound to be disappointed; how could it be otherwise?

A moment of silence, just long enough to be uncomfortable, and then she dives into it. Splash be damned.

"So," she says. "All right already, enough with this chitchat." She waves her arms in the air, clearing it; because of the length and the skinniness of her limbs, it is a grand gesture, at once sweeping and a little wacky. Then she cups her chin in one hand and leans forward. "Tell me how you're really doing."

"Great," I say, smiling, looking down to stir my coffee. "So happy that you're here."

"Really?" A real question rather than a rhetorical one, the skepticism in her voice audible.

"Of course," I say with emphasis. "Did you really think I'd be so angry? I'm completely excited about you being here. There's so much we can do, we have to—"

"No, silly," she says, breaking in. "I mean, are you really doing great? What's really going on?" She examines me almost hungrily, searching my face for details. "You love your job, your parents are doing fine, and you're in love with this guy, this magician, right? So why aren't you happier? Come on, out with it, you know you want to tell me." Then, as if to undercut her own seriousness, she takes a huge bite out of her muffin, getting crumbs all over her face.

"You have crumbs all over your face."

With the back of her hand, she swipes unproductively in the general direction of her mouth. "Schgone?" she asks, her speech impeded by muffin.

Sighing exaggeratedly, I reach across the table and brush off her face with my napkin. "You're as bad as my students. There, that's better."

Her eyes on me, she finishes chewing, swallows. "Did I tell you," she says, "that you haven't changed one whit?"

"Did I tell you," I say, "that it only seems like that because you haven't yourself?"

We smile at each other across the table.

"Whaddays say," she says. "Let's blow this joint. Finish our coffees and go for a walk."

WE ARE ON COMMONWEALTH, two blocks away from the café, when she stumbles. There is no apparent reason for it: the sidewalk is dry and relatively smooth, and there is not even much of a crowd milling about. We are walking, chatting about the neighborhood, a light breeze on our faces and the sky flawless above—Boston in late September, such an unexpectedly wondrous place to be—when she falls to her hands and knees. She gets up quickly, laughing, of course, and makes a crack about her old tendency to walk into doors, about how in that respect, too, she has not changed. In all the important ways, she adds cheerfully enough, she is, to her chagrin, exactly the same person she was at seventeen; no progress made here. I smile as I give her a hand and help her to her feet, and I chatter about the numerous perils that await city strollers as we brush off the front of her dress together, but all I can think is that I have no recollection of her walking into doors as a child.

It is easier to talk while walking, because there is so much other than our faces to look at. It is partly that her gaze is so disconcertingly sharp. But mostly, I think, it's that even though she seems much younger than thirty-four, when I look at her it's hard not to be reminded of all the years that have passed, of all the milestones and crises and love affairs that we have had to go through alone. Her face is so thin now, in a way that accentuates those lovely, slanted eyes (which I used to covet, and which I, when it comes right down to it, still covet); they seem perhaps paradoxically both brighter and more black than they used to be.

Seventeen years, I remind myself: what is surprising is that I could recognize her at all. Her face, so familiar and new all at once (is that wishful thinking on my part to believe that the tightness of her skin over her cheekbones is a consequence of her age rather than of the state of her health? No, probably not, surely not, she was always thin, and her mother also got thinner as she aged), makes me feel shy.

Her voice, though. A different matter altogether. It has changed too, of course; it is deeper although it is still very clear, maybe even unusually so for a voice so low. It is also easily as musical as her mother's now. Yet in spite of these changes, the patterns of her speech have stayed the same—the rat-tat-tat rhythm of it, and the quick intake of her breath in the pauses of her sentences—so that if I close my eyes while I listen to her speak, we could be teenagers still, speculating on the endless mysteries of sex.

"So," she says.

"So," I repeat, dreading and steeling myself for the onslaught of her questions.

We have arrived at the entrance to the Commons. In a couple of weeks the trees will burst into color, but for now they are just tipped with yellow. We cross the street and, without needing to discuss it, head toward the entrance into the park; soon we are surrounded by a stream of people, mostly mothers with small children or babies, prattling and laughing. The day is almost heartbreakingly beautiful, in the way that it is in the fall, with the cool of the air a subtle but persistent reminder of the imminent approach of winter.

"So-o, I always wish I could take my cats out for a walk," she says. "Show them off, let them run around a bit."

Had she managed to pick up on my dread? "I had a cat too," I volunteer shyly, "for a while."

Her reaction is what I expected, and more. She stops walking, her hand placed over her heart. "You wouldn't kid me about this, right?" When I shake my head no, she throws her head back and, there is no other word for it, howls. "Hallelujah! Hallelujah!" she sings, belting out the words in her own idiosyncratic version of Handel.

So, still a warbler like Vikrum after all.

"You don't know how happy that makes me," she says in her speaking voice. Reinforcing the auditory demonstration of her approval with a visual one, she executes what she used to call her happy Snoopy jig right here on the sidewalk. While her feet are not the same blur of motion that they used to be during this dance, her nose still points gleefully upward in the prescribed Peanuts fashion.

"It's about time you claimed your birthright as your mother's daughter," she says, when we fall into step again. "I always thought you were a closet cat person. What was her name? Or his?"

"Orson."

"That's a lot of name to live up to."

"Well, he was a lot of cat."

"So what happened?"

"Diabetes. Three years ago."

"Ah." After a respectful pause, she asks, with delicacy, "Ever think about getting another?"

"I can't," I confess. "I think he's haunting my apartment. It sounds crazy, I know, but you'll see when you come over."

Rei nods, carefully considering my revelation. "Still. Surely even feline ghosts appreciate feline company, no?"

"Maybe. But," I say, dragging out the words, "Vikrum's allergic, besides."

"Go to his place," she says promptly. "That's what I did when I had a boyfriend who was allergic. Of course, since all my clothes are covered with cat hair, I just ended up contaminating his apartment.... That didn't last long, not surprisingly. We were pretty much doomed from the start, I guess."

"We can't go to his place. Ever. That's part of the problem."

"Oh." She hesitates, and then begins speaking in a rush. "Do you not want to talk about it? Does it feel weird talking to me after so much time? If you want to tell me later, when we've gotten more used to each other, that's okay too. I can understand—"

It is then that the question I had not meant to utter during this—a reunion I had wanted to be both celebratory and lighthearted, as it has been thus far—slips out. "Why *has* it been so many years?" My voice cracks a little as it rises, and I have to remind myself of her illness. As it is, there is no doubt that were it not for that, I would be saying far more than I am saying, and at a higher decibel. "How come you wrote so few letters; why didn't you come through on your promises to visit?"

What was I expecting? An outburst of tears, or an only partly exaggerated bit of groveling? She had been an impulsively affectionate child, capable of extravagant displays of emotion. What I get instead is a pair of serious eyes turned toward me.

"I'm sorry," she says. Then she is quiet, hoping, perhaps, that I will step in with words of comfort.

I wait.

"I know that saying I'm sorry doesn't come close to covering it," Rei eventually continues. "I'm going to spend the next fifty years proving to you that I've changed. Heck, the next one hundred years, if that's what it takes. I was a different person seventeen years ago: feckless and heedless, like—well, like my mother. But I'm different now. All reformed, completely full of feck and heed." She is trying to inject a note of jocularity, one based on the kind of wordplay that my father has always loved. But while she sounds cheerful, she is chewing on her upper lip, a nervous habit that she has inherited directly (in a line of descent that would seem skewed to anyone not in our family) from my mother.

"I'm not a saint—I'll make mistakes again, I'm sure, although I'll do my best never to hurt you again," she says now. "But I'm not my mother's daughter either, and—"

"Not her daughter? You don't really think that," I say, interrupting. "Think of all those stories you told me about her. And then you made the decision to be a painting conservator, restoring and preserving for posterity art like your mom makes."

"Still, I'm not at all like her, am I?"

"No," I say. "No, you weren't when you were young, and you aren't now either."

If I had told her, back then, that she was not like her mother, chances are high that she would not have looked relieved.

"I wasn't reliable back when we were kids, at least not in the way that you were," she says. "But I want to be like that now. I even thought that just maybe I could help you for a change. Not now, or at least not yet, but someday. You can lean on me, you know—I'm sturdy as a rock. Just think of me as a walking shoulder to cry or lean on."

She speaks with touching confidence, but she looks pale and gaunt, too weak to support even a corpulent albeit incorporeal cat such as Orson, let alone my weight. "Maybe someday," I say, but gently.

"Okay," she says. "Just remember: it's a standing offer."

This conversation cannot be any more pleasant for her than it is for me. Yet she waits, attentive and patient, as I struggle to find the words.

"I do need to know," I say at last, "why you disappeared for so long."

"It's complicated," says Rei. "A mess, in fact. But I'll try." She rubs and then scratches the base of her throat. "We were the poor relations. We lived off Henry's bounty, and then we became the poor relations who broke our benefactor's heart. I know, I know"—holding up a hand to ward off my protests—"we were all family, and you never thought of us as parasites. But we were, and it was horrible, and I was ashamed of us.

"And then too much time passed—I became ashamed of myself just as much as of my mom.

"Also," she adds, with a quick glance at me, "you probably didn't really want to see me, at least during the first couple of years. You were hating me then for what my mother did. How could you not?"

My head moves back and forth on its own in an almost automatic gesture of denial, yet she is right, of course. Rei watches me, her eyes shrewd, and then nods to herself, reading my answer in my silence. "Claw, you might still resent me now—it's the least that I deserve. But just remember this: I always wanted to see you. I never stopped wanting to see you. And I'm going to be by your side for the rest of our lives, or as long as you can stand me. Okay?"

"Okay," I say, nodding slowly, wishing that I could answer her with more certainty: it will not be easy for me to let go of these past seventeen years.

"Now then," Rei says, her tone suddenly brisk, "you were thinking about telling me about Vikrum."

Her mood shifts are so much the same, I have to smile. "I do want to tell you about him," I say. We briefly part in order to pass a woman pushing a stroller with two babies. I turn to look as we pass: twins, blue-eyed, with matching mats of dark hair. "I'm just worried you're going to judge him."

"Aha," she says. "That might be a valid concern. Is he not treating you well? Because I'll kill him if he's not."

"He treats me really well," I say. The way he looks at me! I shut my eyes for a moment, hard, to get him out of my head, so I do not disappear altogether from this beautiful day with my long-lost stepsister in the park. I open them in time to see a squirrel, a cheeky fellow, scurrying across our path, mere inches away.

"But he's—well, he's married. With two children, a boy and a girl."

Rei stops walking, so abruptly that a small boy runs into her. She looks over her shoulder absentmindedly to see what hit her, then wheels back to face me. Her eyes are once again on me, but while her gaze is still sharp, it no longer seems disconcertingly so; her face, more narrow though it is now, already feels more familiar.

"Does divorce come up?"

"Vikrum comes from a really traditional family," I say, turning my head to look at the path ahead. "Traditional enough that his marriage was arranged; divorce isn't really an option. But even if he didn't come from that kind of background—" I shrug. "He adores his children, and he takes being a father very seriously." As my father did as well, though to a clearly lesser extent. "His devotion to his kids is one of the reasons I fell in love with him in the first place. Kind of ironic, isn't it, that it's also why we can't be together?"

"And his wife?"

"It's not much of a marriage—they haven't slept in the same bed for years, since their son was born. She drinks. It's nothing too serious, but it's enough of a problem that he's glad her mother practically lives in the house with them. He also says that she's cold, that she never cared for him, but I'm never sure if he's telling the truth there." Because, of course, how could you live with someone like Vikrum and not care for him?

The wind picks up and the trees above us and around us stir; a single scarlet maple leaf comes drifting to the ground at our feet. I stoop to pick it up and twirl it in my fingers. The leaf is dry to the touch, its lines delicately etched. I wish, not for the first time, that I had the talent Hana had; I would try to preserve the memory of it on canvas.

"So no matter what, he can't even think about divorce until the children are out of the house. Which means, let's see," I say, as if I have not done these calculations a hundred times already, "Vikrum should be free about a decade and a half from now, give or take a year."

"Oh, Claw," Rei says, and then suddenly her arms are around me.

She's so thin I feel as if I need to hug her carefully, but her hold on me is strong. My God, did I really get through seventeen years without her?

"Thank you," I say.

"Here," she says, rooting around in the pocket of her jacket and pulling out a couple of tissues. She hands me the less rumpled one, then uses the other to blow her own nose. "You're as bad as your students."

We have to walk against the traffic to get to a trash can to throw away the used tissues, a project that takes time as well as patience. When we get there we linger for a few moments, watching the people pass by.

THE TWO OF US racing ahead to the old graveyard at the top of the hill. How old were we that day—eleven, twelve, thirteen? Young enough, in any event, to want to play running and hiding games among the tombstones (although by that standard, we could have been much older; we are talking about Rei and me, after all). Hana and my father following, hand in hand, lingering behind; Kei even further back. We were in Vermont, where we sometimes went for a week or two during the summer (always, always bypassing Boston on the drive there and back, to my secret disappointment); it was a sunny day just on the cusp of being too warm.

It was an annual ritual for us, as a family, to hike up the hill and read the dates chiseled on the stones. The graveyard was old, the oldest one, perhaps, that Rei and I had ever seen, with cracked and crumbling stones dating back to the late 1800s, the inscriptions barely legible, overgrown by weeds but sometimes with fresh bouquets of wildflowers—remarkably similar to the ones that we always made sure to gather for them—placed by their side. Those flowers left by descendants, we thought, great-great-great-great-grandchildren, born of a family who had never left the area and, really, who could blame them—was there anyplace more glorious than this hilltop, where the green fields rolled out in a grand sweep beneath us like the finest silk?

When the Parents, and that slowpoke stuck-up nuisance of an older sister, Kei, made it up to the top, we would marvel all together at the small stones that had been erected for children and babies, as we did every year. We would exclaim over the couple who had both managed to live into their eighties in the nineteenth century, and wonder what miracle diet they had subsisted on (oatmeal for breakfast and red wine with every dinner was my father's guess; a Japanese-style meal plan of fish and rice, Hana's). Small wonder Rei and I loved that graveyard so: it seemed tailor-made to transform death into a concept both benign and unimaginably far away—a game of hide-and-seek, the second date in a fading set of two, a gathering of stones glinting in shades of white and gray under a bright noonday sun.

"I'd like to be buried here"—my stepmother's lilting voice, pitched low and sweet—"with you." She was speaking to my father, of course. They were private words, not meant for our ears but caught and carried up the hill toward us by a stray breeze. Heard only because they arrived during a lull in our game, they abruptly silenced us.

What did my father say in response; did he second the motion, reproach her for her morbidity, or ask if she wouldn't rather be cremated, as all of her relatives had been? I turned my head and saw him fold his long body toward Hana as he replied, but the breeze was gone and so his words never made it up the hill.

"Don't you dare cry," I said, whispering, to Rei.

She gave me a look. "I wasn't planning to," she said. "Why, are you?"

I was a little taken aback by what she said, so seldom was it that our reactions differed, and more than a little embarrassed. Rei had exposed me: I was a coward to be frightened by the thought of my father dying, and I was a sap, or worse—possibly even *the* worst, a girl like Kei—to be moved by Harlequin-romance sentiment.

Still (I told myself), it was not so long ago that Rei had lost her father. Maybe she had not shivered, as I had, when she first heard Hana's words; maybe she had not felt a chill when she realized that death could be far more immediate and personal than a moldering gathering of stones. Moreover, and more to the point, Rei lived with my father and her mother, so she of course saw far more of them than I did. Perhaps she already knew, as I had not, that Hana loved my father so much that as long as they could be buried side by side, the thought of death did not scare her.

My father had met Hana in a hardware store one cold day in March. He bought a monkey wrench he did not need, just for the chance to stand in line with her. While this was not an anecdote that I enjoyed hearing or even thinking about, even I had to admit that it constituted the start of a love story, and one that seemed to have brought its hero and heroine to a state of contentment.

Maybe, someday far off in the future (I thought grudgingly, as Rei and I resumed our game of tag), I would not hate my step-mother quite so much for breaking my mother's heart and for turn-ing my father into a shadowy presence in my life, a tall figure I glimpsed on the path behind me for three nights a week and a week or two in the summer.

I looked back again. Hana and my father were walking so close together that in spite of the height difference between them, it was impossible to tell where one started and the other left off. I sighed then, acknowledging to myself that it did not matter how kind she was to me, or how much she loved my father, and he her, or even how close I was to her daughter. I would always hate Hana.

And while one might think that loving a man with a wife and two children for nearly two years would have changed the way I feel, it hasn't.

WHAT I WANT to convey to Rei is the strangeness of it all—that decades after a childhood plagued by Hana, the thought of her is once again making it hard for me to sleep. There is no one who would appreciate the precise nuances of this predicament more than Rei. But she does not need to be reminded of the havoc that her mother wreaked upon my family.

"Can you believe it?" I say, with more surprise than bitterness. "After a year and a half, I still can't. I'm the other woman. The potential home-wrecker. The bitch."

"I wouldn't have guessed that, no," Rei says slowly. "It's not the fate I would have predicted for you, of all people."

She links her arm through mine, and we begin to walk again. We are quiet, threading our way with care through the throngs of women and their children. I sneak a glance at her. Her head is bent, her eyes on the path ahead of her, and I wonder if she, too, is thinking about her mother.

Chapter Eight

IN THE KLEIN–WATANABE HOUSEHOLD, A RESPECTFUL silence surrounded and protected the subject of Hana's paintings. This silence could in fact be described as wary: perhaps taking their cue from Henry, with his wide-eyed, almost always speechless admiration of Hana's work, the children were afraid to speak about the colorful paintings that flowed in a steady stream from the studio at the top of the house. This was true even though Hana herself seemed casual and hardly intimidating on the subject of her art, asking their opinions of different works and listening with care to what they said.

Maybe, Kei sometimes thought, their silence wasn't so surprising, given that they could only intellectually (and often, Kei mused, just barely at that) understand the urge to apply paint to paper in order to give shape to the inchoate images of the mind. Whatever the reason, they never spoke about the paintings if they could avoid it.

Hence their collective failure to ask Hana what she was doing when she first began painting the same object again and again.

They initially thought that it was a silhouette of a woman: a figure huddling under an umbrella, seen from the back. So indistinctly rendered was this figure that this initial thought was in fact just a guess; the silhouette was really little more than a shape with what might have been a large, domed hat over it. Still, the idea that Hana was painting someone under an umbrella persisted, perhaps because of the angry streaks of rain visible at the edges of the painting.

But the question of what Hana was painting was easily subsumed by one that was more pressing: why did she paint so many versions of this not exactly riveting silhouette? To think that they had once taken it for granted that her paintings would cover a pleasingly diverse array of subjects! Flowers, bees, landscapes, boats adrift on the sea, and countless portraits from memory of her aunt Sachiko. Kei hadn't known how much they would all miss it, the fact that they never knew what Hana would paint, until this parade of what was, in retrospect, a spectacularly various range of images conjured up by the wand of her paintbrush abruptly came to an end.

Kei was seventeen. Tall and poised, with a boyfriend who was now in college, but she could have wailed like a child, in a way that even Rei no longer would, for those pictures, especially the portraits of Aunt Sachiko, that pensive, war-scarred woman.

(Why was Sachiko—Kei suddenly wondered, as she had many times before—so much more dear to Hana than her own mother? Could it be for the same reason that Rei believed Henry to be the finest of men—out of gratitude, as well as simple affection? If so, that's one way, at least, that it's easier to be a stepparent, or an aunt, than a mother or father: the expectations are lower, and so a small dose of kindness will go far indeed.)

One day, it seemed, Hana woke up and began to paint this umbrella-like shape, an angry red against a dark gray background. The next day she painted another one, but this time the shape was black, the background, forest green. Then she painted a yellow shape against blue, gray against blue, blue against purple, gray against black, and black against black. Then she painted even more, in an endless variety of colors.

For weeks that turned into months, she reproduced the image of the umbrella, and she became increasingly quiet around the house as she did so. She worked at what was for her an unusual velocity, sometimes producing two paintings in a day. Her productivity was particularly remarkable given that she painted as she always did, placing her brush and swiping it across the canvas with a bold, even reckless assurance, but then going back and revising almost every one of these strokes with an obsessive care. As soon as her paintings were dry, she stacked them facedown against the wall, neatly in order, until even her spacious studio—the converted attic, the largest as well as sunniest room of the house—began to seem cramped and small.

As she had not since her school days, when the thrill of painting had taken hold of her full throttle, like first love, Hana began to be careless about how the paint made its way onto her body, so that her face, arms, legs, and of course her hands seemed to be perpetually covered with it. Once Kei came down and caught her cooking with paint on her fingers. Horrified, she took over the filleting of the fish while her mother scrubbed her hands under her strict supervision, but since Kei's track schedule kept her from checking on Hana every evening, who knew how much paint-laced food they were taking into their mouths? In private, Kei warned the others, so that they began turning their food over with care for traces of exotic color.

Whereas Hana had once spent her nights reading the papers or watching television on the couch with Henry, she took up the practice of heading toward her studio as soon as dinner ended. There she worked until midnight, when Henry came and stood at the foot of the stairs on the second floor, tilting his head upward so that his glasses winked with the light, to call her to bed.

SHE STRUGGLED AGAINST IT, but in the end Kei came to the reluctant conclusion that she would have to ask the question that was troubling them all. She loved Henry, of course, gentle soul that he was, as Rei did, but perhaps because she remembered their father, their one and only *oto-san*, as her sister, younger than her by four years, couldn't, she was (she told herself) understandably a little more skeptical of this benign, very tall presence in their lives. She could see, for starters, how Henry was rendered almost ineffectual by his adoration of his second wife. Kei was fairly confident that he would not ask Hana about how strangely absorbed she had become in her work, and that even if he did, he wouldn't tell her daughters what she had said.

And Rei and Claudia—the steptwins or stepbrats, as she'd begun calling them, to their equal delight—were all too wrapped up in their own private world of past stories about Hana, the most romantic ones, such as the almost fairy tale about her and the prince, to notice what was happening to her now, let alone inquire about it.

No, it was up to her to find out what was troubling Hana, and then to find a cure for it. Kei didn't like it; she in fact flat out dreaded the prospect. Almost adult though she was, she too would have liked nothing more than to bury herself in a world made up of the sweeter stories from her mother's strange and often troubled past. Yet her *oto-san*, with his easy laugh and deep voice and the sprinter's stride that she had inherited, her special pal just as surely as Claudia was Rei's, was long gone, so what else could she do but leave that world for another far less romantic?

Kei knew that the stepgirls saw her as a worrywart, that when it came to having fun, they had written her off as a lost cause. That they thought so stung a little, young and idiotic though they were. If it weren't beneath her dignity to do so, she would have sat them down and explained to them the reason she tended to frown, watching Hana, far more than she smiled or laughed.

Her father would have wanted her, he would have *expected* her, to take care of her mother. Indeed, every morning when he left for work, that was what he used to say to Kei—*Take care of your mother*—the fact of Hana's vulnerability, a fragility that seemed at odds with her single-minded dedication as an artist, a secret that they shared. While unacknowledged, this secret had bonded Kei and her father together and marked them as kin, as surely as did their ability to outpace all others in the field and their love of the wind on their face as they ran.

So even though her *oto-san* never had a chance to say good-bye to her, that was the charge with which he left her, and the one that she would at all costs fulfill. She would take care of Hana.

If only she knew how.

KEI WOULD LATER COME to think that it was because she panicked that she blurted out the questions in the way she did—at Sunday brunch, over pancakes and cereal and tea, when Claudia as well as Rei was there, and Henry too, anchoring the table with his quiet presence. She panicked for a simple, stupid reason, one that probably would have disappointed her father badly if he'd still been alive: because she realized, sitting at brunch, that Hana was the linchpin to their gathering that morning.

Technically, of course, it was Hana's relationship with Henry that brought them all together. But he always seemed the passive partner in the enterprise known as their marriage—who knew why? Perhaps because it was Hana who, at least according to family lore, pursued him. Or was it merely because it was she who called them to this table? What did seem clear was that if they did make up a family—and while Kei was almost superstitiously careful about including the *if* before that phrase, after four years of living with Henry even she could admit that she could drop that preposition if she chose—then it was Hana's presence at the head of the table that conferred that particular title on the gathering.

They were a motley group. Rei and Claudia might be equally rumpled and disheveled, and yes, they were wearing pajamas with matching patterns, Rei in blue and Claudia in violet, but whereas Rei was dark and quick and far too thin, her steptwin was another story altogether, fair-skinned, stockier, and slow-moving, gazing out at the world with those large, mild eyes. Then there was Henry, ludicrously long, always looking a little sloppy, even when dressed as he was today in a long-sleeved shirt and khakis, and Hana, tiny and chic even in her paint-streaked sweatshirt and pants. Then, finally, there was herself. Kei straightened, angling her butter knife so that she could glance at her reflection on its surface. Dressed in black, her best color; hair brushed and styled; mascara and a trace of lipstick on her face.

In terms of both fashion and biology, they did not form a cohesive group, as anyone peeking in through the window would realize. Yet there they were nonetheless, sitting together during that most intimate hour, ten on a Sunday morning, crowded around a table that was at least two places too small, dipping their knives into the same jar of jelly, diving their spoons and unfortunately alltoo-grubby fingers into the same bowl of blueberries.

A family, if you will.

Kei shot a quick look at her mother, who was absorbed in sliding the lid of the jelly jar in a small circle on her place mat. Lying untouched beside her was a plate of pancakes—they were made by her, so, predictably, they were soggy in the middle and burnt around the edges, but when had Hana ever cared about what she ate? The diminishment of her appetite these days was striking, her weight loss, worrisome. She was becoming steadily more unbalanced, as she had for the year following Seiji's death; that was obvious. Kei felt a surge of fierce protectiveness toward the group gathered around the table, innocently chewing and swallowing, unaware that their comfortable existence as a group was under threat.

The fate of the family resided in Hana. It went beyond the question of whether she would become so obsessed with her work that she would lose interest in Henry and decide to leave him, or, more implausibly, whether he would leave her. Hana *was* the family. What Kei feared was not the prospect of losing yet another father, but the possibility that she would lose her mother.

"WILL YOU COME TOO?" Henry turned to Hana, looking at her with what seemed to his daughter, at least, to be more than a hint of wistfulness. He had been discussing the day's excursion, a walk up the highest hill in the county; Rei and Claudia and even, for once, Kei had all agreed to come.

So quiet had Hana been, and so busy too, rising to get butter, brown sugar, blueberries, and then more butter again, it was unclear how much of the conversation she had heard. Standing now at the refrigerator, she turned around. She gazed down at the carton of milk in her hand, shook it a little so that it sloshed, and then came and sat down. "I think I'll stay home today," she said. In the years to come, her daughters would wonder, with more than a trace of guilt at their long-term aversion to speaking Japanese, whether Hana's inclination to state the obvious was a direct result of the fact that she was a woman who'd grown accustomed to being misunderstood, even—or was that especially?—by the members of her own family. Here she didn't even slow down to tack on a note of explanation that was, for the people seated at this table, hardly necessary. "I want to paint today."

The group was still for a moment; Rei may have sighed. No one asked, because it was no longer a matter of debate at this point, whether Hana would paint more pictures of that curiously bulbous shape.

It was then that Kei asked her questions. Discussing this moment later, Rei and Claudia would agree that to her credit, Kei managed not to express either annoyance or exasperation, even though, knowing her, she was probably feeling both.

Kei herself was appalled. Even as she opened her mouth, she was aware that when she rehearsed these questions in her mind, she always sounded mildly inquisitive, and humorous too, and that, furthermore, they always came at the end of a long, meandering, and most of all private conversation about art and work. But when she actually spoke them—when she, let's not mince words, actually blurted them out—the best she could hope for was that she didn't sound too aggressive. "What are you trying to do with all of those hat shapes? Don't you want to paint anything else anymore?"

Hana bent her head forward. Her lips were apart; her gaze was rapt. She cleared her throat, and then she looked up at the small group gathered around the table.

Yet as she looked at each of them in turn, the brightness in her face gradually faded. When she spoke, her eyes were cast down again, this time focused on the sugar bowl. "I want to paint," she said, taking the lid off the bowl and peering into it, "the eternal mushroom." Then she stood up and moved to the cabinets to replace the sugar.

Kei pushed her plate—of blueberries, and nothing more; she was still thin, but you never knew, and it never hurt to watch what you ate—away from her and frowned. She glanced over at Henry, who adjusted his glasses higher on the bridge of his nose and looked, she thought suddenly, old, far older than he usually looked, older even than his really very considerable years; had he always had those lines around his mouth, and if so, when had they become so deep?

But Rei and Claudia just squirmed in their chairs and thanked their lucky stars that they were seated next to each other and so could not catch each other's eye. The *eternal* mushroom? Maybe they wouldn't have worried about dissolving into laughter if Hana had chosen another adjective. Maybe, in a pinch, they could have respected the desire to reproduce an image of the *perfect* mushroom, even if they wouldn't have understood it (a fungus, after all, a creepy, unnatural thing, thriving in the dark and the damp and hating the sun), but that wasn't the phrase that she used.

It was her English, of course, strange and stilted even after years of living in America with two American-born daughters and an American man. They were all used to it, and generally kind and patient about both her mistakes and her accent. Still, it was hard for Claudia and Rei, thirteen years old at the time and, as such, perhaps inevitably prone to parental mockery, not to giggle at the phrase, and probably asking too much to think that they would not joke about it later in private: Hana's Quest for the Eternal Mushroom or, as they would quickly come to say, her Quem.

LIKE HER ELDER DAUGHTER, Hana had known that she was not saying what she meant to say even as she spoke. What she had wanted to say was that her old childhood nightmare of the cloud had begun to recur, that she couldn't sleep for dreaming it. What she should have explained was that her hope was to capture the image so perfectly that she could banish it from her mind.

She'd wanted to tell her family that with the only tools she had at her disposal, her paint and her brushes, she hoped to trap the cloud on paper, to pinion it like a butterfly so that it could no longer hover on the edges of her mind throughout the day, fluttering its wings and distracting her. She had wanted to explain how bright this image was, how it was almost blinding; she had wished to say that she had become afraid to drive, let alone conduct even the most casual conversation, because she was sure that at any moment it would fly out in front of her, revealing itself to everyone.

Perhaps it was, yet again, a problem with her English. The eternal mushroom, such a stupid phrase: what on earth had she been thinking? Could it be a lack of vocabulary rather than the sheer lunacy of the ideas that she had wanted to express to her family that had kept her from speaking out? Perhaps if she had the words, and the eloquence with which to string them together, she could have said to them that although her paints and brushes had never let her down before, she herself was another matter altogether. That no matter how hard she worked, and how many hours and days, her talent was meager, and that she despaired of summoning the necessary skill to pin down on paper the image that tormented her.

Yes, maybe it was just a question of language. If it weren't for that barrier, maybe she could have told them (how she had wanted to tell them! sitting in expectant silence, their faces turned toward her, wearing that expression she knew so well, polite bafflement coupled with a keen desire to understand), and they would have nodded and understood, that she had circling in her head in an endless loop a nursery riddle, perhaps American, perhaps Japanese, that she had heard somewhere: how do you catch a cloud?

The answer being, of course, that you don't. That you can't.

Chapter Nine

New Jersey, 1974–82

"WHEN SHE WAS YOUNGER, MY MOTHER WAS OBSESSED by the role that luck played in every person's life. That was because of what had happened to her aunt Sachiko," said Rei, looking down at the ground. She never needed to check whether her audience of one was paying attention. "My mother always used to say that if it hadn't been for her youngest aunt, she might have felt differently about the possibility of marrying the prince. And that, even more, she would have led her life as a whole very differently." That the life Hana led would have been a different one altogether, with a whole other set of decisions about love and children and career and travel made at every step, paled in significance when compared to this fact—her approach to and indeed her whole attitude toward life was different because she knew her aunt Sachiko, as well as what had happened to her.

What had happened to Sachiko was this: during the morning of a hot summer day, exactly a month and a day before her twentieth birthday, she made the decision to step outside to let her hair dry in the sun. She lived then, as she would until the end of her life, in a suburb almost two kilometers away from the city of Hiroshima, and that day—August 6, 1945—the annals of her small town, like that of all towns in a hundred- and, for all she knew, perhaps even a thousand-kilometer radius of the city, would become filled with stories that chronicled the most minute of people's actions and movements, with particular attention paid to the chain of events (random, quotidian, and in retrospect, jaw-dropping) that led to their being in a certain place at a very certain time.

An elderly man who stopped to admire a cherry tree he had planted that spring and so missed his train by no more than a minute: had the leaves of the tree seemed less lush that day, or were he just a little less careful in his admiring inspection of its growth, he would not have lived past that morning. A pregnant woman who was traveling all the way from Kyushu, where she had moved with her husband and child, to visit her cousins and her grandmother. Because her son had been ill with a fever, she had not planned to leave Kyushu until the sixth, but when he showed signs of improvement and her grandmother slipped on a puddle outside her doorstep, breaking her left hip and ending up in the hospital, the young woman changed her plans and left instead on the fifth. After spending the night at her cousins', she left for the hospital, which was located in the dead center of the city, at six-thirty A.M. the next day.

By her own account, Sachiko's story was not as dramatic as theirs. What she had gone through wasn't even on the order of what had happened to Mari-chan, the little girl, her hair always in pigtails, who was the younger sister of one of Sachiko's old classmates from school: at 8:14 in the morning of that day, the boldly colored spine of one of her father's books caught her eye. Perhaps partly because she was not supposed to touch them, Mari-chan could not resist; her hand outstretched, she was almost at the bookshelf when it fell on top of her, putting her in a wheelchair for the rest of her life.

No, Sachiko had been one of the lucky ones, as she herself was well aware. The bomb had neither marked nor damaged her body. When she remembered what had happened to so many thousands of others—and how could she forget, when some had been her neighbors, and others her classmates—she knew she had little right to complain, or even to be surprised at the way the life she'd loved had changed forever in an instant.

But for Hana, eight years younger and not a resident of a Hiroshima suburb, astonishment and anger at the sudden way in which Sachiko's life had changed seemed the only reactions that would ever make any sense.

IT WASN'T EVEN the usual time she washed her hair. Because her hair was long and difficult to wash, she usually ended up reserving that particular chore for the evening: Sachiko operated on the premise that unpleasant tasks should be put off for as long as possible (which meant that her nights tended to be very full). Besides, she liked to stay in bed in the mornings, past nine as often as she could manage it.

This week, though, sleeping in late was impossible; a peaceful morning was not an option with Yuka visiting from Nagoya with her three children. When the baby began to wail at a quarter past seven, Sachiko had opened her eyes and then found that she could not get them to stay closed again no matter how she tried. Giving up at last, she sighed, sat up, and stretched.

It was while she was attempting to muster the energy to put away her futon that she ran her fingers through her hair and noticed that the ends of it felt sticky. After feeling it again more carefully, she realized that it wasn't just sticky; there was an *ame*, one of the sucking candies that Hana, her oldest niece, loved, stuck in her hair. The candy was bright red and shiny, and judging from the fact that it was less than half of its regular size, its edges worn smooth, it had probably been sucked on for some time already.

Wincing as she tried to wrest the candy free, Sachiko cast her mind back (while just one night back was all that was required, it was still hard for her, so swiftly did her days pass, and so full did they all seem to be): Hana had nodded off over her homework and Sachiko had picked up the tiny girl to take her to bed; the candy must have dropped out of her mouth then. Sachiko wrinkled her nose. How could she have missed it; how could she have actually spent a whole night with that thing weighing down her hair and pulling it down, and doubtlessly staining her pillow red? And then she laughed.

That's what Sachiko-san was like back then (Hana would tell her daughters decades later in halting, accented English, shaking her head in wonder, her voice catching a little as she tried to reconcile the image of the older woman she remembered with that of the lighthearted girl who now only existed in stories). Before that August, Sachiko would find something to laugh about even on a busy morning in the middle of the war, even if it was a piece of candy spat out by her niece and tangled up in her hair. It didn't matter that she had slept poorly, her stomach upset by the family's wartime diet of soybeans and cabbage. So what if she was deeply worried, as all her neighbors and friends were, about the possibility of a mass raid on Hiroshima, which aside from Kyoto was the only large city that had not yet been attacked by the B-29s, or B-san, as they were known? She could still throw her head back and let out a hearty peal of a laugh.

It took Sachiko a good three minutes to get the *ame* out of her hair. Then she dressed herself in a cotton kimono, folded and put away her futon (moving with a briskness that was not customary to her; the thought of her mother trying to feed all those children made her feel a little guilty, although she herself was the first to admit that how much she could help was another question altogether), and went to the bathhouse to wash out her hair.

SHE WAS THE YOUNGEST of five siblings. The next one up, her brother Motohiko, was eight years older and already married, his second child on the way; Sachiko's oldest sibling, her sister Yuka, was thirty-seven in 1945, almost a full generation older.

Sachiko had come as a complete surprise to her parents, a gift that arrived in their later, more tranquil years, when they not only had more money but also more leisure, and their attitudes toward child-rearing had changed. They were (as they told themselves as well as each other at her birth), old hands at parenting by this point, able to anticipate well in advance any problems that would come up in the process of raising a child. Surely they could afford to let up considerably on disciplining little Sa-chan, who, poor thing, wouldn't have brothers and sisters of her own age as playmates. After all, their four oldest children had grown up fine, with barely a knee injury among them.

That Sachiko's parents spoke to each other of the need to be lenient toward their youngest child was probably unnecessary. The family would soon come to agree on the fact that being stern with Sachiko was not a possibility. As the oldest, Yuka remembered what all her siblings were like as babies, and Sachiko was different.

"The happiest baby ever," pronounced their mother, crooning as she cradled Sachiko to her.

And despite a momentary pang of jealousy, Yuka had to agree.

IN THE BATHHOUSE, Sachiko removed the wooden planks that rested on top of the bath and kept the heat of the water in. Humming one of the songs that her sister Yuka sang to her children, a ridiculous jingle that she hadn't been able to get out of her head all week, she took off her kimono and hung it on a nearby hook.

She thought of Takuro as she dipped one of the containers stacked in the corner into the steaming water and raised it over her head. He was in the army now, as all the young men were, but even though it had been four months since they'd met, it had seemed lately as if he was always in her mind, infuriatingly catchy and as difficult to forget as a child's jingle. What if they had (here Sachiko allowed herself a small smile as she blushed, the hot water spilling over her face) a daughter of their own who was partial, as so many children were, to sweets? And then what if one morning Sachiko woke to find a piece of hard candy spat out by her daughter caught in her hair: how would Takuro react? Perhaps he'd be fastidiously revolted; perhaps he'd laugh at or with her. Or would he cluck his tongue and gently tease the candy out of her hair?

She didn't know him well enough to say for sure, of course. Yet even in the one brief, formal encounter that they had had, she had been able to see the snap of humor in his eyes, and so she strongly suspected that if he saw an *ame* swinging from the ends of his wife's hair, he, too, would throw his head back and laugh out loud, forgetting for one sweet, precious moment that their country was in the midst of a great and terrible war.

SOMETIMES WHEN SHE TALKED about her aunt Sachiko to her daughters, Hana would interrupt her own narrative.

"In Japan back then, women didn't have a lot of decisions to make," she'd say, her face uncharacteristically stern and her gaze focused so intently on Kei and then Rei in turn that they wondered if she was thinking about the unfolding of their fates rather than that of the doomed figure of their bedtime stories, their mother's youngest aunt.

"Choosing a husband was important. Every woman married and

had children—they didn't have a choice about that." Then, as she looked at the eagerly attentive faces of her American-born daughters, Hana's voice would soften. "Not having choices—you don't know about that," she'd say, not needing to add—because someday, if not already, they'd be saying it too—thank God.

It was when Hana came down with tuberculosis, the year that she turned sixteen, that she first began to appreciate not only what her aunt Sachiko had gone through and continued to go through on a daily basis but Sachiko herself. Until then, Sachiko had been all too easy to ignore, a pale, far too thin woman who smiled a lot but said little. While still the darling of her parents, doted upon and spoiled more than ever, she lived like a permanent houseguest in one of the small bedrooms in her parents' house; it was hard not to see her as a highly favored maid of the family. Hana knew Sachiko's history, but although it made her a tragic figure in her eyes and, as such, an object of some interest, she personally seemed rather dull, silent for lack of anything to say rather than because of grief or any hidden depths.

Hana's tuberculosis kept her bed-bound and in isolation, in a room that was separated from the rest of the house by a long corridor. Her year would have been unbearably lonely were it not for the fact that a quarter of the way through it, Sachiko took the train down to Nagoya and moved in. Replacing the maids, she nursed Hana and, even more importantly, provided her with company, reading her books, playing her records, and sitting in the room with her for hours, when Hana's mother did not dare to do more than call out to her from the hallway once a day.

Hana was too weak, even, to hold up a paintbrush, and certainly not a book. Lying in her bed throughout that long year, a quietly companionable Sachiko sitting by her side, she stared at the ceiling (and for variety, sometimes the wall) and pondered the importance of having and making choices.

In the end, the prince probably wouldn't have wanted her anyway (she'd tell her daughters); after all, she'd had tuberculosis (turning her face here and lowering her gaze, so that they thought that it must have been hard indeed for her, shut up alone and shunned by her family—even her mother!—and friends; they wondered if the memory of her sickness, even now, caused her shame). As a person who had contracted that dreaded and highly infectious illness, she would have been judged a poor candidate for marriage by many middle-class Japanese men, let alone by the crown prince's handlers and family.

Yet the prince never got the chance to pursue and court Hana actively, for when she met a man who offered her a life that was less glamorous, perhaps, than that of an empress, but also far more free, she decided quickly, even spontaneously, that she would marry him.

RETRIEVING ANOTHER CONTAINERFUL of water from the bath and closing her eyes, Sachiko began the long process of trying to rinse the soap out of her hair. When had she decided that she would marry Takuro? Much as she tried, she couldn't remember. One morning almost three months ago, she had woken up and there the knowledge was, lodged as securely in her mind as the candy had been in her hair today (and greeted by her, perhaps not incidentally, with the same combination of surprise and laughter): Takuro was the one she wanted to marry. And given that a proposal had arrived from his family and her parents had raised no objections, he was the one she *would* marry.

The matchmaker had arranged for her to meet five men all told, all of whom came, as she did, from respectable, well-to-do families; Sachiko had liked them well enough. But sometimes, she had to admit, it was hard to tell whether she had liked the man or the meeting itself. The possibilities of these meetings fascinated her;

she liked to look at the man sitting across from her and imagine the life that they would lead together, the talks over dinner and the evenings they'd spend reading over the *kotatsu* and, most of all, the children that they would someday have.

But the fifth meeting had been different. Takuro she had liked for himself—how soft his eyes were! a deep brown, with the hint of laughter always dancing behind them—and not just for the fact that he would give her a life that she could imagine and anticipate with pleasure.

She tossed her hair back and blinked the water from her eyes, and wondered if it would rain soon—her affection for the cool misty gray of clouds, the initially soft but then growing roar of raindrops, and the messy but also strangely satisfying act of splashing through puddles a trait that she shared with Rei, her American-born great-niece.

When, in less than half an hour, she would step outside and see a great light flash across the sky over the city, Sachiko would be too startled to be afraid. Even from where she stood, she would be able to feel the force of the blast, but although she would sway and totter back a few steps, she would catch herself in time and not fall. She'd know that this explosion was not a B-san. The light was so strong and blinding, it had to be the sun itself that had swooped across the sky. She would think that the white-faced, green-eyed American demons had turned the life-giving brightness of day into their own personal agent of destruction; they had managed to harness and also subvert the power of the gods in their attempt to destroy her country.

She would be stunned speechless when she saw the flash of light, but when she saw a huge, dark cloud form over the city, she would cry out. The fact that the cloud was in the shape of an umbrella—a benevolent object, one used for protection from the rain and the sun—would convince her once and for all that the Americans had rendered the forces of good into something dark and un-recognizable.

Sachiko combed her fingers through her hair, checking to see if any soap remained. Thinking of the candy that had been caught in it, she smiled once more. She would find time around her chores later this morning, she resolved, to fit in a game of tag with Hana and her younger sister.

IN THE 1940s Hana lived in Nagoya, almost six hours by train from Hiroshima. Although she and her family happened to be visiting the small town outside of Hiroshima in which Sachiko lived with her parents on that first week of August, 1945, Hana did not know her mother's youngest sister well then, and so to her lasting regret she would have few memories of her aunt, prewar, to pass on to her daughters. Her descriptions of Sachiko as a woman who would throw her head back and laugh during the middle of the war because a sticky piece of candy was entangled in her hair came secondhand to her, from her mother and grandmother, these recollections becoming heirlooms, possessions that were prized as rare jewels, the passing down of which elicited not only awe but sadness.

The woman Hana remembered as Sachiko was a different person: mild-mannered and gentle, cheerful enough but certainly not quick to laugh. Furthermore, even though the sight of the mushroom cloud—ominous and almost unearthly—would be fixed in Hana's memory until the day she died, years afterward she would tell her children that she could not recollect the rash that her aunt developed along her hairline, nor how lethargic the usually lively Sachiko became. In any event, Hana and her family returned soon enough to their home in Nagoya. She would say later that she seemed to remember hearing her parents whisper of what had happened to Sachiko, and seeing her mother cry over a telegram that contained the latest update on her health. But Hana's mother cried so often those days, it was impossible to know for sure.

That Sachiko showed signs of radiation sickness after that day came as a surprise to the doctors who saw her. Given that she was so far from the city center, the exposure that she, a grown woman, had suffered upon walking out of the bathhouse should not have been enough to create a risk. The fact that the doctors did not initially believe Sachiko could have developed radiation sickness gave her and her family hope at first, but in the end it only served to point out to them how little the medical community knew about the effects of the bomb and the strange illness that it could cause. For there was the rash and the fatigue that was more intense than any she had ever experienced and then, when she was tested at the hospital, there was her low leukocyte count—unmistakable symptoms all. Not a severe case, the doctors finally pronounced, but a case nevertheless.

Before that day, Sachiko had thought that her current existence—living at home with her parents, helping them out around the house and with their visitors—was not meant to last long. She was in an interim stage, pleasant enough in itself but not anything, she was optimistically sure, compared to what would follow: a home and children of her own. This so-called transitional phase instead became her life, as the symptoms of radiation sickness that she had were not only unmistakable, they were also impossible to hide. Reports of the unlikely fact of her sickness spread, and one by one, the offers of marriage that had come for her were hastily withdrawn, with the family of Takuro Tanaka, the man she had most preferred, being the first to pull out.

PULLING HER HAIR BACK from her face, Sachiko gathered it into a long, black rope and squeezed it tight, wringing it. She dressed herself quickly in her kimono and slipped her *geta* on, enjoying how cool the wood felt against her feet. There was a lilt to her step as she walked down the hallway from the bathhouse toward the door leading to the garden; she could almost have been dancing.

She held her damp hair clenched in one fist, like a bouquet (she thought with a smile) of black, bedraggled seaweed. Would Takuro laugh, too, at the idea that she held her tangled wet hair like flowers? But at least it smelled clean; at least it was no longer sticky.

With that she stepped outside, turning around only to pull the door shut behind her.

Chapter Ten

Claudia
Boston, 1999

"SO IF YOU TWO ARE SO CLOSE, KINDRED SPIRITS AND mirror images and sisters-in-all-but-biology and all the rest of it," says Vikrum, his eyes narrowed as he watches me, "then how come you haven't seen each other for so many years?"

We sit on a bench on the banks of the Charles, surrounded by geese. In the way of all geese, or at least of all the geese I have ever met, these birds look plump but act famished. I throw a handful of bread crumbs at them; it's good to see how hungrily they eat. There is always one goose in the group that stands guard over the others, and I have, as usual, saved a few extra crumbs for him. I toss them in his direction, but he does not even deign to look down at where they fall; his neck stands proud and tall, at the top of which his head swivels slowly, vigilantly surveying the world for possible predators. Is it an honor to be designated the sentry? Was he happy when he received the secret tap (bestowed by a beak, perhaps, on the base of a left wing) that let him know he had been chosen, or did he sigh, at least at first; did he groan and mutter audibly to himself and everyone else in his vicinity?

I throw my last handful at him; my aim is better this time and the crumbs land at his feet, but still he ignores my offering. I am impressed, of course, by how seriously he takes his responsibilities, and I certainly do not want him to shirk them in any way. Still, it seems highly unlikely that he is getting enough to eat.

Vikrum nudges me. "They probably take turns. He'll get to eat later."

My laughter makes one or two of the geese hop away and a few more flutter their wings; the sentry sharply swivels his head toward me. I swallow my laugh quickly and lower my voice. "How'd you know what I was thinking?"

He smirks. "I'm a magician, remember? Trained in the ancient arts of mind reading." He takes my hand, now empty of bread crumbs, and interlaces my fingers with his own. "But enough about me, and it's definitely been enough about geese. How about we talk about why you and Rei haven't seen each for so long instead?"

It might just be my imagination, but it seems as if in the last two months or so, Vikrum has been getting increasingly reckless. Across the shining swath of the river lies Cambridge and, beyond that, the town of Medford, where at the end of a street there stands a crumbling but well-patched Colonial house, the top two floors of which are occupied by a shiny-haired South Asian woman and her two children. More to the point, perhaps, it is just past four, and while the geese outnumber the people now, the balance is about to tilt the other way very soon; on such a beautiful day, it would take an avian assault of Hitchcockian proportions to counterbalance the throngs of joggers, walkers, and Rollerbladers that can be found on the banks of the Charles at the end of the human work-day. I carefully disengage our hands.

At the beginning of our relationship, the fact that Vikrum and I could not touch in public gave us an erotic charge. We would sit together in a restaurant, a proper six inches between us, aching to touch. It became a challenge, a game that we used to play, to see who could hold out for longer in that state of longing, as sharp and dazzling as sunlight reflecting off a blade. One of us always gave in, standing up abruptly in our prearranged signal of defeat, before we had time to do more than sample our food and, on one or two occasions, before it had even arrived. We compared the feeling that that game gave us to the thrill of being handcuffed by a lover to the bedpost; there was the same inability to act, the same need to submit, helpless in the current, to our desire. We even made jokes about it (stupid ones that only struck us as funny at the end of our game, when we were clawing at each other with relief, but then they made us laugh until we could not breathe), such as: who needs handcuffs when we've got restaurants?

Less than a year has passed since either of us has made a joke about handcuffs, but it feels as if it has been far longer.

I turn back to the geese. Having picked over the crumbs thoroughly, they are beginning to wander. "Why do you keep asking me about Rei? You've got a bee in your bonnet on the subject."

"You don't know, do you." It is a statement rather than a question. "She disappeared on you seventeen years ago, and you didn't know why then, and you still don't."

The breeze is picking up. I turn my face toward it; the rush of air is pleasant in the unseasonable warmth of this late September day.

"Vikrum?"

"Yes, love."

"I've been thinking a lot about Hana lately," I say. "Because of Rei and all."

"Sure," he says. If he is confused by the shift in the conversation, he does not show it. "That seems natural enough."

"And I was wondering if you could do me a favor."

"Anything," he says. "Name it." The nature of his reply, as well as the promptness with which it came, a mark of his trust in me: his certainty that I would not ask him something he could not do, no matter how much I wanted it.

"I want to meet your children."

He blinks. "Claw, you know I'd like nothing more. But you also know how kids are," he says. "They'll blab about their dad's new friend—"

"Five minutes," I say. "Please. We'll set it up as an accidental encounter. I'll say hi, maybe shake a small hand or two, and move on." When I came up with the idea of asking Vikrum for this favor, a scant two minutes ago, I had resolved not to beg, but I had not known then how dearly I wanted it granted. "Please," I say again. "I'll skip the paw-shake, if you want. All I want is a chance to say hello to your daughter and son. That's all I'm asking for. It's not much, really, is it?"

Vikrum closes his eyes for a moment, and then he shakes his head. "No," he says, his voice muted. "It's not much at all."

"Thank you," I say. He is quiet for so long that I reach out and pluck at his shirtsleeve: despite my best intentions, it is a gesture that turns into a caress, and I quickly drop my hand. "So you were asking me about Rei."

"I was, wasn't I."

"So ask."

"Okay," he says, rousing himself. "Right, then. But only because you're demanding that I do so. Why did you and Rei lose touch for so many years? Do you even know?"

"Why do you have to ask me if you're so smart? Not to mention trained in the ancient arts of mind reading yadda yadda?"

Shaking his head at me, Vikrum smiles so sweetly that I cannot help but smile back.

If I told him about the cancer that had been in the center of Rei's left hand, he would almost certainly stop pestering me about her. Yet that is not my secret to tell. Suppressing a sigh, I turn and face him. "It was her mother's doing."

He is still, waiting for me to continue.

"Hana fell in love with someone else. Naturally she wanted Rei and Kei—that's Rei's older sister—to look at this new man as their stepfather. And she decided that the best way to do that was to make a clean break with her old life."

"You're saying that she actually forbade Rei to see you?"

"Yes."

"I thought you said she wasn't an evil stepmother."

"She's not, really. Don't get me wrong—I hated her, always have and maybe always will, and it was horrible and cruel to separate us. But in terms of helping her new husband fit into the family, who knows, she might have been right not to let me and Rei see each other." The explanation trips off my tongue: hardly surprising, given that I have made it to myself so many times over the years. "Rei really loved my dad. She looked at him as a father, and he thought of her as a daughter. The new guy didn't stand a chance with me around as a constant reminder of her old life."

Moving as one, perhaps at some hidden signal that I have once again failed to catch, the geese begin to waddle toward the water. The sun is sinking; Vikrum should be getting home soon.

"I can't imagine you hating anyone," he says. His right arm has crept up onto the back of the bench; while it remains discreetly out of reach of my shoulders, his fingers hold tightly to one strand of my hair. "She must have really hurt your dad."

"She did. Very, very badly. But I hated her long before that. Besides, sometimes I think I can't really blame Hana for falling out of love with my dad. She was still grieving over her first husband, Rei's dad, when she and my father met. Hana and Seiji—now, that was a real love story."

With a tenacity that I would under other circumstances term admirable, Vikrum ignores the bait and sticks to the story at hand. "Your stepmother—what was she like?"

"You know how I always brought home sick animals and so many of them died? She used to give me bits of her jewelry to bury with them. Something beautiful to accompany them into the land of the dead, she'd say. Rhinestone brooches and the like. In retrospect, it was environmentally appalling, but it was kind. While she wasn't much of a cook, she'd remember what foods I liked, hummus and eggplant and pumpkin pie, and she always made sure to buy them for me when I came to stay there for the weekends. Even so, she was kind of—well, she was kind of absent. My mom's absent-*minded*. She'd forget to pick me up or make me lunch, and it's a miracle she hasn't burnt the house down, she leaves so many pots burning on the stove."

"Ah," says Vikrum appreciatively, and I know that he is squirreling away this acorn to add to his store of information on my mother. He loves to hear about her, and he is convinced, circumstances notwithstanding, that they are destined to be great friends.

"But Hana seemed almost secretive. For all that she was a really dutiful mother and stepmother and wife, her heart wasn't in it, ultimately. It could have been because she was an artist, but who really knows? Nothing she did ever really made sense to me." Beginning with why she showed no interest in the possibility of marrying a real live prince and ending with why she never told my father the precise reason she was leaving him.

"She was born and raised in Japan?"

I nod. "She always liked it better here, though. After her first husband died, she took Rei and Rei's sister back to Japan with her. Then, after about a year there, she bundled the kids into another plane. They headed for New Jersey, where she found a job teaching art, and eventually hooked up with my dad."

There is a short silence. "Wow," says Vikrum at last. "She must be tough as nails."

"You think?"

"Are you kidding? For a Japanese woman of that generation to do all that on her own? She probably didn't have much support from her family to become an artist, for starters; I'm betting her parents also weren't thrilled with the idea of her running off alone to some crazy country on the other side of the world, their grandchildren in tow. And then she finds security in the form of another husband, and leaves him to boot. That's a lot of broken rules right there."

Mixed in with the grudging admiration that Hana often seems to inspire, at least in me, there is a hint of what sounds like envy in his voice. The first time that Vikrum saw the woman he eventually married, she was in a photograph proffered to him by his parents. In my presence, at least, he has never railed against the way in which his family establishes and controls the parameters of his life; indeed, he has not once uttered a word of complaint on the subject. Sometimes I think that he just does not want to give voice to his anger, but usually I know that the welter of cultural expectations placed upon him is so much a part of him that he is afraid what will happen once he allows himself to begin to resent it.

Still, that does not mean he is altogether free of resentment. Is it possible that a very secret part of him envies my stepmother for the coolness with which she walked away from her family and, later, from a marriage? Or is it just wishful thinking on my part to wonder if that is so?

"It's a real twist that after Hana left your dad, he and your mom got back together," Vikrum says suddenly. "It makes Hana seem more—more guilty, somehow, a real home-wrecker. It's weird enough for you, but it must be really weird for Rei."

I look away again, forcing myself to focus on the two women speed-walking by the river, their elbows swinging freely back and forth. When Rei and I get older, perhaps we, too, will wear baseball caps and go speed-walking along the Charles. But then my concentration snaps away from them like a rubber band.

Is Vikrum right; would the news of my parents' remarriage strike Rei as strange and even intolerable?

So, there it is, the unbidden guest who squats squarely in my view—the thought that I have been trying to dodge for the past week with more than modest success. I should have told Rei about my parents' reconciliation right away, the day that we first met up.

And then, hard on the heels of that thought, comes its inevitable and even more unpleasant corollary: I will have to tell her soon.

I shake my head quickly, clearing it, and turn back to face Vikrum.

His brows have inched together. "Aside from being a home-wrecker, though, your stepmother really doesn't sound so evil. Wait a second," he says, electric in that infectious way that he has when he gets an idea. He was known as one of the more inspiring teachers in his graduate department at Columbia, and it is not hard to see why. "Something's not right here. How do you know that Rei's vanishing on you is her mother's fault? Did Rei say that to you when you two got together?"

"Well, no. In fact, she said it was her idea. But I know she's just protecting her mother—"

Before I can finish the sentence, he is nodding.

"You see, it just doesn't add up," he says. "She couldn't have just disappeared because of her mother."

"But she did," I say, speaking politely but with emphasis. I lean my head to the right so that Vikrum is forced to let go of my hair. "I'm telling you what happened: Hana decided we shouldn't meet, so we didn't. Rei felt guilty about the way Hana treated Dad. She felt so ashamed, she went along with the whole plan in part to punish herself. That's how it happened." That's how it must have happened: there is no other possible explanation. But Vikrum is caught up; his eyes are gazing into the distance and he does not seem to hear.

"Let's just think it through. After all, you were both seventeen by that time, on your way to college. It's not as if you needed your parents to bring you together. Maybe there's another reason that—"

"Rei would never, ever have betrayed me! We were so close, and she could never be so cruel—"

"Whoa," Vikrum says, holding his hands up. His eyes are on me now, and they look bewildered. "Why are you yelling? And how can you possibly even suspect that Rei would have betrayed you? Why would anyone ever do that to you?"

For a second I cannot speak. In a moment he will leave to go and have dinner with his family. But then I realize that he is only speaking the truth: it is not me being betrayed, of course, but them. I clear my throat. "I thought you were implying—"

"I wasn't."

"Oh. Right."

"I'm sorry if that's what you thought."

"Me too. It's getting late, you need to go home soon."

"I know," he says. "I'm going."

We sit. Arms folded, I look out across the water. Moving their oars in enviable unison, a crew of eight streaks by. Off to the left, the Harvard bridge, by far the most prosaic of all the thoroughfares across the Charles, with neither the airy grace of the Weeks footbridge nor the impressive dignity of the Longfellow, shimmers hazily, rendered lovely by the change in light. "Go ahead and laugh if you want to," I say at last. "I don't see what's so funny, but I wouldn't want you to choke."

"I'm sorry," he says again. "I don't think I've ever seen you get quite this huffy...."

"I'm delighted that my indignation is fodder for your entertainment."

With that, Vikrum lets out a shout of laughter that is worthy of Rei. "You are such a goose, do you know that? I'm not laughing at how mad you are. It's just that you worry so much about everybody.

Your students, your family, me...the goddamn geese on the Charles, for crying out loud."

Then, suddenly, his arms are around me, my face placed firmly against his. The pathways in front of us are teeming with people, any of whom might be a colleague of Vikrum's, a parent of his children's friends, an acquaintance of his wife; far beyond them lies Medford, invisible to our sight but no less present. I should be disentangling myself from the warmth of his embrace and the familiar smell (clean and masculine and tangy) of his body; I should be scolding him for his growing recklessness in the past two months. But it takes all of my effort just to utter six words. "You need to go home soon," I say once more.

He sighs so deeply that the rise and fall of his body rocks my own. "I know," he says, as if our prior exchange had been a rehearsal, this the main performance. Then, very gently: "I'm going."

We sit locked together as the shadows grow more steep, the air cools, and the sky to the east turns a deep blue. When the wind picks up around us, the crumbs left behind by the birds scatter and tumble until soon they are all gone.

Chapter Eleven

"GROWING UP, MY MOTHER ALWAYS HAD PAINTBRUSHES rather than dolls," Rei would say to Claudia, who'd nod: they, too, disliked dolls, preferring Frisbee or books or, better yet, stories such as these. "She never thought about having children." Hana was too busy thinking about colors and shapes, about the lines of the tree branches outside her window and the way the sunlight slanted down on the ragged pink sweater lying on the sofa. Her parents liked to tell the story of the first time she ever got hold of a paint set: Hana had dabbed blobs of blue and green onto her sister's and brother's faces and arms until they were both completely transformed. Throughout her childhood, Hana's paintbrushes and paints were her most prized possessions as well as her most constant companions. So used to holding a brush was she that on the rare occasions she took a break, her right arm felt mysteriously too short. She used up all the pencils in the house until they were stubs and dried out the ink in all the pens with her doodling. During the war, when paper was scarce, she covered old newspapers, her sister's clothes, and even the neighbor's sweet-natured white dog with the outlandish images that leapt out as if long pent up from her hand.

It was at the age of sixteen that she put into words the goal by which she resolved to live the rest of her life: to try to put as much beauty into the world as she got out of it. It wasn't a goal that could be achieved, of course. It was absurd even to think of trying, when, even after the war, even after most of the city around her lay in ruins, there was beauty to be had for the taking wherever and whenever she looked: the soft gray of the evening sky; a clump of dandelions growing in a crack in the road; the profile of her silver-haired grandmother as she sat, knitting in hand, and gazed at the floor in a moment of contemplation.

Yes, it was a ridiculous ambition. Yet when Hana thought about devoting years to achieving that all too clearly unattainable goal, she was unable to imagine a life that would be better spent.

PAINTING CONSUMED HANA, perhaps, she was forced to admit, because a part of her always remained unsatisfied with what she did. Her dissatisfaction stemmed partly from her own inadequacies as an artist—it seemed as if she were continually cursing the clumsiness of her hands and her lack of technique and craft—but if that were her only problem, she would have been fine: whenever she was confronted with yet another dismal product of her labor, she just vowed again, with all of the fierce determination that was perhaps her defining characteristic, that she would work even harder, and that someday, somehow, her eyes would be sharper, her hands more deft, and her lines more sure. No, what proved a far more insurmountable obstacle was that while she struggled to paint pic-tures as Sasaki-sensei, her art instructor, said—an exact copy of na-ture—she never wanted to; the pictures in her head, vague and ill-defined though they were, seemed always far superior to the ones that appeared on the canvas in front of her and, more to the point, to the ones that appeared beyond it, the lake or the sunflow-ers or the bowl of peaches or whatever it was that Sasaki-sensei wanted her to reproduce.

But if not lakes, if not peaches, if not even sunflowers (her fa-vorite flowers, their colors so vivid and their shapes so bold, but at the same time almost ugly, their giant heads drooping a little with their own weight), then what was it that she wanted to paint? Hana wasn't sure. She admired but at the same time had no desire to par-ticipate in the delicate, ephemeral arts of Japan, the flower arrange-ments and the tea ceremony and the painstakingly careful folding of origami. She herself wished to create art that would shout out she was here long after she was gone. Her wish to make art that was both substantial and strong was such that, despite her love of the limitless array of colors that could arise with the mixing of paint, she thought sometimes that what she really wanted to do was sculpture: something that would slash against the landscape, loom up and create shelter, and cast shadows in the grass.

Yet sculpture was a path that Hana would never pursue, because one day as she wandered through the galleries in Nagoya, she fell in love. The artist's name was Setsuko Migishi—a woman, unusu-ally and impressively enough, and a Nagoya local too, although she had lived almost half of her adult life in France—but it was her work that captivated Hana. On canvases that were as tall as Hana, Migishi painted flowers and mountains, yet they were barely rec-ognizable as such, constructed as they were out of triangles and rectangles that had little to do with the way that the objects actu-ally appeared; they were, moreover, made with smears of paint, so thick that they formed clots on the canvas. If Hana peered close—

and she did, for so long that her head began to feel light—she could see the swirls of Migishi's brush stroke. While the colors were dazzling, gorgeous, and varied enough to satisfy even Hana, they were not beautiful paintings: indeed, two or three of them were just short of crude. But all of them had power, so much so that they had no need for the heft and size and extra dimension of sculpture to create the same monumental effect.

It was Hana herself who called the feelings she had about Migishi's paintings love (and later, when she told her daughters about the first time she saw Migishi's work, she would again characterize the attachment she formed in romantic terms, as a passion that developed quickly, but one that changed her for good, so that they would fidget and yawn, wishing she would hurry up and get to the juicy part of the story, her romance with a man—their father!—rather than with dabs of paint upon a canvas). Hana based her self-diagnosis on the chatter of her school friends. If a racing heart, an inability to concentrate in school because of a preoccupation with the beloved, a tendency to go up and down in moods in a way that was calculated to drive your mother mad, and sleeplessness were symptoms of a crush—well, then she had a bad case of it indeed.

IT WAS CLEAR TO EVERYONE, friends, family, teachers, as well as Hana herself, that at the age of twenty-six, she was well on her way to becoming a bona fide eccentric, bookish and perhaps overly fond of solitude. Forgetting what she had been like as a girl, Hana's mother believed that it was her firstborn's long and lonely bout with tuberculosis that had turned her into a dreamer, a woman obsessed with becoming an artist, of all things, who had insisted on attending a graduate program in art, who showed absolutely no interest in boys, and who refused to take seriously the possibility of marrying a prince. And it was true that Hana's long stint away from society during her illness had created a rift between her and her friends that she had not felt the need to bridge; it had almost certainly exacerbated her natural inclination toward solitude.

Yet the fact that she had spent a year alone but for the company of a quiet aunt was hardly the only reason for Hana's lack of interest in the society of both women and men. There was her temperament, for starters: she had always been independent, and while tolerant of the giggling and gossipping favored by her girlfriends, she had never been keen to join in, so that many of her classmates believed her to be supercilious. Then there was her resentment at what she considered the gross injustices done to her aunt Sachiko, and then, too, there was her single-minded pursuit of form and color—all factors that had conspired to keep her curiously incurious about the world around her.

She'd almost bumped into the crown prince of Japan five years ago, sure, and she had been struck then by how soft and white his skin was. But she would think later that she never even really looked at a boy until she was thrust into the middle of a crowd at the opening reception for a new art gallery in town.

She had looked at the art in the gallery and had liked it, especially the two Migishi paintings in the corner, but the crush of people was overwhelming and she had been wishing that she had stayed at home to paint instead when she saw him. He was standing stock-still, apparently transfixed, in front of the smaller Migishi work, the one in deep crimson, a picture of a field of poppies, or was that a sea at sunset? As Hana watched, an older woman bumped into him, hard; he moved out of her way and even bowed an apology, but his eyes did not leave the painting for more than a moment.

Hana watched him for a long time, ten minutes or more, as mesmerized by him as he was by the painting. She watched him until he finally looked away from the canvas—was it her imagination, or did he sigh as he did so?—glanced down at his wristwatch, swiveled around, and began to walk quickly away.

He was a young man, but not an attractive one. Hana was an artist, after all, trained to note form and proportion, and she saw that the pieces of his face fit poorly together, that his nose and forehead were too large, his mouth strangely wide, and his eyes too narrow and small. Still, he moved with an athletic grace, a kind of physical self-confidence bordering on swagger, that she liked and that she wished she knew how to capture on canvas. He looked up and caught her staring, looked away, and then looked back. As he approached, he held her eyes with an effrontery that made her catch her breath. He brushed by her so closely that even though he wore a light jacket and she a sweater, she felt his arm pressed against her own.

As he walked away, Hana closed her eyes and shivered deep inside herself. She would eventually come to see the rest of her life as flowing out of that moment: the few seconds, brighter even than the most vivid colors of her palette, during which he touched her as he walked by.

ALTHOUGH HER ART INSTRUCTOR scolded and her classmates were bewildered, Hana began trying to make pictures as Migishi did, clumps of paint in shapes that came out of her most feverish dreams rather than nature, plastered forcefully on the largest canvases she could find. She worked hard, as she always did, but with what she was the first to admit was dubious success. Still, she eventually managed to produce a number of works that even her teacher was intrigued and perhaps impressed by, and she felt justifiably proud when one of them was accepted for the student exhibit held during the summer at her school.

It was one of her friends who reported, giggling, that Hana had a fan. A young man, no less, who made all the other girls blush and giggle too, so what if he wasn't strictly speaking handsome. He had come and stood in front of her paintings, for almost half an hour every evening, three days in a row. Hana thought immediately, and with an unfamiliar sensation of light-headedness, of the man whose arm had brushed against hers—he so clearly loved Migishi's work; that he would also like a painting in the same school only made sense. For weeks Hana had been looking for him in different galleries throughout the town, and a number of street corners besides, hoping for another chance encounter. How ironic, and perfect too, that he would turn up here, in her very own exhibit hall.

She staked out her painting every evening for the rest of the week, but it wasn't until the end of the last day of the exhibit (a detail that always made Rei and Claudia shudder—fate clearly liked to play it close), when the large, well-lit room was empty and quiet and she had just about given up hope, that she saw him again. She'd thought she was alone when an all but imperceptible noise made her turn, and then there he was, just a step behind her. At the sight of him, Hana felt neither surprise nor relief.

"It's you," she said, as if she had known him all her life and he had just stepped out of her sight for a few moments, as if she had been expecting him to be there when she turned.

Surely he also should have been surprised by the way she addressed him, at once so familiar and bold. Still, he, too, seemed calm, as if young women he didn't know talked to him every day.

The very first time she saw him, Hana had thought that he seemed slightly dangerous, perhaps because of the swagger in his step, and that impression had been confirmed by the way he had stared at her and how he had walked up to her so closely they had touched. So she was taken aback at his fine accent when he spoke to her and that he used the honorific and bowed low.

"I'm Seiji Watanabe," he said. "Pleased to meet you."

She may have been flustered, and perhaps a little disappointed too, but she was a well-brought-up girl, and she bowed politely back. "I'm Hana Kawabata."

"Ah," he said, smiling, and Hana remembered belatedly that the cards on the wall bore the full name of each artist. Seiji nodded at the oversized picture behind her. "So this is your painting."

His mouth, already outlandishly wide, grew even larger as he smiled, but it was a pleasant smile, kind and warm. Still, his eyes were intent; Hana was acutely conscious that he was watching her closely. He looked back at the painting, and Hana braced herself for the inevitable question about what it was supposed to represent or, even more annoyingly, what it meant.

"What I like about your painting," he said instead, "is that you've really caught the way in which birds beat their wings."

Birds? It was a picture of her aunt Sachiko at the piano; there was nary an animal of any kind in sight.

Giving the young man—her first fan!—the benefit of doubt, Hana squinted hard at her painting, trying to see how he could have come up with birds, but she came up with nothing.

"You can see how they flutter their wings here"—he gestured at the space where Hana had drawn her aunt's hands in motion—"and how much they love to soar. They're so graceful in their flight, it's almost as if you can hear them sing."

So maybe he wasn't deluded; so maybe she wasn't completely devoid of talent.

"I'm going to be an artist," Hana said abruptly. She spoke with something approaching desperation, feeling a need to remind herself of what had been, up to now, the focal point of her life.

"It seems to me that you already are," Seiji said, looking past her to her painting again.

Was she already an artist? She had always thought she had such a long way to go. Hana straightened her back. "Are you an art student yourself?" she asked, to cover her own confusion rather than to find out the answer. What else could a man who lurked in galleries and university art shows and stood spellbound before Migishi's paintings be?

"No," he said, briefly smiling again and glancing down at her. "I just like art. I'm a banker."

Given that she had guessed wrong about him in almost every crucial respect, it was only natural she felt off-balance. "I plan to live in Paris someday," she said, her words running together, "and I'd like to paint there—"

"—like your idol, Migishi. Of course," he said, his words measured and his eyes still on her work. "I'm going to America, probably in the next three months. My bank is sending me." Then he turned his gaze back to her. "I understand they have a good art scene in America too."

Hana gave him a long, steady look, but she hesitated only momentarily. "Yes," she said, "I believe that they do."

SHE WOULD MARRY THIS STRANGER with what her friends and, especially, her royalty-obsessed mother would consider to be undue haste, and she would never look back. Together they would move to America, find and settle in a brownstone in Boston, and have two children and almost, heartbreakingly, a third.

It would be Seiji who chose the names Keiko and Reiko for their daughters. Years after he was gone, the girls, outraged by the thought that the *ko* attached to the end of their names meant *child* and that, even worse, such an ending was a convention peculiar to female names only, would contemplate officially becoming known by the easy, American monikers they had been using since their late childhood, Kei and Rei. Independently of each other, they would both come to decide against making the change unable to bear the idea that they would have names that their father had never called them by.

Long before that, though, Hana would find that she was right in her initial assessment that Seiji was in many respects an unusual man. Partly in an effort to placate their parents, who implored them weekly to come home, he did give their children proper, even slightly old-fashioned Japanese names, but he himself was anything but traditional. Hana would soon learn that her husband's taste for the avant-garde encompassed far more than art and that he had an unbridled, almost childish enthusiasm for anything innovative. Seiji read up faithfully and avidly on the latest scientific discoveries; the antithesis of the conservative banker, he came home daily, it seemed, with the latest in gadgets, transistor radios, tape recorders, video cameras, lawn mowers, and one day even an electric meat slicer, never mind that Hana hardly ever cooked meat.

Seiji's embrace of the new could also be seen in the fact that he was a progressive thinker. To take just one crucial example, there was the fact that if he felt disappointment, as almost any Japanese man of his class and upbringing would, when they had daughters rather than sons, he never betrayed it. And even though he denied it, saying that it was all about his work, Hana would always wonder (to herself, and also out loud, years later, to Kei and Rei) whether Seiji was fully and immediately supportive of her suggestion that they extend their stay in America at least in part because of his daughters—because he saw and did not like that women had narrower lives in Japan, their possibilities at once more limited and scant.

To the very end he would love America, its uninterrupted sky and its wide, endless streets, the taste of its hot dogs, the loose-limbed friendliness of its people, and the possibilities that floated down its rivers and swung like lanterns from its trees.

WHEN REI FINISHED telling Claudia the story of how her mother and her father, a man whose face she could barely recall, met, there was always a short silence. How easy Hana and Seiji made love look, how simple, direct, and quick! Who would ever have guessed that it would make itself felt so strongly and, perhaps even more shockingly, so soon; who would have known that a look held in a crowded room, a press of the arm, and the exchange of a smattering of words was all that it took? Perhaps, Claudia would worry out loud, she had already passed by the boy she was destined to love and marry and had failed to recognize him. Which always made Rei laugh—maybe it's that guy crossing the street three blocks away, you'd better run if you're going to catch up with him, or could it be that boy in the backseat of that car that just whizzed by?—even though she tried more often than not to be sympathetic to all of Claudia's concerns.

But the real lesson of this story (the stepsisters agreed) was not how suddenly love could make itself felt in your life, nor even how vigilantly you have to examine every chance encounter to guard against its passing you by. So was it the fact that happiness lay in choosing love over a more glamorous match—that love, which might just be life's ultimate goal, was captured by Hana only because she could see that the handsome, glamorous Emperor-in-waiting offered less than the banker with the oddly mismatched face?

An obvious point, not to mention an almost disappointingly clichéd one: fairy tales are not about finding a literal prince. And, in this case, inaccurate besides. For while Hana had indeed chosen a match that offered her love rather than wealth and glory, while she opted to live in a brownstone with the man she loved rather than in a palace with the one she didn't, it was far from clear that she had seen the decision that confronted her in those terms, as love vs. wealth and glory, or even that she had seen marrying the prince as a viable option at all. Five years had passed between her encounter with the prince and her meeting with Seiji, after all: what had really happened was that she had chosen being single over the prince, and then Seiji over a lifetime of being single. Perhaps Hana just instinctively knew that she would have been miserable cooped up in a palace, with her primary responsibility being the bearing of sons. What else had the example of patient, lonely Sachiko and the experience of being quarantined for a year taught her but that she wanted to roam about and breathe?

Hana had wanted a life in which she would have decisions, in which she could be the kind of artist she wanted to be, and she had gotten that; she had wanted passion and love, and she had gotten that too. So perhaps (Rei and Claudia tentatively asked each other) the lesson to be derived from the story of Hana's and Seiji's romance was a somewhat dangerous one—that one should set one's priorities and then shoot for the moon, never settling for less? Perhaps that was it.

While both Rei and Claudia knew that there was one more possible lesson that could be teased out of this story, it was one they could not bear to say out loud, even to each other. It was also one that they would have struggled to articulate, since it involved a slippery concept, one that they, as children, necessarily grasped only poorly—regret. Hana married Seiji and, the story went, never looked back. Still, how could she not? Sure, she also fell in love with America as she fell more in love with her husband—one love affair, at least, that would last her all her life. It was also true that she possessed the necessary steel in her character—that determination that had served her so well in her career as an artist of modest fame—to hold herself as well as her children together after Seiji died. But given that her marriage gave her ten years of utter happiness but nothing more, didn't she look back at least once or twice to contemplate, maybe even with regret, what would have happened if she'd chosen the prince instead?

Perhaps she sometimes suspected and often half believed, as Rei and Claudia were wont to do, that happiness was apportioned to everyone in equal measure but that how or whether you rationed it out was a decision left up to you. And if so, then wouldn't she also have to wonder, as they did, whether she should have doled out her allotment of happiness slowly, in teaspoons over a lifetime, rather than dousing herself in it all at once, and for all too fleeting a time?

Chapter Twelve

Rei
Boston, 1999

LIKE AN ATHLETE AFTER A WORKOUT, CLAUDIA HAS A towel slung around her neck. It's a dish towel, orange and red with a picture of a teddy bear on it, but she wears it as an athlete would, with comfort and grace. She is washing potatoes, chatting to me as she does so, her voice raised to carry over the sound of running water. She turns, empties the potatoes from the colander onto the cutting board, takes out a very shiny knife from a drawer, and begins to peel them. Her fingers move so fast and the knife looks so sharp, it's difficult for me to watch. Which is ridiculous, since if nothing else, I should remember that much about her—the girl knows how to skin a potato. Still, I look away from her hands, up at her face.

Her cheeks are flushed, and I'm not sure why. Claudia is so fair, she's practically transparent. Veins as delicate and finely etched as calligraphy are visible on her temples, and when she is hot or feeling emotional or working out, you can actually track the course of the blood as it spreads up and across her face. Talking about Vikrum would seem reason enough for the high color of her cheeks, but then, too, the kitchen feels warm even from where I sit, and she's the one who has been hovering, chopsticks wielded like a pro, like a native Japanese, over a steaming wok on the stove.

When Claudia was younger, she thought her veins were disgusting, and she hated that she blushed so easily. I used to tell her that there was no way on earth I was the only one who noticed and admired her skin. She would make her you-are-so-crazy-you-know-that? face at me, the one where she lowered her head and looked at me from under raised brows, her mouth pursing up so tight her lips didn't show. She was all eyes when she made that face; it always made me laugh.

That was, to be fair, back when we were teenagers, in the early eighties, when people clad in strips of cloth and pieces of string marinated themselves with baby oil, lay on reflector mats, and allowed themselves to be cooked by ultraviolet rays, when it was considered far better to be the color of well-done meat than of the inside of the bun it came served on. So it wasn't all that surprising that Claudia thought her skin was ugly. I was one of those people turning slowly on that spit, aiming for and achieving that even brown—a fact that I've had plenty of opportunity of late to rue; Claudia, who went from white to painful pink and then right back to white again, who laughed at herself in a bathing suit, wasn't. Still, even in those days of raging tan worship, I noticed her skin, and I don't think it was just me; it wasn't just some latent Japanese adulation of white skin that made me remark on it.

As I sit at the counter of her cluttered, comfortable kitchen, lazily nibbling on cashews while she tosses odds and ends, peas and pineapple and even peanuts ("It's going to be a p-curry," she says, "made up of foods beginning with the letter p—I wish I had a pumpkin too"), from her refrigerator into the wok, I realize that it all comes down to the transparency of her skin in the end. That, and those big gray eyes. They are the reason she has such an enormously expressive face, the reason the emotions flit across it like block letters formed by a child's hand—large, clear, and so nakedly readable I want to cover her face, hold a red and orange striped dish towel over it so only a trusted few can see.

IT WAS ALMOST ALWAYS the other way. I talked, she listened. Before I met Claudia, I never thought about whether my life was eventful or not. Some time after that fateful encounter, I came with some regret to the conclusion that I had a streak of drama queen in me. What passed between us wasn't just the stories, some complete fantasy and the others less so, about Japan and my mother that Claudia always wanted to hear, but also the ones that were harder to tell and, surely, harder to hear—about the death of my father, say.

She is older than me by just five months. But if we go by the somewhat suspect proposition that the quantity of time logged on this earth is a measure of who is more grown-up, and by yet another proposition, equally if not more suspect, that the more grown-up should look after the less so, then it might just as well have been five years, or fifty. Or at least it felt like that back in the good old days, when we were all part of one family. It was always she who took care of me.

My first day at her school, for instance, when I was, finally, on my way home, and a circle of girls surrounded me: "Chinese, Japanese, squinty eyes, dirty knees..." Does Claudia remember the fight she got into? Probably, almost certainly, even though it was more than a quarter of a century ago, even though we never did speak of it afterward. It's not the kind of thing one forgets.

Given this history, it feels good to be able to do something for her for a change. Even if that something is, paradoxically enough, not doing: not moving anything more than my lips, upward, as she talks, not allowing anything more than an occasional hmm and an uh-huh to escape from my throat.

Bite your tongue, Rosie used to say, whenever Claudia and I swore. I had never heard that expression before, and so the first time I heard it I thought, What a strange woman Claudia has for her mom. But I liked her, curious and unsmiling though she seemed, the woman Henry had once been married to, and so I tried to do what she said, biting down so hard that tears came to my eyes, and Claudia asked, Why are you making such a funny face; are the cookies I made so bad?

Perhaps today, as on that day so many years ago, if I open my mouth as I stand in front of a mirror, I will discover that I have two tiny red marks on the tip of my tongue.

Because she deserves to have this evening; she deserves to relive every delicious detail (her story as tasty as her p-curry, whipped up with her own special touch) in her own recounting and reimagining of it, like any other girl in love. And because scolding wouldn't serve any point. Claudia has been scolding herself, and far worse, for a long time now, for easily as long as she has been with Vikrum. That, too, is written in a child's block letters on her face.

SHE NOTICED HIS BICYCLE FIRST. In retrospect, she may have even fallen in love with it first; at the very least, it greased her later headlong descent into that state. She was locking up her own bike and saw that there was only one other bicycle locked up outside the post office, which was not surprising since the sleet had only recently started to lessen. It was February, and cold and wet.

("Are you still riding . . . ?" I ask hesitantly, unwilling to bring up a potentially painful subject.

"What do you think? You didn't really think I'd trade her in, did you?" she asks, her eyes wide with horror that is only partly mock, and I'm overcome with mortification that I asked such a question. I quickly but only partly effectively reassure her: I thought maybe Stella had broken down, or been stolen—never, ever traded.)

Stella is Claudia's old gearless bicycle, a hand-me-down from Henry. Seventeen years ago, it was so old that it was impossible to tell whether it was black by virtue of paint or age or rust, but it worked well enough. And, too (Claudia reminds me now), it's so heavy it's difficult to steal. Actually, I'm thinking, if the bike thieves do leave it alone, what's at issue is probably not Stella's weight, impressive though it is: after all, the old bat does come with wheels. But I keep my mouth shut, for I don't want to impede the flow of her story, and, besides, what do I know from the bike thieves of Boston? From what I can gather, they're like the New York thieves, a none-too-picky group.

The other bicycle parked outside the post office was like hers, black and upright, ancient and so rusted that at first she thought it was abandoned. But then Claudia noticed that it was locked up with a heavy chain and lock, the almost-thief-proof kind that she herself had. In the midst of scooping the rice onto plates, she turns to me for emphasis as she recounts this last detail, her face lit up with a smile, and it takes me a second to realize that her glow comes from pride, and the pride from the fact that her lover is— can you believe her luck?—a man who treasures his old bicycle.

I can see my stepsister taking a moment out to nod approvingly at the well-locked old bicycle outside the post office, her uncovered head cold and wet in the sleet. I can picture her shaking her raincoat out with care so that she will not further contribute to the spread of the doubtlessly already treacherous puddles on the floor of the post office. I imagine the way she tries to smooth her matted hair out before giving up with a shrug, how she hikes her knapsack, heavy with books for teaching, higher on her back, and how her head is bent forward as she slowly makes her way up the ramp toward the door.

IT WAS A SATURDAY, middle of the afternoon, a busy time at the South Station post office. Standing at the end of the line, her birthday package for her father (a wool hat and two mysteries) tucked tightly under her arm, Claudia was lost in cataloging her to-do list for that day and so did not notice for some time the hands of the man standing a little way up in front of her.

There was no particular reason she should have. The room was filled with people, and he was not one to stand out in a crowd ("Not that he's bad-looking," adds Claudia to me hastily, "not in the least"). A dark-skinned, South Asian man, he was on the tall side but not unusually so. He was dressed in dark and quiet clothes, a black leather bag slung over his shoulders, and he wore a pair of large glasses that were patched together on one side with Scotch tape. A graduate student, probably; there are so many in the Boston area. Perhaps he was a man who had traveled a great distance to pursue his passion—in philosophy, maybe, or classics; religion as an outside chance—in this red-brick university town.

This man was one of the few in the room engaged in lively conversation; an old man standing just behind him was chattering away to him about what Claudia thought was his dog, or was that his wife? They talked together using the large gestures and the hyperclear enunciation that signified a first encounter. But the conversation itself was also not why Claudia noticed the young magician: he wasn't actually talking himself, his role in the dialogue that of listener only. (Once she did take notice, though, Claudia was impressed with the way the student held up his end of the conversation. He listened in a way that went beyond courtesy; tilting forward a little toward the old man, his gaze fixed upon him, the student seemed genuinely interested and even absorbed in this man that he seemed to have just met.)

No, what made Claudia notice this young man was that his hands were busy, incessantly so. He pulled a red bandanna through his fingers, back and forth, and this is what made Claudia blink and take notice—as he did so the bandanna vanished, then reappeared, vanished and reappeared.

Abracadabra, eye of newt, toe of frog.

Five more minutes in line, five more minutes of steady, almost hypnotically rhythmic vanishing and reappearing of the bandanna. And then the conversation between the two men began to change. The magician began to talk, and because his voice was unexpectedly loud, carrying easily in the cavernous space of the room, Claudia could without difficulty overhear what he said. Yes, I'm married, with two children, a boy and a girl. Ages two and four. Actually, I do have pictures (and with those words, he stuffed the bandanna unceremoniously into his jacket pocket and began rooting around in his bag), right here.

That's my daughter and my son. No, she's the handful—he's actually an angel. Oh, do you think she looks good? My wife—her name is Lakshmi—doesn't like that picture of herself, but I don't think it's so bad. . . . Yes, I did take it myself, thank you, right in our backyard. I'm pretty proud of the shot.

The magician was smiling now, animated and lively; other people standing in line began to turn toward him and ask him questions, their faces reflecting his smile, their voices catching some of the excitement in his. Claudia had half a mind to reach for the pictures herself—what was it about this man?—but there were now three people exclaiming over them and another four waiting their turn. Instead, she turned away. Watching him, she had pegged him as an adventurer or a scholar. A wizard. She tried but could not help feeling crushed (and at this point in the story Claudia begins to laugh, disappointed in herself as much as in this not-so-mysterious man) that his accent was as banal, completely standard-issue American, as the words he uttered.

Still, of course, his pride in his young family was sweet. She had no problem there; she was not, of course, jealous. Of course.

Because Claudia was in love herself, and very happily, thank-you-very-much. For two years and counting, with Doug Foreman, a very nice man, once a teacher like herself and now the principal, no less, at the public school she worked in. Doug, with his honest face and large, flat hands ("farmer's hands, peasant's hands," he'd always said), who had grown up in Pennsylvania, just over the border from New Jersey, a mere half hour from Claudia's own hometown. Doug had gone to Brown, too, two years ahead of her; they had taken a number of the same courses, almost but never quite at the same time.

People said that it was a wonder she and Doug had not met earlier. They themselves said that it was not a wonder but, rather, the strange workings of destiny conspiring in their favor that didn't allow them to meet until two and a half years ago—when they were in their thirties, ready for love, ready for each other—on Claudia's first day at Parker School.

WHEN HENRY GOT SICK, Claudia tells me now, she didn't have nightmares about losing her father. Instead, she dreamed regularly of walking out into the bright sunshine and seeing only rows and rows of new, brightly colored bikes. If she were lucky, she woke up after finding her lock chewed cleanly through, as if it had been rope rather than metal, and the bike gone; if she were not, her dream would continue with her roaming the streets of Boston, calling out for Stella (yup, just like Marlon Brando, she says, nodding, beating me to it), peering into dark alleys as if for a lost cat.

Yet when she stepped out of the post office that day, it was without a sense of outrage that she noted the young family man leaning over her bicycle, tinkering with her lock.

"Excuse me," said Claudia, trembling a little; the wind was bitter. "I think that's my bicycle."

He looked up. The lenses of his glasses were lightly splattered with sleet, and the Scotch tape on the frame was peeling in the damp; behind them his eyes were very dark. For a second he stared at her.

"Oh, so that's why my key isn't working," he said. His words may have been rueful but he spoke with an easy confidence. "That's my ride over there." He nodded his head over at the other old bicycle, on the other side of the rack. He didn't even have the grace to look embarrassed, smiling instead, trying hard, Claudia thought (too hard, annoyingly hard), to be charming; his lips were turned upward in a smirk rather than a smile. "I wasn't trying to take your bike, of course."

"Of course," she repeated, tight-lipped but still Claudia, polite as ever.

"They look alike, no?"

At this her eyebrows, already arched by this point, shot up further still on her forehead. She spoke with uncharacteristic crispness: Stella, it needs to be remembered, is an heirloom. "If you know nothing about bicycles, yes, they do."

His smile, she noted with a burst of pleasure so sharp she could almost taste it (for Claudia, this was more than uncharacteristic, it was downright bizarre—how disappointed in him had she been?), slipped off his face like melting slush. He opened his mouth—to apologize or placate, perhaps; already she knew this young man well enough to guess that he was not about to retort—and then, looking away, closed it.

A gust of wind, and with it an extra scattering of sleet. Claudia involuntarily shuddered. She thought it was the cold but was not sure, because just as the wind blew, two facts of overriding importance had suddenly become clear in her mind: first, that she hated to see this man that she had just met looking like this, and second, that she would do anything to call a smile—so what if it was closer to a smirk?—onto his face once again. ("In retrospect, it was a historic moment," she says to me dryly. She scrapes the jalapeño peppers she has just minced off the cutting board and into the wok, then stands on tiptoe to retrieve the curry powder from the cabinet above her head. "The establishment of a lifelong pattern: he pouts, I die.")

"Never mind about the bike," she said. She extended a gloved hand and smiled; doubtlessly she flushed as well, the high color rushing into her face and transforming it. "I'm Claudia; it's good to meet you, even under these circumstances."

He took her hand, clasped and held it briefly. "Vikrum," he said.

"So are you a magician?" she asked. "I saw you with that handkerchief in there...."

He threw her a quick sideways glance. "A magician? I wouldn't say that, no."

Claudia waited. The wind no longer seemed as biting, her to-do list for that day not as long.

"I just—how should I put it?—have a talent, a small one, for finding things. Unfortunately, my gift doesn't seem to extend to my own possessions." Here he nodded at his bicycle. "But I do okay with other people's stuff. For example..." Taking his bare hand out of his pocket, he reached down and ran a finger beneath her bicycle bell (where were his gloves?—she felt an urge, suddenly, to scold him for forgetting them; as if he were one of her students, she wanted to hold his hands between her own and to rub them and so make them warm) and then plucked out a quarter, shining and new. "Aha. So that's why you like your bicycle so much. The goose that lays the golden eggs. Look, there's more." He fished out another from one of the tassels that hung down, matted and bedraggled as Claudia's hair, from Stella's handles. "Fertile little bird, isn't she?"

Then the man held the quarters out to Claudia on his palm.

"You should keep them," she said, shaking her head. "Not to put down your considerable talents, but I understand it's been a rough year for magicians, and—"

"It's okay," he said, smiling kindly. "I have a day job."

She peered at him doubtfully. Her feet were getting cold.

"I do," he said, seeming to read her silence correctly as skepticism. "Really. I'm a neurobiologist." Then, as her silence continued: "I'm presently working on the theory that the human race originated from one common sex. Because why else, really, would men have nipples?"

Claudia flicked him a look filled with only thinly veiled suspicion. Was he a liar, a creep (the reference to nipples), or, even worse (after all, she's Henry's and, especially, Rosie's daughter, brought up to prize rigor of thought), a real scientist who spewed crackpot theories? Then, abruptly, she gave in. "I always thought men had nipples so they could pierce them," she said. "But what do I know? I'm just an elementary-school teacher."

Vikrum looked at her for a second, and then he laughed. He had a full-throated laugh, terribly pleasant to listen to (thought Claudia, who had completely forgotten about her feet), and deep. When he stopped, he said, "I should tell you that I'm lying. I am a biologist, but I'm not working on that theory. Although I did think, until I heard yours, that it's probably right. I clone. Genes, not sheep." He looked closely at her, and smiled. "Just so you don't think I'm a crank," he added.

"I see," said Claudia. "Well, I should be off."

"Don't forget your quarters," he said.

She looked down at the coins, hesitating.

"They came out of your bike, didn't they?" Vikrum said. "Oh, wait, I'm sorry—maybe that came out of mine. You'll have to forgive me. As I've been told by a very reliable authority, when it comes to ascertaining the ownership of bicycles, my judgment is severely impaired."

Trying not to smile, Claudia took the coins and pocketed them. "Thank you."

"You're welcome," he said.

"I DON'T KNOW IF you realize it," Claudia says to me, pausing in her story, "since you just moved here. But the meters in Boston only take quarters. And same with the washing machines in my building."

"Ah," I say. "Light dawns. You got together with Vikrum for reasons pertaining to personal hygiene."

Dinner is ready. Claudia walks carefully to the table, two steaming plates of p-curry balanced in her hands. Placing the larger portion in front of me, she looks up, her eyes grave.

"That's not fair," she says. "The parking meters were important too. I am a law-abiding citizen."

IT WAS COLD ENOUGH that she could see her own breath when she talked. She could not see his, and she wondered if that, too, was a magician's trick.

"I teach second grade. At Parker," she said. "Maybe you can come in one day and perform for my class."

"Maybe I can," he said.

She asked if he had a card; he nodded and gave it to her. She said she would be in touch.

"I'll look forward to it," he said.

IT IS AT THIS POINT that the story shifts.

Claudia picks up our plates and carries them back into the

kitchen. She tilts one above the garbage can and scrapes it with her fork, places it in the sink. Then the same to the other.

Up until this point, the story has been a treat for Claudia and me alike, sweet and savory all at once, something for us both to smack our lips over and take in with joy. At this moment it changes into something else altogether—or is it that I only become aware now what it was all along?—a story that's hard enough to get lodged in the throat, and bitter besides; a narrative that has nothing to do with pleasure.

What Claudia is giving me now isn't an excuse, exactly. It would probably be best described as a plea for understanding. An attempt to explain how it came about that she, Claudia Klein—a girl who tried but could never bring herself to forgive her stepmother for breaking up her parents' marriage, a girl who always believed in the sanctity of marriage and vows as if she were a refugee from a simpler time—took the first halting steps toward embarking upon that oldest of clichés, an affair with a married man.

The main course over, Claudia puts the kettle on. She takes a pint of ice cream, an old favorite, rocky road, out of the freezer and begins scooping it into beautiful blue bowls that I recognize: my mother gave them to her for Christmas, more than twenty years ago. Back then, Claudia kept them shut in a box that she never opened.

THE SLEET HAD ALMOST completely stopped, yet the wind was still sharp. Claudia took her time unlocking her bicycle so she could watch Vikrum as he wheeled his bike out, swung his leg over it, and pedaled away. He was slow with his lock too. As he left, he turned to wave at her, twice.

Shivering in the cold, she stood and watched him go. She would be friends with this man, she told herself, why not? She could do with a friend like that. Heck, she *needed* a friend like that; she had been looking for someone who rode an old bicycle and who could pull quarters (remember her overflowing hamper, remember those two parking tickets she had gotten just last week), shining and sparkling new, out of the sleet and fog.

Chapter Thirteen

"WHEN MY MOTHER FIRST MOVED TO AMERICA," BEGAN the story that Rei most liked to tell her stepsister, "she carried a *daikon*, a Japanese radish, with her in her purse." Hana called it a purse, but it was for all intents and purposes a carry-on bag, designed to hold far more than a wallet and sundries. Still, capacious though it was, the purse was overstuffed, and so it did not quite accommodate the *daikon*, which was huge— long and white, and of a giggle-inducing phallic shape.

The tip of the radish poked out like an overweight hitchhiker's thumb from a corner of the purse. The vulnerability of that exposed tip, combined with her sense that this was in all probability the last *daikon* she would see in years, made Hana reluctant to let the purse out of her sight even for an instant, so that even though the journey was to last for more than twenty hours all told, she woke herself with a nervous start whenever she began to nod off, and she could only bring herself to flip through the pages of the English dictionary she had bought at Haneda Airport with the purse tucked firmly under her arm. When her dinner was served to her, she insisted on keeping her bag on her lap, even though the red-haired woman who brought it gestured that she should put it away, even though it meant that Hana had to sit in a very cramped position.

It also meant that she could only see what was on her dinner tray by craning her neck, but that didn't matter: after taking one look at the chicken on her tray and then, even more unfortunately, getting one whiff of it, Hana realized that her purse could in certain circumstances be a useful obstacle. The one bite of iceberg lettuce that she had—where was her usually healthy appetite? gone along with her hitherto unflappable stomach—she had managed to spear on her fork only by dint of luck and guesswork.

Taking her purse to the bathroom would usually have been accomplished with a minimum of fuss. Indeed, given that it held her wallet and passport, the argument could be made that it was the more prudent course of action. Yet this simple act was made incalculably less so by the fact that Hana had to go often to the bathroom, because she, a first-time flyer, was sick to the stomach. Her bag was, furthermore, loaded with books and paints as well as with the *daikon*. Still, she hoisted the bag up on her shoulder every time, excuse-me'd her way past the none-too-patient passenger seated on her right, and trudged as quickly as possible down the narrow aisle, hurrying to beat the rise of gorge in her throat, with the bottom of the bag banging against her side. A day later, resting in the disappointingly shallow bath of her new home, she would discover bruises all along her left hip.

She always made it to the bathroom in time, although it was very close more than once. Squatting on the floor after gagging into the metal toilet, Hana looked up at the *daikon* tip, cheekily begging for a ride from the depths of her conservative black bag, and felt comforted.

The *daikon* was a present for Seiji, her husband of fifty-one days, who flew out to America two weeks ahead of her. In the only phone conversation that they had since then, he had yelled to tell her over the static that he liked their new home, the bottom floor of a brownstone in beautiful, red-bricked Boston, and she had felt a chill reminiscent of a fever's creep over her as she listened to his tinny voice, so many thousands of miles away: who was this man she had married, how could she have thought she knew him at all? She had chosen him based on a chance encounter, a moment of heat that had passed between them in a crowd. From something tense and alert in his stance as he walked toward her, she had thought he seemed dangerous, a rebel of some kind, so that when she met him and it turned out he had a job at a local bank, she had felt herself inwardly sigh.

Given that she had misjudged him so badly at first, she could not expect anything different now. And she would receive help and solace from no one. She knew nobody in America other than this stranger, her husband. Her family was unimaginably far away—she had craned her neck over the kind woman on her left to watch Tokyo turn into a toy town and then vanish in a swirl of ultramarine blue—her aunt Sachiko even quieter than usual, her mother perhaps even now drying her tears and getting on with her life in the wake of the departure of her oldest daughter.

Sitting in the plane, the feverish chill (or was that another bout of nausea? Never again, she vowed, would she set foot on a plane; she would swim back to Japan when it was time) creeping over her again, Hana gripped her purse handles tight. She had packed Seiji a number of presents, chocolates and gourmet crackers and a new shirt and even a few books, but it was within her purse that her salvation was contained. Grated *daikon* ranked number one on the list of Seiji's favorite foods, and by carefully grilling him in the days before his departure, Hana had ascertained that the pale radish was not a commodity easily come by in America, exotic land of hamburgers and hot dogs rather than of fish, of pasta and bread rather than of rice. Her plan was simple but infallible; her body might be failing her but her mind was clear and strong. She would smooth her husband's hair back and grate the *daikon* into clouds flavored with soy sauce. She would feed it to him by the sweet spoonful and so cure her marriage, fifty-one days young and already ailing.

IT WAS NOT UNTIL HANA was standing in line at border control, her legs cramped and her head light from the long sleepless journey, her hands trembling with what she hoped was fatigue but suspected was anxiety (what if he were late to the airport, what if she failed to recognize her own husband?), that the possibility even occurred to her that she might not be allowed to carry the radish with her into this strange new world. She unwound one end of her wool scarf—it was September, and still warm out, but she had taken Seiji's warnings about the cold New England winters to heart—from her neck and placed it over her bag, covering the tip of the *daikon*.

The customs official was a white man, tiny, blue-eyed, and elderly. He stood with his arms folded as he watched the people stream by. Years later, when telling this story to her children, Hana would always laugh at this point, pointing out how she did everything wrong. She tried to move to the edge of the crowd farthest away from him; dragging her suitcases beside her ("and this was before they started making suitcases with wheels," she would remind her daughters), she walked as quickly as she possibly could without actually running, her eyes on the floor.

When the customs official called out, "You there," her head

jerked. She turned slowly, her breath coming fast and shallow, and saw that he was beckoning to her with his finger. She picked up her suitcases and dragged them over to his side. When he held his hand out for her papers, she passed them over to him. He examined her visa and asked her if she really intended to stay in the country for two years. She nodded and he stared hard, eyes narrowed, at her.

Then he pointed to her purse. "What's in there?" he said.

She gazed back at him. Almost delirious with exhaustion, she wondered how old he was: she was not sure if she had ever seen hair so white before, and she was certain that she had never seen white hair over such a relatively unwrinkled face. He was just about eye level with her; she had not known that American men could be so small. She knew he was waiting for a response but found she could neither nod nor shake her head, let alone speak. On her way out of the plane, she had passed by and bowed her thanks to the tall blond pilot, but she had never actually spoken to a white man.

He sighed. He had a slight tic over his left eye. "Empty it," he said.

She was sweating in her winter coat with the scarf looped around her neck. She unzipped her purse and pulled out from it one end of her scarf, the *daikon*, her books, her paints and her wallet. She tried to cover the radish with her scarf, but the official was too quick.

"What's this?" he asked, pointing.

Short though he was, the man in front of her terrified her. Still, she was determined not to cry. She stood up straighter. "*Daikon*," she said.

Accustomed, no doubt, to hearing a vast array of foreign words, he nodded. Then he picked up the radish and put it on the table to his left. "Now open those," he said, gesturing at her suitcases.

Hana wanted to ask what would happen to the *daikon*, whether she would perhaps even be able to take it back and stow it away in her purse now, but she obediently bent her head down. She heaved up one suitcase onto the metal counter and unzipped it. Then she did the same with the other.

The official removed her clothes, neatly folded and pressed, onto the counter. He searched the pockets of her skirts; he checked the lining of her jackets. When he dug toward the bottom of the suitcase, a dozen pairs of socks, each neatly folded into a ball, tumbled onto the floor. He stood, waiting, while she stooped down and gathered the socks onto the counter. After she was finished, he took apart each pair and turned them inside out. He picked through her underwear and riffled through the contents of her books; he uncapped her toothpaste and peered into it. Then he checked her other suitcase. Nothing contained inside it, even the package of gourmet crackers, elicited a reaction from him.

When he finished, he stepped back and nodded. "You can go."

With a hand that shook just a little, Hana pointed at the *daikon*, which was still on the table to the official's left. "Preeze," she said, her voice a croak.

The official was once again watching the travelers streaming through the gates; he did not turn around.

She cleared her throat, and tried again. "Preeze," she said again, more loudly.

When he turned, Hana noticed that the tic over his eye had grown more pronounced. "I could have you deported," he said. His voice was lower but at the same time more piercing; out of the corner of her eye she saw a few travelers, as well as another customs official, swivel their heads in their direction, then just as quickly swivel them away. "Do you want to be deported?"

Hana did not yet know the word *deported*, but the way the official hissed it out made her shrink back and guess at its import. The next day, after Seiji left for work, she would look up the word in the English dictionary she had bought in the airport in Japan. She would first underline the entry and then cross it out, striking it again and again, so that when her American-born daughters leafed through the dictionary in the years to come, they would come across an ink-dark spot where the word should be.

Struggling not to cry, Hana zipped up her suitcases and lifted them off the counter onto the floor. Then she bent down and began dragging her suitcases toward the double doors, beyond which lay the country where she would spend the greater part of her life.*

THERE WAS WHAT SEEMED to be a horde of people standing beyond the doors. Hana heard a cacophony of voices, most in languages she could not even identify. For a second she stood straight up, her back uncoiling and stretching, her head lifting and her hands dangling down empty above the suitcases, as she looked around the large hall.

She recognized him right away. He was standing toward the back of the crowd, and his dark clothes caused him to blend into the background. When she saw him he was looking down at his watch, wondering, perhaps, why she had not been among the other passengers who came off her flight. But even though his face was not visible to her, she had found him; what's more, she knew that even if his clothes had been darker, and he even farther back in the crowd, she still would have known him right away. Her realization of this simple fact was like a jolt of energy, like three meals and a restful night's sleep in a bed all rolled into one. She picked up all three of her bags and lifted them, stuffed full with books and paints and clothes, lightly in the air ("Who needs wheels on their suitcases?" she would say at this point, smiling a little wistfully, when she told this story to her daughters) and ran toward her husband.

She jumped into his arms, her suitcases having miraculously dropped clear, and then they were laughing and talking all at once.

His arm was around her, propping her up—a delicious sensation, as if she were floating, or was that light-headedness again? Being with Seiji again was as easy and natural as slipping back into her mother tongue, and a part of Hana wanted to cry at her treachery in having thought that it would be anything else.

Finally Seiji said that they should get going; why stand around in an airport when they could be in their own new home? Hana hesitated, then looked up at him. "I, I—well, I want you to know that I brought something special for you," she said, the words falling and scattering around them like her socks, "but—"

Seiji stooped, letting go of her shoulders in the process (the loss of the warmth of his arm, temporary though it was, overdressed though she was with her scarf and her big coat, making her shiver inside), and picked up a bag that he had laid at his feet. "I brought something for you too," he said, more shyly than she would have thought possible.

She looked down. Poking out rudely from the bag in his hand was a white tip resembling an overweight hitchhiker's thumb.

Now Seiji's words came scattering out as well. "When we were back in Tokyo, you asked me so many times about whether it was available here that I knew you were worried that you'd miss it. So I went to an Asian food store and badgered them until they managed to track one down. They said it was really hard to get. I'm sorry, it might be the last one you'll see for the two years that we'll be here, and it's not even such a good one, a little bruised, maybe, and not large . . ."

His long speech had given Hana the time she needed to reel her jaw back in from where it had been hanging. "Thank you," she said, accepting the gift in the prescribed Japanese manner, with both hands. "It's the perfect gift, exactly what I wanted." With that, she burst into tears, great hiccuping sobs that threatened to engulf both of them. She did not stop bawling for many minutes, despite the restoration of the warmth of her husband's arm around her shoulders, despite his concerned face, his soothing words.

Later, in the car (the steering wheel on the wrong side, the seats almost impossibly roomy), she explained to him how exhausted she was from her trip, how overexcited she had been from the prospect of seeing him again. "And I think"—she arched her back in a burst of well-being, because she was suddenly sure—"I'm pregnant."

It was worth the long journey, the homesickness she had already developed, the nausea, and even the customs official to see Seiji turn to her in surprise, and then slowly smile.

IN HANA'S TELLING OF IT, this story was a classic O. Henry, even to its end: and then the happy couple went home, grated the *daikon* together, and ate it side by side. She meant for Seiji to eat most of it, since it was his favorite food, yet it turned out to be her first craving in a pregnancy filled with not many others, and so she consumed by far the larger share of it, he watching and nodding approvingly as she swallowed it down.

But in Rei and Claudia's analysis of the story, the O. Henry quality of it was sullied by a fact that got lightly overlooked in Hana's version—that throughout their all-too-brief marriage, Hana never told her husband that their reunion in America should have involved not one *daikon*, but two. She never described to him how carefully she had guarded a gift for him throughout the journey; she never told him of the almost magical import she had placed on it, and how abruptly it had been taken from her by the first white man she ever met.

Rei and Claudia tried but they never could figure out why, exactly, this aspect of the story made it so poignant to them. Did it have to do with the burden that Hana had to shoulder too long by herself, as if her own isolation in her new country made the callousness of the customs official that much more difficult to bear? Or did it have to do with the limitations of even the most happy of marriages; was it the idea that secrets were held, and half-truths told, even in this, a relationship they deemed well-nigh perfect?

Chapter Fourteen

Claudia
Boston, 1999

I SPOT THEM RIGHT AWAY, FROM SO FAR A DISTANCE THAT it should by all rights be an impossibility. They are in a playground, after all, a space where clusters of one figure surrounded by a couple of shorter ones are the norm. Since I am coming from the east at four in the afternoon, moreover, the light shed by the sun setting behind them has turned the entire crowd into dark silhouettes. Finally, there is the fact that Vikrum is not particularly striking in terms of his shape.

Still, I know every line of his body and every gesture that he makes, and I have imagined his children (his daughter, age six, short, frizzy-haired, and dark-skinned, and his son, four, the very image of his father) for so long that I probably could have spotted them with my eyes closed and a hill lying between us.

They are in the middle of what appears to be a family conference, Vikrum counseling or reasoning with his daughter as his son watches from the side. Her hair tamed into two long braids, Padma stands facing Vikrum, her feet planted firmly apart. Her stance looks confrontational, but then she rushes toward him and melts into his body, reaching her arms up to wind them around his stomach.

It is on the cool side, a few degrees short of apple-picking weather, but I am beginning to sweat. I should not be feeling this way, flushed, dizzy, and a little ill—I knew, or at least I thought I knew, that Vikrum was a good father, much loved by his children.

But then again, I am clearly having trouble with the concept that Vikrum is a father at all.

That Raja does not look as much like Vikrum as I had been led to expect seems at first to be one small consolation. His hair is curly, his face round, and his skin almost as dark as his sister's. Yet that consolation proves to be hollow, for when Raja looks up, I see that he has Vikrum's eyes. I am in trouble: if I look too long at those familiar eyes set in that unfamiliar face, I will cry, or worse—snatch him up and carry him away, maybe, either to keep him for myself or to stash him somewhere secret that Vikrum cannot get to, I am not sure which.

Perhaps (it occurs to me now, and not for the first time) I should just keep on walking. It is enough to see them like this, a family.

Indeed, it might very well be more than enough.

Still, I have come this far. There is little point in turning back now.

"VIKRUM?" I SAY, shading my eyes with one hand. "Vikrum, is that you?"

He turns, looks around, focuses on me, smiles. "Oh, hello."

So far, so good. But then I stick my hand out, and after a moment's hesitation he is taking it in his and pumping it up and down.

It's nerves, of course, and even though I am the one who wanted

this rendezvous, even though I know that these are the only condi-
tions under which this meeting is possible, it's also my discomfort
with acting out a lie. Vikrum and I have orchestrated this event
carefully and rehearsed it a dozen times—the accidental encounter; the polite, restrained greeting, as befitting two people
who are acquaintances, and that just barely; the introduction of
the children almost as an afterthought; the quick-without-being-
hurried farewell, instigated by me.

The handshake was never part of the plan, and it almost proves
our undoing.

"How do you know my daddy?" asks the girl attached to his hip,
wrinkling her nose at me. "Do you clone too?"

Standing a little to the side of his assertive sister, the little boy
looks at the ground.

"No, I don't," I say, wrinkling my nose as well, but she gazes un-
smilingly back.

Uncoiling herself from her father, she takes a step toward me.
"So how do you know him, then?" she says, folding her arms and
looking at me and then at Vikrum, and then back at me again.

We are caught, fair and square. When we shook hands, Vikrum
and I had held on to each other a millisecond too long. Our clasp
had been a little too tight, our gaze, a fraction too intimate.

Most six-year-old girls would not have noticed. But her size
notwithstanding, Padma does not seem anything like six—sharp-
eyed and poised, she would not be out of place among the sixteen-
year-olds that my colleagues at school struggle to connect with
and teach.

"Padma," begins Vikrum, "don't you know you shouldn't be
asking—"

Ignoring him, I bend down and begin tying the laces on my boots.

"You're stepping on something," I say to Padma.

"No, I'm not," she says, without looking down.

"Move your right foot and see."

One grudging foot tap. "I told you there's nothing."

I wave a hand over her kneecap. "Now try again."

This time there is a quarter, a little dented and none too shiny, peeking out from under one small sneaker-clad foot.

"Hmph," she says. Her arms are still folded.

Raja casts a quick sidelong glance at his sister's feet, and then drops his gaze back to his own.

"So that's how you know Dad?" asks Padma. "Because you're a magician too?"

"I'm hardly a magician. I'm just starting to learn," I protest, which only in itself is not really a lie.

"*I'll* say," she pipes in. "That wasn't bad, but you need a *lot* more practice."

"Padma," says Vikrum again, but now there is a hint of laughter in his voice.

"Here, I'll show you," she says grandly. Stooping down, she scoops up the coin in one small hand, tosses it in the air, catches it, holds it up so that it catches the light. And then the coin is gone.

"Did you just make my lucky quarter vanish?" I say. "Where'd you put it? Is it here?" I lift her hair and check her right ear.

A six-year-old after all, she begins to giggle and then, when I poke her in the ribs and the belly ("Did you swallow it; do you think you can keep it in your tummy for safekeeping?"), she bursts into gales of musical laughter.

She is Vikrum's firstborn. When he held her in his arms the very first time, he was terrified to think that he had brought someone so tiny and helpless into the world.

"Paaaadmaaaa," comes a voice from the swings.

My lover's daughter turns, her braids swinging out around her head. "Coming," she says, singsong, and then she begins to run toward her friend, almost knocking her brother over in the process.

"Padma," Vikrum hollers, "aren't you going to give the coin back to the nice lady?"

But she is already gone.

"Don't worry about it," I say to him, shaking my head.

Vikrum smiles apologetically, and then there is a short, awkward pause.

"Well, it was fun running into you like this," he says at last. While the dismissal that is contained in his words makes me wince a little, he is right to issue it: I have already stayed far longer than is prudent. He places his hands on his son's shoulders. "This, by the way, is Raja."

"Hello, Raja," I say, squatting down. "I'm Claudia. Nice to meet you."

He smells like chocolate, milk, and pee. It is dangerous for me to be so close to him, and I am about to turn and flee when he thrusts a chubby hand out to me.

I put out my hand and place it around his. When I withdraw it there is a keepsake, dented, warm, and a little moist, nestled inside my palm.

"Thank you," I say, with all the gravity that his offering is due. I pocket my gift and stand.

He inclines his head in what might be a nod and wheels around. There is a swirl of dust, and then he, too, is gone.

Vikrum turns his head toward his children, and smiles and waves. "I'll be there in a second," he calls out. Turning back to me, he speaks quickly and quietly. "He really liked you." Not only do his eyes have the almond shape, the rich brown color, and the liquid shine of his son's, they wear the same expression—weary and sad beyond their owner's years. "They both did. It's just that he hardly ever talks these days."

With that, I have to leave. But the conversation about his son would be over anyway, because there is nothing more to say. Even if we had more time and more privacy, Vikrum would not attempt to solicit my professional opinion on what it means when a four-year-old child stops talking almost completely, for the simple reason that he does not have to.

He knows, just as well as I do, that Raja is exhibiting completely normal behavior for a boy with a mother with a drinking problem and a father who might love him but, what with the competing demands of work and a mistress, is not very often at home.

IT IS WHILE I AM WALKING HOME, the magic quarter clutched tightly in my fist, that I face up to the fact that I have been dodging for the good part of the last two years.

Never mind that she never gave birth to me, that we look nothing alike, and that I only lived with her during weekends for just eight years of my life. It does not even matter, perhaps even more unexpectedly, that I have hated her for much of my life for what she did to my mother and me.

I am my stepmother's daughter.

Chapter Fifteen

Rei

Boston, 1999

WE TAKE OUR FATHERING WHERE WE CAN FIND IT. DOES Henry, his speech slurred by the stroke, still love to play with words? I glance over at Claudia, trying to see if I can read the answer in her profile. It's the perfect time to ask her. She has been preoccupied today, still a bit shell-shocked, no doubt, by the encounter with her lover's children three days ago, but as we move through Cambridge at her leisurely pace on this gray afternoon, a silence as comfortable and companionable as an old sweater has wrapped itself around us. Yet in my quest for the answer to this particular question, her profile is as far as I go; I have to believe that Henry still plays his word games. The alternative—that he's unable to, or that those around him can't understand when he does, or even when he doesn't—is too unbearable to contemplate.

Back when Henry was my stepfather, picking up my

mother's accent on certain words gave him unending pleasure, "jet rag" and "flied lice" being his particular favorites. But what he most reveled in was scrambling like-sounding words. "Let's adjoin to the adjourning room," he'd say after supper, and "I'm ravishing, my ravenous one," to my mother before it, and when Kei and then Claudia began to date, "So will that imminent fellow of yours be arriving eminently?" making them blush and then glare. My mother didn't get the joke, such as it was, very often, but when she did, she would smile but also admonish. "You're going to confuse the children," she'd say, not bothering to add, because it didn't need to be said, "let alone me." And she was right. Even now I have to think carefully about whether my departure is imminent or (as I fear everyone considers it to be) eminent, whether the model in the magazine is ravishing or (the poor skinny girl!) ravenous.

Despite what might very well be a lifelong confusion over certain words in the English language, I wouldn't trade those years with Henry for anything. When Claudia and I were young, we spent so much time talking about my mother that we never really got around to discussing her dad. The few times he did come up in our conversations, I always referred to him as Henry. Claudia did the same; not once were the words *my father* spoken by her in my presence. A certain familiarity with a parent's first name might be one of the hallmarks of children who are close to their stepsiblings, but in Claudia's case it was just another of her many acts of generosity. By forfeiting her claim to sole proprietorship through those words, she allowed me to pretend with someone other than myself that he was mine too.

Rarely ruffled and apparently congenitally incapable of being hurried, Henry had a singular serenity about him. I used to think that it was his height (which seemed outlandish to me, a nine-year-old just back from a year in Japan, when I first met him) that accounted for his air of inner peace: it seemed to allow him to exist in another realm, high above our petty concerns.

Years ago, I once pointed out to Claudia the irony in the fact that Henry was a tall man who'd chosen to be a geologist, a profession that required him to examine rocks and the ground lying beneath our feet. She agreed, deadpan—"You're right! It'd make much more sense if he were an astronomer; someone should tell him, stat"—but I wasn't really joking, and I didn't consider full-time stargazing, for Henry, to be such an unlikely job. Geology always struck me as a curious career choice for him, a man who seemed so poorly grounded, as it were, in this world: a person who not only could not do his taxes but also kept his affairs in such poor disorder that it was up to his wife (my poor mother—lucky she was so organized, with a sharp businesswoman's head attached to that artist's eye and soul) to pull it all together for the accountant.

It wasn't until years later, when I was down at the bottom of the Grand Canyon on a steamy evening in late spring, that I realized that geology and Henry were in fact a perfect fit. My clothes covered in red dust and my legs aching from the steep climb down, I leaned into the long, lean figure of Max (an attraction to tall men and a fondness for wordplay the only legacy from eight years as Henry Klein's stepdaughter) and listened to a park ranger speak about the history of the canyon. The swirl of dark colors, no larger than a postage stamp, that had grown from a freckle on the palm of my left hand had not yet been diagnosed. The air was hot and almost unbearably still and heavy, but I felt unusually and almost strangely comfortable.

The ranger, a short, stocky woman who wore her uniform with visible pride, talked about continental drift, plates of land floating away from each other and then together again, colliding and ever so slowly swinging into something close to the positions in which we know them now. She told us how this unchoreographed, stately dance was responsible for the formation of mountain ranges, how when the plates bumped into each other, the land was pushed upward and boom! the Rockies, the Alps, and the Himalayas came into being. Right here at the bottom of the canyon (the ranger gestured, the sweep of her arm taking in us, the lodge, the woods, and the growing dark outside) are the roots of an old mountain range that was formed almost two billion years ago.

Then, she told us, came the layers of sediment and rock that were carried in by the sea. The earth's climate changed over time, and as its temperature warmed and then cooled, the caps of snow at the poles melted and then froze again, which led in turn to the rise and fall of the level of the sea. When the ocean rose so high that it washed over the land, it brought in limestone deposits, which also contained fossils of strange marine creatures—coral, sea lilies, fish teeth, worms, and mollusks. When it retreated, it left behind deposits of shale, mud, and slate. The ocean had been particularly busy, coming and going, in the area of the canyon, which is why it's made up of so many stripes of color, orange and red and brown and siena and even a shade of green, hues of such variety that I'd need to get my mother in to name all of them.

The ranger talked about how the mighty Colorado River, fed by the snow from the Rockies, chipped away over the centuries at the banks through which it flowed, cutting an increasingly deeper and wider path through the layers of stone. She described how dry the land became and explained that when heavy rain fell, as it did every year, the soil was too parched to absorb the water, which ran into the river and swelled it even further, producing floods that could and did dislodge boulders the size of elephants.

"And then there's the wind," the ranger said. "That plays a part in the erosion too. It's one of the reasons why we don't have any rock layers younger than 250 million years in the canyon. I know it feels real airless down here in the valley right now, but at the top, believe you me, it can blow."

A breeze blows, dust scatters, and one step is taken in a billion-year process.

The ranger ended by saying that the hundred-thousand-plus-pocket-change years that the human race had existed didn't even register in the timeline of the canyon, and that the billions of years that had gone into its formation were inevitably difficult for our minds to grasp. "Geologists work on such a vast scale, yesterday and today and next Thursday become completely meaningless categories," she said. "They have a completely different sense of time than the rest of us." She even had a term for this reconfigured sense, *deep time*, which made me fleetingly smile: in the family that I once had, we, too, had a term for an alternative approach to the passing of hours, *Henry time*, which almost invariably involved being too early or late for events.

How is it that over a span of eight years—not long enough a period to account for a layer of rock in the canyon, perhaps, but enough to formulate and submit a question, or even two—I never once asked Henry about his work? While he'd always been humble or at least quiet about the value of his work, especially in comparison to my mother's paintings, which he held in awe, that was hardly an excuse.

Sitting in the lodge at the bottom of the Grand Canyon, I leaned against my lover and missed my stepfather. The ranger had just asked if there were any questions, and while the audience stirred, I turned around, thinking that I would whisper to Max how I'd once been related to a geologist. I looked at him, the angular planes of his face thrown into relief by the light shining from the lamp on the table beside him, and knew then that he was going to leave me.

I had been wrong about Henry, believing him to be immune to the worries of our world by virtue of his six-foot-five frame. It was silly of me, really. He loved my mother so much that he wanted nothing more than to shoulder as many of her worries as he possibly could. What I had with Max was altogether different from what my mother had had, and had wasted, with Henry.

The next day I would wake up (at four, so we could beat the heat for the long climb back up the canyon) in Max's arms, and I would wonder what had been wrong with me to harbor such doubts about my long-term love. And in fact it would be another month—a month during which I'd learn that my next year would be filled with tests and treatments and retching and mornings in which I'd wake to find locks of my hair scattered on the pillow—before he left. Throughout those thirty days Max was a steady arm around my shoulders, so much so that I didn't allow myself to think that life would ever be anything but the two of us side by side.

But that evening in the valley of a canyon billions of years older than the human race, thinking back to the only father I can remember, I knew.

"I THOUGHT ABOUT YOUR MOTHER a lot," says Claudia abruptly, her words coming slow and heavy, large rocks up a steep incline, "in the days before I began sleeping with Vikrum."

With that, she stops talking. We are walking toward Harvard Square, and we go another three blocks, which means, at her pace, considerably more than a few minutes, in silence. I am just about to prompt her ever so carefully when she begins to speak again.

"Did you know that you don't have to teach babies how to walk?" she asks. "What's really incredible about it is not only that they can figure out how to stand and put one foot in front of another on their own, but that they *want* to figure out how to stand and put one foot in front of another on their own. They're born with the desire to learn to walk. They'll keep struggling by themselves, grunting away, until they succeed. And think about what it takes to succeed: balance, strength, the coordination of a large variety of muscles, knowing where you want to go and also that you want to go.

"Talking happens the same way. Just by listening, they'll pick up a language. Without even trying. And you know what kind of effort that takes for any regular adult, and how many years; you've studied a foreign language. Don't you think that's incredible? To think that just like that"—she snaps her fingers—"babies learn how to move the tongue and the lips, how to produce certain sounds and pitches and inflections, how to conjugate and pluralize and use irregular verbs and the subjunctive and the pluperfect, whatever the hell that is, and God knows what else. It must be the most amazing thing to watch."

This brief lecture on babies, arriving as it does apropos of exactly nothing, leaves me without much to say. I turn my head to the left and then to the right, looking for the inspiration to this commentary, but I can spy nothing to make me erase my belief that this commentary is a complete non sequitur.

"There," she says, pointing with her chin to a spot directly in front of us: the source of this outburst had been in my line of vision all along. Held in the arms of a curly-haired man, the baby is positioned so that we can just make out the upper half of its face.

"Right," I say. We trudge on.

Maternal, adjective. Of, relating to, belonging to, or characteristic of a mother: motherly. In the most recent version of the dictionary of my mind, this definition is accompanied by a picture of my stepsister, age thirty-four. But in the older versions of this lexicon, Claudia also figured in this definition; her picture was found beside it even when she was only nine, a child who could easily have been the object rather than the subject of the verb *to mother*.

Where does she—a teacher of small children, sure, but as childless as I am, and not even an aunt—collect all this information about babies? More importantly, why does she persist in doing so; why does she torture herself, collecting and brooding over information (like a miser, like a frustrated hen with borrowed eggs) that she cannot use?

And, finally, what does this all have to do with Vikrum and my mother, and do I really even want to find out?

PARTLY BECAUSE OF (and not, as one might be tempted to conclude, in spite of) her pronounced maternal qualities, Claudia has always enjoyed a solid and remarkably easy popularity with men. Remarkable to me, anyway, at least when we were fourteen. You're *too* interesting, she explained to me as she looped her hair into a high ponytail, saucy but also serviceable, before going out on yet another date. You're smart and you have a personality and, most of all, you're pretty in such a completely unusual way that these stupid high-school boys are intimidated.

Resigned to another Saturday night spent reading or playing Scrabble with Henry, I just smiled, letting Claudia think that that explanation had achieved its intended goal of making me feel better. Which it maybe would have, if it had not been for my sister, Kei, also cursed or, in her case, clearly blessed with completely unusual looks, who four years earlier had captured the imagination of what seemed like every single boy in her high school. Every day at least one of them, and sometimes three or four, called to ask her out. If no one was calling for me, whether or not my looks were unusual had nothing to do with it.

Claudia's success with boys was less spectacular than Kei's, but it was arguably more solid. Whereas Kei went out with a succession of boys, many of whom did not seem to like her in the end, Claudia's stuck by her. It was partly because of the kind of boys Claudia chose to go out with (she was nonplussed by Kei's taste for the pot-smoking, black-leather-clad type and, at least back then, particularly mystified by her interest in other girls' boyfriends), but it was mostly because of the ones she attracted and how she made them feel.

Yes, the boys liked Claudia in high school because she was a nice girl, brainy but unpretentious, and always kind and sweet. Yet they also liked her because she was a nice girl etc. who had a healthy appetite for sex and who saw nothing wrong with indulging said appetite as much as possible. At the age of fifteen, three years before I even kissed a boy, she lost her virginity with a minimum of fuss, and then, having lost it, she practiced the moves that had accounted for its loss as many times as the opportunity presented itself.

Her popularity was such that the opportunity presented itself often.

"Before Vikrum, I'd never made the first move with a man," Claudia says, breaking a medium-long silence. "Let alone asked anyone out."

Again with the non sequitur. This time, though, I am too startled at the way our thoughts as well as our feet have kept pace that I can't be bothered to search for the inspiration to her comment. Besides, this comment might just be the preamble to the next chapter of her romance with Vikrum. "Never?"

She shakes her head. "Pathetic, isn't it? So unfeminist of me."

"You only didn't because you never had to," I say, "because they always beat you to the punch." I pause and then add, "So to speak."

Claudia smiles. "Maybe. Still, I should have gotten a punch in there somewhere, don't you think? You have, haven't you?"

"We're not talking about me," I say, scolding. "Don't change the subject. Why do you think you never got a punch in?"

"I think that maybe I've always liked men too much. I've always liked the idea of men . . . but none of them in particular, if you know what I mean." With that, she stops walking and begins to rummage in her bag. "It's starting to rain. I brought two umbrellas—you should take this one."

"There was Doug, though," I say. It's a mist rather than a real rain, so refreshing and light I want to dance in it, yet I take the umbrella from her without protest. She opens hers, and once again we fall into step. "You were with him for a number of years—you must have liked him in particular."

"There was Doug," Claudia repeats. "That's true."

"But?"

"Was it so obvious there was a *but* there? Never mind, don't answer that. I actually loved Doug in particular. But I didn't make the first move with him. But I wouldn't have cared, honestly, if nothing had ever happened between us—if we'd only stayed friends." She glances at me and says, gently, "But you're supposed to open the umbrella."

"But it's barely raining." Still, I pull it out from under my elbow and open it.

Tilting her own umbrella back, Claudia smiles at me. "I'm a nag, I know. It's just that we still have ten minutes more to go, and if you're soaked, it'll detract from our shopping experience."

She must have packed an extra umbrella for me this morning. How could I not at least listen? If only I could dance my way through her story: a swoop to the left and a twirl to the right, and then before I knew it I would be on the other side.

"So," I say, leaden as my feet are now, one step forward at a time. "So was it different with Vikrum? Did you actually want him enough to make the first move?"

CLAUDIA HATED MY MOTHER, of course. I say of course even though she used to beg me for stories about the girl who gave up a chance to become a princess, and the woman who remained devoted to a ruined, melancholy aunt.

My mother tried hard to be kind to Henry's only child. When Claudia came to stay for the weekend, she slept not on ashes or even the rickety fold-out in the den, but in the best twin bed in the house, set up in a room that was reserved just for her. She was never asked to help clean up after supper, or put out the garbage, or even make her own bed, as was expected from Kei and me. Furthermore, my mother was always civil and even friendly to Claudia, taking a real interest in how her classes and flute lessons and soccer practice were going, exclaiming with real pride over her good grades, and buying her so many knickknacks and special outfits that sometimes Kei and I ended up feeling like the unwanted stepchildren.

Still, Claudia hated her. When her father moved out and her mother buried herself in her numbers, who else was there for her to hate? At times, it was true, she hated her mother; once or twice, maybe, her father.

But her stepmother she hated all the time, and no one was the worse for it, other than my mother and me.

"DOUG CALLED THIS the boyfriend chair," Claudia says, fondly tapping one of the arms of a large, upright wooden chair tucked away in the corner of the shop. "He'd sit here, glowering away, his arms folded and his face red, while I shopped." Leaning close to me, she adds, sotto voce, "The skimpy clothes and lingerie in here really embarrassed him. You should have seen how red he got when these skinny young things would be trying them on in front of the mirror."

She's shown me pictures. A big man, tall with a fair amount of flesh on him. Square head, square jaw, square shoulders; nice-looking in an unassuming way. In all the photographs that she has of him, and there are a great number, he looks as if he's not quite comfortable. I would have chalked it up to the clothes that he had on, except that Claudia has photographs of him in a considerable variety of outfits, from T-shirts to tuxedos and swim trunks to down coats, and it seems unlikely that he's uncomfortable in all of them. So maybe it's having a camera on him that does it.

Based on the pictures and the little she's told me about him, I can imagine him sitting in this tiny shop with its low ceilings as we look around. He'd be a quiet, reassuringly pleasant presence, a large man trying politely to make himself small. Maybe a little easy to forget about, patient and uncomplaining in spite of his red face.

When it came to shopping with Claudia, his patience wasn't actually tried all that much. Although her familiarity with this particular store might suggest otherwise—and although, perhaps, Doug might even beg to differ—she doesn't really like to shop. She didn't when we were younger, and while she has literally dragged me, pulling me by the arm, into this store filled with vividly colored, beautifully textured clothes that she loves as much as I do, I can tell from the way she's acting that that has not changed. While she pretends now to be interested in the scarves, holding them up to herself and checking the tags, she's not fooling anyone (least of all the women who work here, who studiously ignore her)—it's for my benefit that we're here.

Big-boned and perhaps inevitably self-conscious about it, Claudia has always thought of herself as plain. A teenager no longer, she's not really bothered by this, but out of years of habit she slouches still, carrying her body as if it were an unwieldy parcel that she had been asked to carry by a stranger, and a stranger of dubious provenance at that.

And since we were little, she has admired my lanky frame as well as my dark skin and black hair.

Does she know how much I covet the health and solidity of her body now; could she possibly fathom the depths of my envy?

"One time," she continues, still lost in memories as we move toward the rack of dresses, "the boyfriend chair was taken up by some other woman's boyfriend and that open space over there was taken up by some boxes, so he had to stand. There was a sale and it was crowded, and he ended up being squeezed up against all these lacy clothes, and all these women had to reach around him and over him to get at what they wanted. And he's so big, and self-conscious about being big on top of that; naturally he felt horribly awkward."

"How could you have subjected him to that?" I say, marveling. "Claudia Marianne Klein, you shock me. To think that I thought I knew you."

"Wait, it gets worse. We were only here a few minutes that day. But I couldn't resist: before we left, I yelled across the store to him that I had to spend another hour here, just so I could watch him squirm." Extending her arms out in a luxurious stretch, she sighs with satisfaction. "Those were good times."

"Well, not for him, maybe."

"No, he thought it was funny too. That whole big-lug-of-a-guy was something of an act. He knew he was a little like that, and so he exaggerated it and laughed at himself for it."

Not so easy to forget about after all. Clearly my understanding of human character leaves much to be desired. "And yet you gave him up."

"And yet I gave him up," she says, the tone of her voice perhaps determinedly light.

No, Claudia doesn't know—she shouldn't know, and I will do my best to see that she never will—how much I envy her life.

In this respect, too, little has changed since we were young.

Chapter Sixteen

New Jersey, 1974–82

A FAMILY; A ROAD TRIP; AN ACCIDENT WITHIN A STONE'S throw of the Canadian border. This, too, was a story Rei fed to Claudia. At times she thought she should bring herself to circulate the narrative more widely; the details of the trip alone made it worth telling. Nowhere else in the entire history of the Watanabes was there an image that gave such a wholesome, quintessentially American face to her family.

It was the car, not unexpectedly, that served as the cornerstone to this idealized image. As if it were not enough that they were on the first leg of a cross-country road trip, on their way to see no less a cliché than Niagara Falls, the car they were riding in was a station wagon, and a Ford at that. Bicycles and luggage were piled in the back and, in what Rei would later characterize as the figurative as well as literal crowning touch, a few suitcases rested on the roof of the car, where they made alarming creaking sounds when the wind blew. Seiji drove while his wife, three months pregnant and dreamily absorbed by it, sat beside him, strapped in by her seat belt. Their two daughters squabbled with varying degrees of seriousness in the backseat.

It was the picture-perfect image of American domestic bliss. Never mind that Seiji hated American cars and had complained almost without cease through Massachusetts and New York about the heap of junk that this one was. Never mind that he dreaded driving and did so only now because Hana was tired after having spent the day before behind the wheel. Never mind, even, that they had returned from their two-year sojourn in Japan just this spring; that Seiji was complaining, Hana was dreaming, and the daughters were squabbling in Japanese; that they viewed themselves as foreigners, as year-round tourists in this country of uninterrupted vistas and pleasantly wide highways; and that they were worried that Seiji's bank, as well as assorted visa complications, might force them to leave this country in another ten months. Their Ford station wagon, with their luggage wobbling above it, conferred upon them the stamp of Americanness, as surely as if their ancestors had arrived on the banks of Plymouth—as if their forefathers had crawled, like the first amphibians, up onto those shores in another great moment in the annals of evolutionary progress—fresh off the Mayflower.

Rei was five; Kei was newly nine, and uppity about it. Their bickering could not last forever, though, and a temporary cease-fire was at hand (Kei lost in the pages of the Japanese translation of *Anne of Green Gables*, and Rei singing to herself) when one of the suitcases slid off the roof of the car and landed with a thump on the ground. With that thump, Kei lost her place in the novel, Rei stopped singing, and Hana woke from her reverie. Seiji steered the car over onto the shoulder and stepped on the brake. They all looked back and there, on the side of the highway, they saw the suitcase.

It was a sturdy, well-made piece of plastic and nylon—one of the wheelless suitcases that Hana had lugged with her from Japan, it had managed to survive the fall without bursting open. An attractive shade of light purple, it lay on its side on the road, glinting faintly in the sun.

Seiji muttered a curse. Hana turned to him, the beatific smile of a young madonna on her face. He looked back at her and then, suddenly, he smiled, rueful about his own bad mood. He turned around and chucked his older daughter under her chin, tousled the younger girl's hair. Then he opened the door. As he stepped out of the car, Rei picked up the song, this time under her breath, from where she'd left off; it was an American song that she had learned recently in school, and one that she particularly liked.

"...ninety-six bottles of beer on the wall..."

Her mother, who was more musical as well as more artistic than anyone else in the family, but of course did not know the words to the song, easy as it was, hummed an accompaniment from the front seat.

"...ninety-six bottles of bee-er, take one down..."

Her father was not a handsome man. Kei might marvel almost daily at the unfathomable depths of Rei's stupidity and ignorance, but this much Rei knew. His facial features were laughably mismatched: his nose bulbous and squashed; his eyes so squinty they were barely visible behind thick glasses; his teeth small and crooked.

When he walked down the street with her beautiful mother, people often stared at him as well as at her, in bafflement at his luck.

"...pass it around..."

Rei turned to watch him as he ran out onto the highway. He was not a handsome man, her father, but it was impossible to remember that fact when he was in motion. He had the loping grace of a cat; his stride was strikingly easy, and effective too, good enough to have made him the Japanese equivalent of an all-state sprinter in his youth. He was still young, only thirty-seven, even if he seemed impossibly old to his younger daughter then—even if he, with his job in the States and his two-and-a-half children, probably seemed old to himself—and he looked like a boy as he ran, stretching his legs out with some eagerness after the long hours spent cramped in the car.

They were traveling eastward, and it was midmorning. The sun, which was particularly radiant that day, hit him full in the face. He held one arm up to shield his eyes from its light as he raced back to retrieve the wayward piece of luggage.

FOUR YEARS LATER (a month before Rei turned nine, half a year before Henry came into their lives), Kei learned that her younger sister remembered only one half of the most momentous event of their lives. Trying to fill in the blanks in Rei's memory, she told her of the stretcher on which their father rested, a sheet, the red stain on it visibly seeping outward, that covered him to the top of his head, and of how they had been ushered into a police car while their mother, who had remained dry-eyed and self-contained until then, began sobbing hysterically on the shirtfront of an embarrassed paramedic.

Kei said (incredulous at her sister's lack of memory, but trying, for once, not to scoff) that Rei, too, began to bawl then, and would not stop even though the policeman that was with them picked her up and held her in his lap during the ride to the police station, even though he reassured them both that their daddy could not have felt any pain, as the truck had hit him too fast.

"Were the sirens blaring?"

Kei nodded vigorously, hope in her eyes. "And the lights were flashing. You remember that?"

Rei shook her head slowly, sifting through her memories. "No."

THE SUN HURT HER EYES TOO, and Rei turned her head forward again ("...ninety-five bottles of bee-er..."), away from the sight of her father. Kei slipped back into her book. Hana opened the window and tilted the side mirror toward her; she had been eating a muffin and she needed to see if she had poppy seeds caught in her teeth. Five more seconds ("...take one down, pass it around..."), and then a loud screech of brakes from behind made them all jump. With a swiftness that would not have seemed possible for a woman so dreamy, Hana turned. Rei had a blurred impression of her mother's face, the eyes dark and huge and the lips parted, and then she could no longer see: Hana's hand was covering her eyes.

"Don't turn around," said Hana. "Don't look."

Rei wanted to protest that there was no way she could, with a hand blotting out her vision. She wanted to say that her mother was hurting her, that her grip was too tight. But there was something in Hana's tone that commanded silence as well as obedience.

Telling this story to her stepsister in the years that followed, Rei would find herself stunned anew by the traits exhibited by her mother on that day: the lightning-quickness of her reflexes, and the strength of will that made it possible for her to remain calm and quiet, covering her daughters' eyes, while she gazed out at her husband's broken body.

"YOU REMEMBER HIS FUNERAL, at least, don't you? You and I cried so hard that Mom almost didn't have time to cry herself."

Kei sounded so uncharacteristically anxious, so desperate to dredge up a shared glimmer of recognition, that Rei thought momentarily of speaking up. Instead, she shook her head again.

"What about afterward? You couldn't sleep at night because of the bad dreams. Mommy had to sit up with you."

"No. Nothing."

She had been only five, after all. Who wouldn't believe that the memories she retained of her father's death stopped there, with the tight clasp of her mother's hand over her eyes, and the picture, shot through with sunlight, of Seiji running with his easy, loping grace?

Chapter Seventeen

Claudia
Boston, 1999

"HOLY MOTHER OF GOD," REI SAYS, HER VOICE HUSHED
with awe. "Would you look at this sandwich."

"Yup," I say, "that's the Hi-Rise Bakery for you. I always
figured the people who work here are engineers
or architects rather than chefs."

"Because it would take a fine sense of spatial relations
and maybe an advanced degree in applied science
to build a sandwich that combines so many
elements and still manages to tower so high?"

She is so poker-faced I have to smile. "Something
like that."

The sandwich is not only tall, it's huge as well—calculated
to make a girl add flesh to her frame. Or so I
hope. Rei eats and eats, so why is it that she does not
gain weight? But then again, perhaps I am being too
impatient. After all, only a few weeks have passed
since she and I met up; maybe a little more time is

needed before all the food I have been making her eat shows up on her body.

Time or no time, though, it would help my cause immeasurably if she would stop admiring her sandwich and take the first bite out of it instead.

Tilting her head far back, Rei drains the last bit of water from her cup. She wasn't in the mood for anything but water, she said; it did not matter how eloquent I waxed on the subject of the Hi-Rise juices.

"Didn't you say you were going to tell me about how you got together with Vikrum when we stopped for lunch? Not to hint or anything," she says, chewing on her unused straw.

Even when she was little, Rei had to be coaxed into eating. If she needed movies (more, even, than butter and salt) to go with her popcorn back then, why not a story to go with her tuna and avocado sandwich now? "I did, didn't I? Let's see, where to begin . . . What do you think of as romantic? In terms of a seduction."

With a cock of her head, she eyeballs me. "Are you planning to seduce someone new? Ah, and here I thought Vikrum had it so good."

"Just trying to lay the foundation to my story. Come on, help me out here: ingredients for a romantic seduction. I'll name some if you do."

"Let me think." Removing the straw from her mouth, she—finally!—picks up her sandwich and takes a large bite out of it. "Atmoshphere," she says, her mouth half-full. "Damn, that's a good sandwich."

"Be more specific. About the atmosphere, not the sandwich."

"Hmm. Moonlight?"

"Starlight."

"Candlelight!"

"How about," I say, swallowing with a gulp a bite of my own sandwich, "no light at all? Some of the sexiest encounters I've ever had have been in pitch darkness, under the covers."

"That's good," says Rei, nodding. She pushes her sleeves up her arms, and then picks up her sandwich again. "Darkness is very good. Although sexy is different from romantic, isn't it?"

"Maybe. Probably," I say. Like the other women of her family, Rei has unusually slender wrists, so much so that she regularly has to have an extra notch put into the bands of her wristwatches to make them cinch tight. Her forearms are so skinny now, it takes a real effort to focus on what she is saying. "Okay, what else?"

"Another ingredient for a romantic seduction?" Rei asks. "I've had so many, it's hard to remember details of any one of them in particular; they just all start to blur in my mind...."

She sounds as if she's kidding, but it is impossible to tell. "How many have you—" I begin.

"We're talking about you, remember?" she says. "Or we're supposed to be at least leading up to a talk about you and Vikrum. If it'll help you get there faster, I'll give you a list of what else I think is romantic, with the caveat that it's probably going to expose how banal and girlishly sentimental I am at heart. There's champagne. Balconies, beaches, cars speeding along deserted highways—basically anywhere there aren't too many people. Rain. Not buckets of it, but a mist or a light patter will always do it for me, maybe because I like the idea of huddling under an umbrella together with someone."

I always used to wonder why Hana's aunt Sachiko, that wraith of a woman, loomed so large in the tales that Rei wove out of her family's past. Sure, Rei's mother adored her aunt, but Rei herself barely knew her, and Sachiko was only a bit player in the drama that most transfixed the two of us, the ups and downs and unlikely twists and turns that characterized Hana's life. Yet for all that Hana's favorite aunt hardly ever took center stage, she was a persistent presence, lingering in the background in many of the stories, like the moon on certain sunny days: a faded white mark, out of place and out of its time, serving no apparent function. A compelling figure in her own way, without a doubt, but was Rei haunted by her at least in part because she resembled her so closely? When I looked at their family album, the only way I could tell their pictures apart, aside from the quality and the age of the photographs, was that my step-sister never wore a kimono and she was not quite as thin. Now it would be that much harder to tell.

I give myself a small shake and force myself to sit up and look directly at Rei. "Well, what you're saying confirms it. It's what I thought. What Vikrum and I had was an antiromance."

Chewing meditatively, she observes me with grave eyes over the top of her sandwich and waits for me to continue.

"We got together in the middle of the day, under fluorescent lights," I say. "We were surrounded by people. Neither of us had drunk anything—champagne, wine, beer, or even water for a few hours; come to think of it, we were both pretty dehydrated at the time.

"So that's it. The End. I warned you, didn't I? It really is such a disappointing story."

And it is. The story of my romance with Vikrum is, in fact, so disappointing that were I to think much more about it, it would overwhelm me. So perhaps I should be grateful that all I can think about is how once, long ago, Rei described Sachiko's wrists as being so thin that they did not look as if they could bear the weight of her hands.

Chapter Eighteen

Rei

Boston, 1999

"WAIT," I SAY. "WAIT, WAIT, WAIT. YOU'VE RUSHED THE story way too much, haven't you?"

Claudia looks up innocently. While we've sat here having lunch, the rain has stopped and the clouds have cleared. Backlit by the sunlight trickling in through the windows, Claudia's outline seems hazy, her hair shot through with gold. The light enhances her look of innocence. She's a religious icon waiting to happen, and I'm a fool and, even worse, a cynic for thinking that she was trying to hold something back.

"I have?" she asks.

"Definitely. Rewind, please. Much, much further back. I need to know what happened after the post office. How did you meet up after that; did you contact him, or did he somehow find you? And what was happening with Doug?"

"Okay," she says, putting down her coffee cup. "Fine. After I met him at the post office, I called him. We became friends. In a completely aboveboard way—his wife knew about me, and Doug knew about him.

"It was a bad winter—the clouds and the snow seemed to be hanging on and on, and you remember, don't you, how blue I get when there's no sunshine—so we used to meet often."

I have to smile. To think that I could actually have forgotten how she hated bad weather! It's been a long time, of course, but still. Her aversion was striking because she hardly ever complained about anything other than the cold and overcast skies, but then she complained a bucketful. I told her that as soon as she could, she should light out for southern California, where the temperature never dropped below freezing, palm trees lined the streets, and the skies were blue all day, every day. Even back when she was ten, though, she just shrugged at that and said Boston was where she'd like to live. Why Boston? I asked, guessing what she'd say, and sure enough, she hesitated only briefly before answering as I'd been expecting: because of the way that it sounds in your stories.

In my stories, tranquil Boston was an enchanted city, the setting for the long honeymoon that was my parents' marriage. It seemed very flattering that Claudia would want to live there based on how I'd described it, but considering how mythologized Boston always has been in my family, that she had set her sights on making it her home in spite of a deep aversion to the cold seemed neither misguided nor surprising.

When we left Boston for good, I was five, too young to remember it with any real clarity now. In some ways, I still can't believe I've returned to it. I never thought I would ever live in Boston, mostly out of some perverse sense of loyalty to my mother—perverse in that she wouldn't have minded at all if I did. Just because she herself can't bear to live here, it doesn't mean that she's stopped loving the city; in fact, she would have relished the chance to hear what I said about it.

It astonishes me, really, how misplaced my loyalties have been.

VIKRUM HUMMED WITH ENERGY. He sang with it too, often and loudly and sometimes even tunefully, with or without cause. That, Claudia tells me, is what she liked about Vikrum when they first became friends. His energy was contagious: if she didn't exactly hum and certainly didn't sing, she did find herself striding briskly through the streets of Boston ("Can you imagine, me striding?" she says, at which image I can only shake my head in disbelief). He spurred her on to a renewed mental vigor as well, so that even the ambling rhythms of her speech speeded up to keep pace with the increased production of her thoughts.

Were it not for his apparently boundless store of energy, she would have felt guilty about taking up as much time as she did. They were, in fact, spending a lot of time together—four or sometimes even five hours at a shot, two or three evenings every week. His energy was the reason he managed to have time in the day for all that he wanted to do, and then some: cloning, magic, mornings and evenings with his family, and long hours at the coffee shop arguing politics and life with Claudia. Tireless, efficient with his resources, and blessed with a rare ability to focus on whatever he was doing as if it were the only matter that concerned him in the world, Vikrum could see her for ten-plus hours every week without his research suffering, the precision of his magic tricks slipping and, most of all, his children having to give up one iota of their daddy's attention.

He was, Claudia knew, adored and even worshiped by his children. A dad who could produce flowers and rabbits and even a tricycle or two with a wave of his hand and a few muttered words:

how could they not? And he, in turn, adored and even worshiped them back. Claudia didn't have to worry that she was taking up time once allotted to them, because Vikrum himself was vigilant about excising anything in his life that might come between him and his daughter and son.

Or so she told herself, anyway.

THIS NEW IDYLL in Claudia's life was broken short when she fell victim to a particularly virulent case of the flu ("Exposure to every strain of virus that mankind is prone to," she says with a resigned air, "of course being one of my greatest occupational hazards") and found herself bed-bound. Racked with fever, shivering with chills, and aching in every limb of her body, her nose dripping and her throat swollen, she was able to call Vikrum to cancel their next coffee-shop rendezvous but could not tell him when they might meet up next.

When she heard a knock at her door an hour after she had hung up the phone, she only went to answer it because she thought it might be Doug, coming over to take care of her in such a hurry that he had forgotten her house key again. Her apartment was littered with used tissues. She was in her pajamas; her hair was matted and dirty, her nose a vivid shade of crimson. Her eyes teared with the fever.

When she opened the door and it was Vikrum, she squinted up at him without surprise, believing him at first to be yet another flu-induced hallucination. He had never been to her home before, and she could not remember if she had ever given him her address besides, and surely he was supposed to be at his lab now—wasn't it mid-afternoon on a Tuesday or Wednesday?

He had brought her chicken soup and orange juice; she tried to thank him but the hallway was tilting at alarming angles. After half leading and half carrying her back to her bedroom, Vikrum sat down on the edge of her bed and fed her the soup spoon by spoon, ignoring her laughing protestations that she could lift it—it was just plastic, after all, nothing as heavy as metal—by herself. When the soup was all gone, he took out the orange juice and helped her lift the cup so that it slid easily down her inflamed throat. Before, they had always crammed every second of their time together with conversation. As he wiped off a few drops of juice from her chin and tucked her back into bed, as deft as one would expect a father of more than four years' experience to be, she reproached herself for having contributed to their fervent pursuit of words, the silence between them was so sweet.

Then he took off his shoes, bulky hiking boots with shards of ice still clinging to them, glittering and dripping, from his walk to her apartment, and began to climb under the sheets with her.

For some time, Claudia had known that there were at least a dozen very good reasons why she and Vikrum should not be in bed together. Much, much later, it would almost seem funny to her that, faced with the imminent possibility of this happening, she came up with the reason that she did.

"You'll get sick," she warned. Then, as if to drive her point home, she sneezed.

Vikrum paused, his head cocked, considering. "I'll take the risk," he said, and handed her a tissue that she promptly used and discarded among the others on the floor.

She lifted her head up, and he slipped his arm under it in a manner that was reassuring to her in that it seemed brotherly rather than sexual. She laid her arm on his stomach and familiarized herself with the contours of his ribs and soft belly.

She would come to think it was her fever that had been responsible for her calm acceptance of this married man in her bed. Search as she might, though, she would never be able to come up with a satisfying explanation for her heartless indifference to the possibility that Doug might walk in at any moment and the docile way in which she opened her mouth to take in the spoonfuls of chicken soup (which she, a vegetarian, had not tasted in five years) and the sour orange juice.

HAVING SEX WITH VIKRUM (Claudia announces to me now—it's a proclamation, lacking only the blare of trumpets and the waving of flags) was a revelation. From the very first time. She had never understood what real desire was before him. She'd read about it, seen it acted out in movies and television, and discussed it with me and others. Heck, she herself had told countless lovers over the years that she desired them, not realizing that what she'd felt was only a pale shadow version of all that lust could be. It was as if she'd only seen those paintings of ice cream, made by that guy who's famous for it, what's-his-name—

Wayne Thiebaud?

She nods. Being with Vikrum (she continues, without stopping for a breath) was as if she had only seen Thiebaud's paintings and not known how creamy and cold and sweetly delicious ice cream actually is in the mouth.

But (I say, breaking into her reverie in an attempt to steer her back to the matter at hand) that first time—that wasn't on that afternoon, right?

No. They didn't even kiss that day (she says, shaking her head at their foolishness), choosing to wait instead until they were in a hallway of the Boston aquarium, surrounded by what seemed to be hundreds of screaming children. They would never be so reckless again ("although," she says, suddenly and briefly frowning, "it's the damnedest thing—just lately, I feel as if he's been getting reckless again, and I don't know what to do about it"), but that day they would stay in that hallway for an hour or more, until Claudia finally pulled away, tucked her hair behind her ears, and silently took Vikrum by the hand to lead him back to her home.

She's getting ahead of her story again. I am about to give her another gentle nudge when she nods at me, signaling that she's ready to return on her own.

Yet before she continues with the chronological unfolding of her tale, there's one more fact about her first taste of real ice cream that she needs to recount. It's a minor point, a detail that, I imagine, has been fretting away at her, a small but persistent pain like a sharp pebble in her shoe.

"That first time I took Vikrum home—I had to make sure to put the chain lock on the door," she says. It's wrenching to watch her attempt to smile. "For Doug, just in case."

CLAUDIA FELT HER FACE BURN, as if with fever once again.

Eighteen days had passed since that afternoon she had spent in bed with Vikrum. Fully dressed, her hair washed and combed, she stood with him now in the aquarium, which he had suggested as the site for their first encounter in almost three weeks. She was, finally, more or less fully recovered from the flu, a hacking cough and a certain rather sultry throatiness in her voice the only vestiges thereof, but she was far from over the memory of the day she last saw Vikrum. While Claudia loved the aquarium ("and the whale watches," she says, clutching my arm, "we need to go on one of those together, you and me"), her mortification at seeing Vikrum again was enough to diminish even her pleasure in the penguins, who dived into the water and chased each other with what seemed very close to pure joy, and the large, conical tank, where the sharks and the sea turtles swam peaceably side by side.

That there were sea horses and conch shells to gaze at now was a relief, since she had trouble looking at any spot within six inches of Vikrum's eyes. Hard as she tried, though, it was difficult to avoid his gaze: he seemed to be far more interested in her than in the flashes of neon darting through the tank in front of them, enchanting though they were. Still, why shouldn't he want to look her in the eye? His conscience wasn't troubling him (she thought to herself bitterly). If she had acted out of unimpeachable motives, as he had done—and if his eyes were not so large and wonderfully clear; could they possibly be the largest and clearest that she had ever seen?—then she'd be eager, or at the very least able, to look up and meet his gaze too.

When Vikrum had climbed into bed with her, he had been guided only by a parent's instinct to take care of those unable to fend for themselves—the same innocent impulse that had led him to swipe drops of juice off her chin. As for the instincts that had guided her—well, suffice it to say that *innocent* was not a word that could be applied to them. Neither, for that matter, was *credible*. Had she really slipped her hand beneath his shirt and slid it up and down the smooth skin of his stomach? Was it true that she had rubbed her cheek against his chest and listened to the slow pulse of his heart; had she actually tried to see if she could speed up that beat by running her tongue down his torso?

Given the incredible nature of her behavior, it was perfectly understandable that she hadn't been able to stop thinking about that afternoon—the muscles of his arm beneath her head; the heat of his body, which seemed, fever or no, easily equal to that of hers; and the way he had shuddered, his skin rippling and coming up in goose bumps, when her tongue first touched his chest—for the past eighteen days. It was only to be expected that she and Doug would have fought, with him accusing her of being strangely distracted ("I know you're sick, C, but there's something else wrong, I know that too"). Of course her face was burning now.

Vikrum had lain in bed with her for half an hour and then, after depositing a benevolent, perhaps forgiving kiss on her forehead, he had sat up, pulled his hiking boots back on, and left, all without saying a word. Considering what she had done, small wonder he had been so quiet. If the steady rhythm of his pulse had picked up its pace when she licked his chest, as she had maybe wishfully thought, it was doubtlessly out of embarrassment.

Embarrassment for her, seasoned with a pinch of regret, perhaps, at witnessing a perfectly good friendship go to the dogs.

"I'M GLAD YOU'RE BETTER. I've missed you," he said, "a lot."

Claudia counted them in her head. Nine words. Added to the "Hi, Claudia, good to see you," with which Vikrum had greeted her when she walked through the doors of the aquarium, and the meekly uttered "You too" with which Claudia had responded, that made a whopping seventeen words spoken in the forty-odd minutes that they had spent together so far that day.

"Let's walk," she said, turning abruptly. "This next tank is a good one."

Obediently he fell into step beside her.

She cleared her throat. The rattle she made in the process was so deep and loud, the woman in front of them turned to stare and then hurried to gather her children close so that their mucous membranes would remain safe from the air exhaled by the tall red-faced lady.

"Here," Vikrum said, moving toward her. "You're still not all better; you've got to keep yourself warm." He reached out and began to tie the scarf that was draped around her neck. "It's good to see you again," he said softly. "I wanted to come by your apartment again. I would have, but when you didn't return any of my calls . . . It feels like I've been waiting a long time to see you."

"Well," said Claudia, with an attempt at tartness, "you know what they say: anticipation is all too often the best part."

He hesitated. "I don't believe that for a second," he said, "and not just because I instinctively distrust whatever 'they' say." He knotted and cinched her scarf tight.

A long pause. Finally she raised her head and looked at him. For the second time that afternoon, she thought that he had to have the clearest, most beautiful eyes she had ever seen. And for the first time, she realized—or, more accurately, admitted to herself; the knowledge arrived without a shock—that he wasn't just looking at her.

What he was doing was gazing, with real hunger.

She backed away a step, moving cautiously and watching him all the while.

"You're married. With children," she said at last.

She would try to figure out later whether she had been expecting a denial or an excuse, or perhaps both. In any event, she didn't receive either. He stood absolutely still, his arms hanging by his sides and his eyes intent upon her. She couldn't be sure, but she thought he may even have stopped blinking.

She imagined him coming home at the end of a long day, his children skimming across the driveway to greet him. Lifting his daughter with one arm and hoisting his son over his shoulder with the other, walking effortlessly toward the house, grumbling all the while about how heavy they were getting. They rummage through his pockets during the ride, looking for the odds and ends from the grocery store that he's picked up, knowing that later he'll clap his hand to his forehead and exclaim that he's forgotten to go, that he'll have to find what he needs somewhere else instead: a small carton of cream stashed behind his daughter's ear, a whole bag of carrots that the dog has been carrying around, and two lemons nestled like eggs in his son's woolen hat.

"So stop looking at me like that," Claudia finished weakly.

Never less than the soul of politeness, nothing if not respectful, Vikrum immediately averted his eyes. "Sorry," he said.

As soon as he stopped looking at her, she felt something catch in her chest. She cleared her throat again, in the off chance that it was another cough rather than a sob.

She thought of Doug, and the warm solid mass of his body.

"These past three months," Vikrum said, his face turned toward the wall, "with you . . ." Then he shook his head and stopped.

She had never seen him so serious before. Intellectually engaged, sure, but he had always been essentially lighthearted in her company, boyish and playful, verging on giddy.

Claudia moved forward a quarter of a step, perhaps two inches at the most.

Taking a breath in, Vikrum began to speak again. In the deliberate pacing of his speech, she could hear how carefully he measured his words. "If you never want to see me again, I'll understand. These past three months," and here he took another gulp of air in, "with you, I almost wish they hadn't happened. But if they hadn't, well"—defiantly he turned his head to look at her again—"think how much we would have missed."

Another two inches, and yet another pause.

"You're married," Claudia said again, the words an incantation, a spell designed not to protect her from the consequences of what she was about to do but rather to test whether she could be as clear-eyed as Vikrum himself was about what their future held. "With children that you're devoted to." She spoke very softly, almost under her breath; in that echoing hallway filled with children and their parents, anyone farther away than Vikrum was—his face now just an inch away from hers, their noses all but touching—would not have been able to hear her.

Vikrum remained quiet, seeming to know that she was speaking, this time, more to herself than to him. With the shadow of a smile hovering around his eyes, he waited, watching her, until she was ready, until she slowly propelled herself another fraction of an inch forward and touched her lips to his: a magician she might not be, but her incantation had worked.

As they kissed, Claudia felt the room tilt again, and she wondered, but only for an instant, whether the profound sense of vertigo that she was feeling was love or the return of the hot flush of her illness and the delirium that it caused.

"THAT'S A GOOD STORY," I tell her. "Thank you. It wasn't disappointing at all."

"Really?" Claudia asks, shifting restlessly in her seat. The strain is more apparent than ever: her forehead's creased and her napkin has been methodically and neatly shredded into bits. "It seems so sordid to me."

"Bittersweet, maybe. Sordid, no. I just have one last question."

She looks so tired, I'm half tempted to back down. But then she nods. "Ready," she says.

"It's just the obvious one," I say apologetically. "What about children? You've wanted kids for as long as I can remember."

"Yup, that's the obvious one," she says. "Well, for starters, Doug wanted children; he wanted to get married and the whole shebang, but I resisted him, so maybe I don't want it quite so much. Two, I teach elementary school, after all. In a way, I've got twenty-four kids of my own already. And three," she adds hastily, as if to preempt me, although I've made no move to interrupt and have no intention of doing so, "this might sound more pathetic yet, but I keep thinking about your mother's aunt Sachiko, and how she was so happy taking care of other people's children."

"But Sachiko-san couldn't get married," I say, as gently as I can. "She had no choice. You do."

"I know," she says. Her voice is quiet, her eyes clear. "But sometimes it feels as if I don't. Even like this, even though I see him only two, three times a week if I'm lucky, I'm happier now than I've ever been in my life. He fills me up; he's all I want and, I think and often fear, all I ever will want."

We fall silent, and remain so for the journey home, even though there should be plenty for me, at least, to say: while we've been chatting in the bakery for more than two hours, it's Claudia who did all the talking. Can she read in my silence how I'm feeling? It'd be ridiculous to hope that she can't. Still, it's possible that she's only picked up on part of it—a less than ringing endorsement of her relationship with Vikrum, based on the heartache that has to lie at the end of it. Which is to say, nothing that she doesn't already know.

With any luck, Claudia won't be able to tell how at once maddened and relieved I am that she failed to follow through on how my mother figured in her story. Regardless of how close we are, and even if I have made the decision to make her my only family, there are some subjects that will always be difficult for us to discuss.

As we near the river, it starts to rain again, hard enough that without prompting I open the umbrella she brought for me. The first day I arrived in Boston, unbearably early on a September morning, the Charles was like a mirror, clear and still, reflecting in minute detail the lone sculler rowing on it. I thought the town prosaic then, stodgy and overly quaint and dull, its people monochromatic and bland. It's not until today, when the river is windswept and choppy, deprived of any power to reflect by the splattering of the rain, that I can finally see what my mother saw in this poor excuse for a city: the way that it whispered promises of romance and adventure, of a new life and love. If it weren't for the rain, maybe I could hear them as well—promises so sweet and seductive, it's no wonder she fell for them, and that Claudia did too.

Chapter Nineteen

Hana
California, 1999

HANA, AT THE AGE OF SIXTY-SIX, HAS COME TO ACCEPT it: the English language has beaten her. She uses both hands to hold on to the receiver, but the receiver shakes anyway. Her hands haven't been steady for some time; these months of stress have taken their toll. The operator, a woman with a voice almost as deep as a man's, is businesslike but patient while Hana stumbles over her request. It is as Hana waits for her to locate the number for Claudia Klein that she realizes that what she is most nervous about, at this very moment, is her English. This comes as a surprise. Compiling a list of all that she's nervous about right now would take up an impressive amount of time, far more than she actually has. Then there's the fact that for some months, maybe even a year, the number-one spot on that list has been occupied solidly by her younger daughter.

And, finally, language has been a source of concern for her for so long, you would think she'd be over worrying about it.

Hana has tried, but she can't remember at what point she gave up on words. The day that she realized she couldn't even follow the playful chatter of her own small children, maybe. Or one evening when she'd been overtaken by a moment of recklessness and had spoken up, attempting to deliver a pun, no less, at one of Henry's faculty parties. "I think Carter is peanuts to talk about rust in his heart."

Had she really said that; what had she been thinking? She had, word for word, and she knows all too well what had gotten into her that evening—a sudden burst of annoyance, mixed in with a good measure of boredom, at her perpetual silence. If only she could fool herself into believing that time had distorted her memory, magnifying the extent of her humiliation! Everyone in the group she'd been standing in had turned to look at her, a moment of heavy quiet followed by a flurry of talk about something else altogether. She isn't sure, to this day, whether her comment was dropped because of general shock that she, so subdued that the functioning power of her vocal cords was cast in doubt, had finally uttered a sound or because of the far more likely possibility that the sentence she'd blurted out had made no sense to them, both in the context of the preceding conversation and in and of itself.

Henry, who had been standing nearby, to all appearances absorbed in a one-on-one with the chair of his department, saw and heard yet did not flinch. In a few moments, he was standing beside her, his hand light on the small of her back but conveying to her with such clarity that its touch itself was proof of the insignificance, the complete and utter irrelevance, of words in her life: *Never mind, it's okay, I'm here.*

In books, Hana has seen Egyptian hieroglyphs, and she thinks that she might not have given up on English, at least the written version of it, if it, too, were a language made up of stick figures and line drawings of animals and trees. A whole nation that thinks in terms of images rather than words? Bliss indeed. Japanese, she supposes, works along those same lines: so the character for *tree* is a cross with two branches dangling like a skirt from the center of its trunk—a willow tree, she's always assumed, with its tendrils giving it an airy grace. So the ideograph for *rice paddy* is a box cut into fours, geometric and tidy as those she glimpsed from the window of the plane, through a haze of motion sickness, when she first left Japan; so the character for *river* is three vertical lines, ever so slightly bowed, which immediately evokes for her the sailboats made of bamboo leaves that she and her sister used to sail down the stream by their house, and the hushed murmuring sound that the water made.

Then there are characters that encapsulate a concept through an image: thus *trouble* is written as a tree locked away in a box. Back in the distant past when ideographs were first created, perhaps people took it as a religious tenet that a tree's rightful place was outdoors, under the sun and the moon and exposed to the air and the wind and the rain. Perhaps the idea of shutting one up seemed a stark violation of the natural order and, as such, a good example, maybe even a prime example, of trouble.

Growing up in Japan, Hana became used to picturing as she read, not only the characters or the descriptions contained in a passage but also the concepts ingrained in the visual cues of the language itself. She loved reading then, and loved writing too, loved the act of picking up an ink brush and watching the black strokes appear on the smooth white of the paper: a series of images, but one that magically made sense as well, one that transformed itself with little or no effort into a sentence, a thought, a story, an entire world. Not too surprising, really, that she'd derived an almost sensual pleasure from the act, something akin to the fierce explosion of joy she sometimes felt when dabbing her brush in paint, that moment of applying color, a splash or dot or an arcing, soaring line of it, to the pure white of the canvas.

But Japanese is no longer the language she deals with every day. Her chosen lot in life (and one she doesn't regret, despite everything; hasn't life in this fine, easygoing country, where women could be artists and girls, tomboys, been better for herself as well as for her daughters?) is, instead, the slippery cadences of English, with its odd inflections and its enormous vocabulary, and the letters that bear little relation to the images or sounds they represent. There are a few exceptions, which Hana cherishes: the way in which the letter O is written is clearly a tribute to the shape that the mouth makes when saying it; the letter I, tall and proud and solitary, the one and only form possible for the first-person singular pronoun. Could the words *water* and *waves* start with any letter other than W, with its sharp undulations, and doesn't it make sense that the word *yay* begins and ends with the letter that it does, its shape so resembling a figure with two hands lifted up in a glad shout of praise?

It's ridiculous—the height of stupidity, on the order, yes, of a tree shut up in a box—that not everyone speaks the same language. This is a thought that Hana has had more than once before, but perhaps because the thought of talking to Claudia is making her breathe hard (and also, she has to admit, because worrying about Rei might be addling her brain, sending it off in directions that she can no longer control or predict), she feels particularly outraged, and particularly overwhelmed, at the problems caused by there being such a mixture of different tongues in the world. She remembers how excited she'd been when she found that there was a story in the Bible to back her up on this point.

"That's not quite it," Henry had said, smiling with affection, pleased to see that church hadn't made her sleepy for once. Slipping his arm around her, he explained how the Tower of Babel was a story about the perils of reaching too high; he told her that it was a cautionary tale against pride and ambition.

"Oh," she had said, nodding. "Okay, now I see."

But she had thought it over later and come to the conclusion that she'd been right after all. Wasn't the imposition of different languages on mankind a punishment as well as a way to foil them in their attempts to reach high, and didn't that mean that the whole point of the story was the chaos that originates from not being able to communicate?

To put it another way, if everyone spoke the same language, then surely the human race would be able to build a tower high enough to reach God.

"I HAVE HERE the number for a C. King in Boston—"

"No," says Hana, interrupting politely. "Claudia *Klein*. K-L-E-I-N."

When she was Hana Klein, she'd been pleased to find how seldom she had to repeat her name, or to spell it. Her accent must be very bad today: nerves, no doubt.

HANA CAN FUNCTION in this world, ordering fresh tuna from the man at the fish store and having a chat about the latest drought with the best of them, and she's glad about that, of course. But in a way, her very facility undoes her. Her conversational ease makes her seem more proficient than she actually is, so that even those closest to her—which is to say, her daughters—believe that when she sits quietly during a discussion about anything more complicated than the weather, it's because she isn't interested in the topic, or would rather listen than participate.

When in actual fact she's struggling to find the entryway into the towers of words looming around her, when the thought of constructing her own sound structure out of the oddly shaped building blocks of the English language utterly defies her.

If only she were a braver sort. If given enough time and an audience that didn't rattle her, she could form a sentence, or three. She could tell her children stories, for example, stumbling through them though she did, sprinkling in words and whole phrases of Japanese, when they were young. But never when they were older, sharp and sharply critical teenagers who may have tried to be polite but were clearly embarrassed when she spoke in Japanese, heaven forbid. When they asked for stories then and she refused, they assumed she had just gotten tired of telling them the same old tales, never knowing how much she missed having someone with whom to share them.

With Henry, too, the give and take of a sustained conversation about any topic of substance had been beyond her grasp. The times he did take in all that she said, she always seemed to understand little of what he said in response, and the reverse held true as well. It was a mercy, really, as well as a boon that their physical relationship had been what it was. Lying with him had come as close as her brush and paints ever did in terms of stilling her desire for a greater fluency of speech.

But perhaps she'd misunderstood the relationship between her silence and their hunger for each other's bodies. Maybe it hadn't just been a stroke of good fortune that they'd had such a deep physical intimacy, one that not only went beyond words but also took the place of a substantive ongoing conversation (such as she'd once shared with Seiji, such as Henry must have once had with his first wife). Would Henry have been as passionate if she had talked more; wasn't it partly because of his need to communicate with her in some fashion that he had made love to her every night with such an intensity of focus? Nightly his fingertips had roamed over her, touching her everywhere, again and again, as if he had been born blind, her body the one and only book he could ever hope—he could ever want—to read and learn.

Apart from her body, she had given him so little.

Henry was a patient man, and he had been deeply in love with her (as deeply, yes, as she had been in love with him), but even patient men have their limits. She couldn't blame him when he reached his, nor could she admit to any surprise.

No, the only wonder was that he had stayed with her as long as he had.

IN THE YEARS SINCE HER SEPARATION from Henry, very little has changed. While she desperately hopes that she'll be able to get through to his daughter, to talk to her for the first time in, could it be, almost eighteen years, she'd do anything to substitute her paintings for words now. Hana finds phone conversations, perhaps not surprisingly, the hardest context in which to communicate, since she has no visual cues of any kind to rely on; even after more than three decades in America, she still dreads picking up the telephone. She likes to think of the telephone as the idiot box, although she knows (no idiot she) that that's a term invented for another contraption. When she wraps her hands around a receiver, that small, innocent-looking box with pushbuttons and numbers on it becomes a sinister device through which only idiocy is sent forth.

Claudia never liked or trusted her, the woman who'd stolen her father from her mother; throughout her marriage to Henry, Hana couldn't help but know that. Given that Claudia must believe that Hana went on to betray Henry, she has to be thinking far worse of her now.

So how can she persuade Claudia, over the idiot box, to help her find her daughter, when broken English is all that she has?

But then again, it's not as if she really has a choice. She has to find Rei, to ask her forgiveness and to find out if she's safe and well.

And if she is, and if, what's more, Rei could find it in herself to forgive her mother—the letter Y would have nothing on Hana, so high would she raise her arms in praise.

* * *

COMING BACK ON THE LINE, the operator apologizes for the long wait. She has the number, she announces; she's sure that this one has to be right.

Hana writes it down, thanks her, and hangs up the phone. Claudia's in Boston, just as she'd thought. Where was Henry now, and would his number be as easy to locate as that of his daughter?

WHEN HANA THINKS ABOUT the end of her second marriage, which is as seldom as she can manage it, she's grateful for her mushroom paintings. Dislike them though she always has, even she has to concede they did serve one purpose, and that exceedingly well: for a long time, before she was able to place blame where blame was squarely due, they, or at least the nightmares that led to their creation, were a convenient scapegoat for the end of her marriage. The dreams were always the same—a step-by-step reliving of those long-ago days in Hiroshima. When she woke up, her mouth dry, her heart thudding, and beneath her the sheet damp with sweat, the images would be so vivid that, try as she might, she couldn't blot them out of her mind.

Which is why she sometimes wondered if the nightmares were actually preferable to what followed them: the hours spent lying awake, gazing up at the ceiling in the dark. Usually she got up to pace or to brush her hair; sometimes she made the trek up to her studio to paint yet another mushroom—an image that, God knows, she was tired of by that point.

She'd tried, but of course she couldn't keep either her nightmares or her insomnia secret from Henry.

Talk to me, he'd urge in bed, with his touch as much as his voice. *Let me in. What happened on that day in August; what did you see, and how close did you get?*

The first time he asked her that, she had wanted to run away. It was a cool, unusually still night in April ("How strange," he muttered, more to himself than to her, as he pushed open the window closest to their bed. "How odd—how often is it that there's absolutely nothing to listen to outside?"), and she had been feeling relaxed and a little sleepy from her bath. But when he lay down beside her and asked her, first, if she'd done any more mushroom paintings that day ("Two," she had replied, so bored by her own obsession that she was beyond any shame), and then, more pressingly, about her memories of Hiroshima, she felt an immediate desire for flight. It was a bodily response, instinctive and irrational, and familiar to her from when she was a small child in Japan and she'd known, deep inside, a full second before it happened, that an earthquake was on its way.

It was a credit to the masterfulness of Henry's hands, as well as to the strength of the bond that lay between them, that she had managed to stay put. She tensed instead, lying so rigid that he temporarily stopped the soothing and at once almost astonishingly arousing movement of his fingers, propping himself up on an elbow to peer into her face and make sure that, he told her later, she hadn't had a seizure of some kind.

Then, having reassured himself of her seizure-free state, he recommenced touching her. Henry's hands were oversize, his palms and fingertips, strikingly rough. Soon after they met, she'd asked him why they were so calloused, and he'd laughed and said, *Don't you know, I work with rocks?* She had suspected he was joking, since as far as she could tell, his work involved less actual rocks than soil, microscopes, graphs, and books, but she never could be sure, as the mystery of the toughness of his palms went otherwise unexplained.

Wherever the calluses on his fingertips came from, she was thankful for them. His hands on her were a miracle: a combination, she thought, of the roughness of his skin with how gentle he was, and how deft; how did he know so precisely where to touch her, with the exact right pressure, and the perfectly calibrated stroke?

If this was how he touched rocks, she wondered that they didn't split open at the feel of his fingertips, obediently revealing the secrets of the ages for him to study and see.

Which speculation led her to the unfortunate conclusion that she was harder to crack than a rock. Because while her legs obediently—helplessly, even—parted under his touch, her lips didn't; while the feel of his hands kept her from fleeing when he asked her questions about *that day*, even the calluses on his fingertips were not enough to make her open up her secrets to him.

ALMOST A FULL YEAR AFTER that night, Henry would stop reaching for her in bed; defeated, he would, at last, give up on trying to pry her secrets out with the rough tips of his fingers.

Two months after that, he would find the document that made him as chary of speech as she always had been around him. "I don't think I know you anymore," he'd say, standing in the doorway to her studio as she sat on a stool in front of her latest mushroom. "If I ever did." The document was in his hand; a brush, still glistening with paint, in hers. She'd want to protest (*You know me*, she'd want to say, running over to reassure him with her hands and lips as well as her speech, *no one better*), but before she could start moving, before she could gather her thoughts and the words needed to express them, he'd go on. "I'll be better later," he'd add, looking away. "I'll get over this too. But surely you, *of all people*"—she'd humbly accept that dig, as well as the bite in his voice as he said it, as the least of what she deserved—"will understand if I don't feel like speaking now?"

What had happened to her; how could she have lost herself so in her work? Her hair was unwashed, her studio littered with used teacups and the remains of makeshift meals that she had had more than a week ago. She had not left the house for what seemed like days; she couldn't remember the last time she had gone on an outing with Henry, not even to the grocery store or the bank. Sure, he was a scientist and a devoted amateur gardener, spending much of his time at work hunched over his papers and at home alone out back, overturning earth with his hands. But he was, in the end, a social being, as she herself was not. What he loved most about his work was being a teacher, the give and take, the push and pull, of intellectual discussion.

She'd know then that she could never make him happy; she'd realize that it was only a matter of time before he, too, would come to acknowledge that fact.

Then, finally, about a year and a half after the night that he first asked her about Hiroshima, when she and Rei had moved out of the house to a small apartment on the other side of town, Hana would once again find that sleep was eluding her at night. The nightmares wouldn't be troubling her then; she would, at last, be painting images other than mushrooms. It'd be, instead, the thought of Henry that was keeping her awake through the nights and dogging her through the days. Who was stroking his hair back from his face at the end of a long day; who was rubbing his bad back, tucking him in, and making and bringing him the ginger tea that he liked?

So one night in early October, her hair washed, her hands clean of paint, and a thermos of hot, fragrant tea on the seat beside her, she would pull out of the lot attached to her apartment complex and begin driving through town, back to the neighborhood where she had lived with Henry for eight years. She would not get very far on that night, her courage giving out as the streets grew increasingly familiar, but when she embarked on the same journey a week later, she would have steeled herself so well for the trip that she'd be pulling up on the curb outside the house in what seemed like no time at all.

The lawn would be a little overgrown, the leaves of the maple tree they'd planted together a deep red, the house still in dire need of a paint job but dearer than ever. Only the kitchen light would be on, and Hana would strain to catch a glimpse of Henry through the curtains. Was he sitting down over a proper meal; had he lost weight that he could ill afford to lose? Had his hair, like hers, grown grayer in the six weeks that they'd been apart? But nothing would be visible from where she sat.

She'd be sitting at the wheel, giving herself a few minutes to still her breathing, collect her thoughts, and review the apologies that she'd carefully prepared and rehearsed, when, as if in answer to her prayers, her husband would step into view. Hana would see his shadow first; it would grow longer and more distinct as he came closer to the window. Then his arm would reach out, pulling back the curtains and pushing up the windows, first one and then the other; it wasn't a warm night, but he'd always loved the fresh air.

It's when he stepped back that she'd see he had company: a woman leaning against the counter.

Hana would suffer no more than a moment of panic—could he have met someone already, and if so, who, and how?—before she'd recognize Rosie, Claudia's mother. Of course, of course, she must be there to pick up her daughter or drop her off. And she probably was.

But as Hana sat there, she'd observe how Henry's first wife talked. She would see how Rosie at times used the length of her arms, and how at others she thrust her chin forward. She had, Hana knew, a reputation as a dynamic lecturer, much beloved by her students; she was, moreover, a fine scholar, well-respected in her field and in the college where she and Henry both taught. Hana would notice that while Rosie talked, Henry would nod, smiling once in a while. Then, suddenly, he'd shake his head, jumping in with a burst of his own.

Hana would bury her face behind the wheel for as long as fifteen minutes, oblivious to the possibility that one of her former neighbors might come by and tap on her window. When she finally raised her head and turned the key in the ignition, she would see how

Henry leaned forward to make his point; while backing the car out, she'd glimpse how he'd raise one long index finger high, and laugh.

Then Hana would drive through the increasingly unfamiliar streets, the thermos cooling on the seat beside her, her hands clenched so tightly around the wheel that she'd find the next day that her nails had broken the skin on her palms, back to the apartment where her work and her younger daughter awaited.

THAT ODDLY STILL NIGHT in April, lying next to Henry with the ends of her hair still wet from her bath, her body succumbing slowly but surely to his touch, she didn't know and couldn't have guessed all that would happen. If she did know or, even, could have guessed, would she have acted differently? Could she have brought herself to tell him about what it had been like; could she have made herself admit how little she remembered of the most momentous event of her life?

Hana shrugs. Whether or not she could have told Henry is an unanswerable question. What she does know—what she has to live with—is that she wishes she had. *Never tell anyone about what happened in Hiroshima,* her mother had warned. While Hana never had been one to listen to what her mother said, the fact that her mild-mannered aunt Sachiko had endorsed this injunction in unusually strong terms made her loath to disobey it. And then, of course, there was, there is, her own disinclination to speak on the subject.

Her continued silence about what happened at Hiroshima might, she supposes, seem peculiar to some, especially those whom she has met on these shores. She herself has lived in the States long enough to understand, even if she doesn't quite believe, the concept that talking about an event can exorcise it.

But after all she is, in the end, Japanese. In these thirty-odd years of life here, she has at times come close to convincing herself otherwise. She'll be with other people, laughing and talking, so caught up in the moment that she'll have forgotten about her accent or her lack of vocabulary, when she'll suddenly catch sight of herself in the mirror. As soon as that happens, she'll go mute again, struck by how different they look from her: big-boned and long-nosed, their eyes so round, their hair in myriad colors. Yet clearly it's more than her looks that mark her as alien in her own eyes, because otherwise she'd think of her daughters as foreigners in the country in which they were born and raised, and she never thinks that; when she observes them surrounded by others, they look natural to her, fitting in so well that she almost can't believe they're her own children.

She's often thought of aping her daughters' mannerisms, the way they laugh and talk and even blink. If she could do so convincingly, then perhaps she, too, could pass as an American. Of course, it would only be an act. She's not one of them, and she never will be. That fact, for she considers that a fact, serves as a valid excuse as any for why she never bought into the notion that talking about Hiroshima would go some way toward relieving her of its burden.

Still, whether or not it would have been of therapeutic benefit to her is, finally, irrelevant. She should have told Henry regardless. She should have said to him how, for the first couple of days after the mushroom cloud appeared in the east, she'd been at a hospital where she was a witness to the devastation wrought by the bomb, the mangled bodies of what seemed like and what must have in fact been thousands. Or so, at least, she was told. For weeks afterward, she didn't remember any of those bodies, nor could she recall how flattened the city of Hiroshima was, and how burnt, the smoke curling everywhere, whole buildings—along with whatever or whoever had been inside them—reduced to piles of rubble.

She should have told Henry, too, about her mother's reaction to her memory lapse. *What better way for her to keep what happened a secret,* her mother had said, *than to forget about it herself?*

But what about the slow return of her memories? The images and scenes, bright as any picture she could possibly hope to paint in her lifetime, first began to come back two or three months later, when she was home once again in Nagoya. Maybe she couldn't have told Henry about those recollections, and maybe that would have been fine. There was, for instance, the so-called hospital that she woke up to find herself in—a cot in a tent, another child lying in a bed so close to hers that if she'd reached out her hand, she could have placed it on his face. Not that she would have. His head and his left eye were bandaged, and he lay still and unmoving, as if in a deep sleep; her touch would have woken him, she thought at the time, and the boy, who appeared a year or two younger than she was, looked as if he needed his sleep.

Why doesn't she remember what any of the adults in the hospital looked like? While it's possible that she was in a children's ward—or, rather, tent—given how makeshift the hospital was, there had to be some wounded adults nearby, and certainly there were doctors and nurses. But all of the memories that came back to Hana involved children: an older girl wandering around in a daze, her left arm missing from the elbow. Sobbing from what sounded like a young boy—it was so continuous that after the first day, Hana no longer noticed it. Until, finally, it stopped in the middle of the night, and the hush that resulted was so startling that she awoke with a start. Early the next morning, when she saw a small figure, covered by a sheet, being wheeled away, she turned her head to the wall and gave out a sob of her own: she had so hoped that the boy, whom she never had a chance to glimpse, had stopped crying for another reason.

Children of all kinds and ages screaming for water, relief from pain, their mother, their father, their older brother, their teddy bear, their dog.

And, finally, the girl in a cot across the aisle. She screamed regularly, piercing sounds that almost but did not quite form themselves into words. Her face, as Hana remembers it, was covered with a violet-colored burn that looked like a map of the United States. Hana's vantage point, from a cot across the way, was awkward; that she, a twelve-year-old Japanese girl, would know what the United States looked like was doubtful, and her memory of Hiroshima after the bomb fell has already proven to be faulty. Still, there it is; that's one of the memories Hana will always carry with her.

No, she couldn't have described those images to Henry, and she was right not to have tried. They would have been too heavy even for his solidly square shoulders. Some things are better left unspoken; some secrets, best left unshared—a truth to abide by for a lifetime, never mind what they say on talk shows or in the women's magazines she flips through while waiting in line at the supermarket.

Still, she should have at least told Henry about the mushroom cloud itself. While the cloud is the one part of the experience that she has always been able to recall, her memory isn't completely trustworthy in terms of it either, any more than it is about all that followed. In her recollection the cloud has a rectangular border around it, as if seen through a window, which of course can't be accurate, which makes little sense—unless she was, even then, even as it was happening, imagining it as a painting, its horrors transmuted through the powers of her brush into something flat and portable, an object that could be bound and held within the four sides of a picture frame.

She gazed at the cloud for what probably was no more than a moment or two, until she felt the air begin to pick up speed. *How could the wind be so strong,* she had time to think to herself, *isn't it August?* before it grew even stronger and (she was later told) threw her against the wall with such force that it knocked her unconscious for two days. When part of the roof collapsed on her, it was a blessing, since it seemed to have acted as a shield, the doctors first thought, blocking her from the worst of the radiation.

Mulling over the cloud years later, she would see how its shape resembled a mushroom, a question mark, a tree in bloom, a woman huddling from the rain. She would eventually come to believe that the Tower of Babel, before it crumbled, must have been formed in the same likeness.

But on that day, as she gazed at the mushroom cloud, she registered only that it was the strangest, most monstrous thing that she had ever seen.

Would any of that really have been so hard for her to tell her second husband? She had never told her first one, it's true, but since the nightmares had remained safely in check during the years she'd been married to him, the subject had not come up. That Seiji had never asked about it was a relief, since he was, after all, Japanese, with a visceral understanding of what exposure to the atomic bomb meant.

Henry, though, was American. What if she had confessed to him how ashamed she was that although her body was not marked by visible traces of that day, it carried invisible ones, coursing through her bloodstream and buried in her very bones—wouldn't he have just held her? Didn't she know that he wouldn't have shied away from her; couldn't she see that he would have forgiven her for this too, as easily as he'd forgiven her for not being able to follow his puns?

It didn't matter, in the end. The fact that she knew he would have absorbed what happened to her in Hiroshima with kindness and sympathy made no difference. She couldn't have told him; she couldn't have spoken of that day in any kind of calm or coherent way to anyone back then, and she couldn't now either—look how she'd talked to her own daughter about it!

More to the point, even if she had told him, it might not have made a difference in terms of their marriage. At the most, it might have staved off what was surely the inevitable end by a few more years. What chance, really, did a relationship based on touch alone have? She had worried from the start that their days as a couple were numbered. Their marriage would probably have been doomed even if she had told Henry, even if she could have possibly conveyed to him through words rather than touch or images what had happened on that day in August the year that she turned twelve.

Still, even so, how she wishes that she had tried.

HANA LETS OUT HER BREATH SLOWLY: it's a soft sound that no one but she hears. Then she picks up the phone and dials the number for Henry's daughter.

Chapter Twenty

Claudia
Boston, 1999

WHEN WE WERE YOUNGER, REI AND I USED TO TRY TO
trace out the course of our lives in our palms. She was
humoring me; I was the one fascinated by the promise
of reading our hands. In a way that perhaps presaged
how I would one day fall in love with a magician, a
trickster with deft fingers who would pull rabbits from
top hats and make himself vanish—poof!—with a
wave of his hand in a cloud of white smoke, I was consumed by the notion that the blueprint to your life, its
twists and turns, its random detours and pointless
shortcuts, so often accidentally and thoughtlessly
chosen, is inscribed on the flat, square landscape of
the palm of your hand.

I liked to think (and in my more superstitious moments, can still, even now, almost make myself believe) that the palm is like DNA, the lines of the hand
a set of instructions, written in code, that dictate the

events of your life as precisely as your genes calibrate your susceptibility to summer colds and the facility with which you sing in key. The idea was oddly reassuring to me. Life might be cruelly random, but the thought that it had been mapped out beforehand (and as Rei might add, onhand) restored a measure of order to my sense of it. Your life could still change in the instant that you crossed your doorstep, the bedraggled strands of your hair gathered like a bouquet of seaweed in your hand, or in the moment you leaned forward to check whether you had a poppy seed stuck in your teeth, but at least it was a change that had been preordained, one that you could even have prepared for, if only you had known how to read the lines etched on your palms.

Rei's hands were crisscrossed with lines. Not just the three main ones where her hands creased, but myriad offshoots, and offshoots from those offshoots as well; together they formed a fantastical pattern, as weird and baroque—although of course without the colors, at least not then, at least not yet—as one of Hana's paintings. My palms, by contrast, were and still are almost completely smooth, even the three main lines on them not as deep nor as long: a classic example of minimalism, a palm for the twentieth century.

Rei and I were hampered in our endeavors at palm reading by our ignorance about what any of the lines meant. (Many years later, I would ask Vikrum, whose palm lines lie somewhere in between mine and Rei's in terms of wildness of pattern, to read my hand, but acting out the magician divo, the artiste, all he would do was playfully scoff—mind reading, yes, but palm reading? That's for hacks and charlatans; you don't really believe that superstitious nonsense, do you?) I thought I remembered reading that the top line stood for life and the one below that for love, or possibly the other way around, and that the continuity of the crease, as well as the detours that it took and the lines that cut across it and also sprang from it, were all signs by which we could foretell our fate. So the fact that the top line of my palm was short, with a break toward the end, prophesied that at some point I would come close to death and possibly even experience it but then miraculously recover, and that I would die soon afterward. The fact that my middle line was long, straight, and untouched by any bisecting pathway meant that my love life would be simple and straightforward, that there would never be anyone or anything to distract me from my one chosen love.

I shrugged when I read out my fate to Rei. It was so much what I had always expected, I could not even think to be disappointed.

And so, too, with her. She just nodded when I told her what was inscribed on the map of her palm. She had always expected that her life would be long and as adventurous as it had been up to then, that it would continue to take her to places and situations we could not even imagine; she had guessed long ago that her romances would be various, tumultuous but brief, and dizzying in their complexity. My assumptions about her had traversed the same route. Rei was destined to lead a life filled with action, while I would always be on the other side of the stage, sitting in the shadows and watching, leaning forward with bated breath, my neck craned as far as it would go during her crisis moments, and leaping to my feet, hands coming together on their own, when she got through them yet again.

I suppose I still think that.

For the most part she listens quietly while I talk about Vikrum, her eyes seldom leaving my face; every once in a while she will nod or ask me a question, and if I pause, she will prod me to go on. What does she think of my entanglement in that oldest of all clichés, a love affair with a married man; does she pity me, judge me, or take me for a fool? If she feels any of that, she hides it well.

As a child, Rei hated to sit for long. In almost all of my memories of those years, she is either dancing or whirling or running; in the few instances that she is not, she is usually just recovering her breath from having done so, or catching it preparatory to bounding up again. Even though she does tire quickly now, it is clear she is still partial to darting motions and the feel of air rushing by her face; only ten minutes ago, she was twirling about the kitchen, and when she talks, she is like my students, making gestures that require the use of the entire length of her arms and even of her legs, just as she did as a girl. But when I tell her about Vikrum, she is completely still. Only the expressions of her face are ceaselessly at play then, her mouth twitching and then suddenly breaking into that yelp of a laugh at certain points of the story, her brows lowering and her eyes darkening at others. I love how closely she listens.

So for her, I have been putting it all in order, lining up the events of the past two years as neatly as the spices in my pantry and looking them over to see how I have become this person, this woman I cannot like or respect—a potential home-wrecker, yearning to be a real one. And then, and then, and then; cumin and nutmeg and rosemary. It's strange, I hungered for so many years to hear Rei's stories, and I never knew that it worked the other way, that wanting to tell them can be as fierce an appetite. There is a power to the process, a power that seems a little dangerous to me, somehow (perhaps because it is hard in retrospect not to emphasize the role of fate and, in the process, to excuse myself, or is it that I cannot fit my love affair with Vikrum into the box of a story without altering it too?), but it is also intoxicating, and I cannot give it up.

Still, much as I might like the role of storyteller, it is not really mine. I have been waiting patiently for weeks now; it's high time for her to slough off her silence about what is ailing her. Rei just shakes her head, though, when I tell her that it's now her turn to spill.

"This is riveting stuff," she says. "I'm hooked, you can't stop now."

I tell her that at best it's a tawdry story, not even original and certainly not sensational enough to make it to the soaps. I say I told myself for the whole first year that I was with Vikrum that I am not the typical thirtysomething still-single woman who ends up in love with a married man with children, but that I then realized that is precisely what every thirtysomething etc. tells herself. Rei's eyes narrow. Then, crossing her heart with her pinkie, she swears that her life isn't anywhere near as exciting as mine, and when I ask her about why she moved here so suddenly—surely there is a story there?—she shakes her head no very quickly; it was just about the job.

After that Rei turns to look away, across the room, and when she does so there is something familiar about her pose—the lift of her chin and the set of her lips, and the way in which she veils her eyes. When I realize where I have seen it before, I am glad that my hands are busy in the dough, and also that I can use the flour adrift all over the kitchen as an excuse to swipe an arm across my face: even after all these years, I am more disturbed than I should be to be reminded of her mother.

STORED IN AN OLD SHOE BOX that I keep on the shelf at the top of my coat closet, I have a large number of photographs of Hana. In the throes of passion and almost endearingly oblivious to the fact that I maybe would not want them, Dad gave me copies of the best shots of her and him together. Sometimes I think I should throw them away, or at least cut her image out of the pictures of her and Dad together. Still, maybe he knew what he was doing when he gave them to me: I cannot quite bear to get rid of them.

In light of the dozens of Kodak images I have of my stepmother, it seems odd that the picture of her I recall most often in my mind is one that cannot be found in that crumbling shoe box. It is instead a shot from a photo I have lost, or perhaps never had or have even seen—a picture that may exist only in my imagination. She and my father are dressed in light T-shirts and surrounded by lush, colorful flowers, bougainvillea and birds-of-paradise and others so exotic I do not think I have even seen their like in the travel books that I used to love to read. A magnificent blue-green butterfly hovers, caught mid-flight, in the upper right-hand corner of the shot. Hana is in the dead center of the picture, my father standing a little behind her, on her right, his face partly in shadow. He looks down at her adoringly; his arm is draped over her shoulder and his torso is a little curved, protectively, to enfold hers. Skinny as he is, he is so much larger and broader than she is that part of his left shoulder is visible behind hers.

Hana and my father's positioning in the shot, combined with her beauty (so simple but powerful that it puts the blazing brilliance of the flowers and the butterfly to shame) and the way in which she gazes away, to a point far beyond the margins of the photo, makes it seem as if his function in the picture is to be a frame for her, of no greater importance than the white border that traverses its edge. He looks so alive—grinning away, his thick brows, already gray then, lifted in amazement at his good fortune to be with her, the object of his adoration, his former paramour and now his legal wife, in that tropical paradise—that his face throws into relief the absence of any emotion on hers. The effect is of a stillness in the center of the photo, eerily at odds with the rest of it, so bursting and bustling with color and joy.

They are in Hawaii in this shot. That was as close to the Far East as Dad ever got with Hana. He always wanted them to go to Japan together. He badly wanted to meet her mother, who was ailing but still alive during the first half of their marriage, and to talk with her brother and her sister in their native setting. But in the end, Hana said no, that she hated so much to fly that she would not be able to bear it. Besides, she did not really see the point of visiting, now that her aunt Sachiko was gone.

How much did it disappoint my father to be deprived of a chance to visit Hana's childhood home with her? Did he yearn with a deep hunger to hear of her past; did he plead with her for stories, just as Vikrum demands them from me? But then, once she began, was he sorry? Did he hate hearing about her first husband; was he tortured by the story of how she chose to marry Seiji instead of a prince and how she never once regretted it?

It seems obvious, looking back, that Dad never really stood a chance at making Hana happy. The real wonder is why he decided to try—as well as, of course, how he could give my mother and me up in the process.

"I'D FORGOTTEN HOW MUCH I love the smell of flour," says Rei. "It's like old times, isn't it? You baking, and me sitting and watching and being no help at all."

With the dough—white bread, of course, and formed in a braid, a shape that, she tells me, she particularly likes—in the oven now, I can give her my full attention. "You'll help eat it, right?" I ask, trying not to sound anxious. Freshly baked bread was one food that she always had a real weakness for, and surely that has not changed.

"I'll help eat it," she repeats. Her voice is innocent but there is a knowing glint in her eye, and I wonder if she has cottoned on to my resolution to make her gain weight. Given how much food I have been making for her, it would not be a miracle if she has.

"Do you remember how I once tried to make banana bread, and how even that ended in disaster? You had to bail me out." She shakes her head, remembering.

"Rei," I say. I have utterly failed to pave the way for this revelation, but unless I speak up soon, I am going to lose my nerve once again. "I need to tell you something I should have told you before. About two years after your mom left Dad—"

"What was that?" she asks sharply, her head swiveling. "Did something just get knocked over?"

"Just a pile of books. You see?" I say, waving my hand airily toward the back of the room, where there is nothing to see. "I told you: this apartment is haunted by Orson. How could I even think about getting a new cat?"

"You're right," she says, lowering her voice. "Let's see if we can hear him again. Hey, Orson, hey, kitty, come out."

The ticking of the timer is loud in the silence. Through the open window, a late-afternoon breeze wends its way into my apartment, lifting first the ends of her hair, and then of mine. It sifts through the small piles of flour that remain on the counter and riffles through the newspaper that lies on the chair next to Rei's.

"A true cat," Rei pronounces after a minute or two. "He won't come if he's been called."

"Maybe later. Anyway," I continue, "as I was saying before Orson rudely interrupted me, Henry got remarried." I take a deep breath in, but it's no good. My nerve is nowhere to be found. "Two, almost three years after he and Hana split up," I conclude lamely.

"That's good," Rei says, nodding. "Kei and I have been worried about Hana a little, what with her being single and all. It must be a relief for you, knowing that there's someone looking after him. My God, it's a huge relief for me—I was feeling really worried about Henry."

That is the most she has said about her mother for some time, and I leap at it, perhaps too aggressively. "Your mom's single? But she has a boyfriend, right?"

Rei flushes. "She doesn't, actually. And she hasn't since Henry, if you must know."

"Oh," I say. "Right."

There is more to this story than she is telling me, of course, since Hana had to have had at least one lover since my father—why else would she have left him so abruptly? But Rei is looking as remote as her mother again, and adept as I was at getting her to tell me tales of both the fairy and non-variety when we were young, times have changed, and my confidence has slipped. At this point I am no longer sure if I can make her cough any story up. Besides, and perhaps more to the point, I do not have time now for my own particular brand of the Heimlich maneuver (a punch in the ribs, yes, but one specially designed to draw out stories rather than chicken bones); revelations about Hana's love life and even about Rei's health can wait for another five minutes.

I am a woman on a mission. I have a secret of my own that must be divulged.

"So as I was saying, my dad got remarried," I say, and then I stop.

I take so long to resume that Rei looks up. "Yes, you were saying that."

"And . . ." I say.

"And?" she says, beginning to laugh. "You can tell me, whatever it is. It's okay; he and Mom divorced what—almost two decades ago, and by now I'm resigned to it."

"And," I say, reminding myself to breathe, but forgetting to do so right away, so that I have to remind myself all over again, "the woman he remarried—it's Mom."

"Right," says Rei. "Wow." She has turned a shade paler, but she manages a smile, and it is a real one; I have known the girl since she was nine, and there is no fooling me. "That's wonderful."

She's okay. Suddenly I notice that I have been holding on very tightly to my favorite wooden spoon; when I uncurl my hand, it's stiff and a little cramped. Rei is fine with the news; Vikrum was completely wrong about how difficult the idea of my parents' remarriage would be for her. "It happened at least two years after he and your mom split up," I tell her again. Then, to give her time to compose herself, I squat down and rummage through the cabinet below the counter, looking for a utensil I do not need.

Only a few seconds lapse before Rei begins to speak. "You know, I actually wondered for a moment or two way back when if that would happen. They remained such good friends, after all, throughout the divorce. . . ."

Such good friends? Taking advantage of my position behind the cabinet door, I sit back on my heels for a moment. It is true that my parents had sat together at one of my band concerts, but that was only because Dad was late, coming in as the lights were dimming, and had slipped into the nearest available seat. When he came to pick me up or drop me off for my weekend visits, he and Mom chatted, very civilly, mostly about their work and sometimes about me, but they never seemed disposed to linger and in fact always seemed relieved and even anxious to go their separate ways.

Still, maybe Rei is not too far off. Even back then, my parents always kissed each other, albeit only on the cheek, when they met up. No matter how bad it got, no matter how awkward and uncomfortable and sad (Mom smiling valiantly, waving good-bye from the door as I left with Dad to go to his new home—to his new wife, his new children, and his new cat—for our first Christmas as a divorced family; Dad quiet in the car, watching her in his rearview mirror as he pulled away until she was just a dot of red and green), they were always kind to each other, always considerate of the other's feelings.

"... and I'm glad it happened, for your sake. And for your mom's sake, and of course most of all for Henry's." Rei pauses. When she speaks again, her voice is shockingly bitter: "He deserves all the happiness he can get, after my mother."

I am so surprised that I involuntarily jerk my head up and bang it, hard, against the cabinet shelf.

"Are you okay?" she asks, startled, peering over the counter. "That was loud."

"It's fine," I say, waving her away. "That sound was just the cracking of my skull. And, to a lesser extent, of my dignity."

Rubbing my head and once again sitting back on my heels, I look up at Rei across the flour-dusted counter. She gazes back at me, open-mouthed, still, with surprise. Have I ever heard her say anything that negative about Hana, let alone in that tone? She and her mother had always been close. When I would complain about mine, which was often, Rei was sympathetic, but she never recip-rocated with stories about her mother's annoying habits, the myr-iad petty ways in which she was misunderstood by her, or the unjust treatment she received at her hands.

Sometimes I wondered whether Rei was silent on those occasions out of loyalty to her mother, knowing—all too well!—how tenuous my relationship with her was. But in the end I always decided that no, incredible as it might seem, she really just likes her mom.

"Why did you say that about your mother?" I ask.

"Should I get you some ice?" she says, reaching her hand out to touch where I am rubbing. "You're going to have a real bump."

Again I wave her away. "Dad was happy with Hana," I tell her. "Sure, it didn't work out in the end, and he was really depressed af-ter she left. But they were happy together for a long time—almost eight years isn't too shabby."

Shaking her head and muttering something not quite audible about stubborn people who don't take care of themselves, suffering concussions and ending up in comas as a result, Rei pushes her chair back and goes to the freezer to make an ice pack.

"If Hana ultimately ended up meeting someone else she loved more than Henry—well," I say, lifting my shoulders up in a quick, easy motion, "that's the way it goes, isn't it?" That I can shrug about these particular aspects of our parents' shared history is, of course, only made possible by what followed it. If my mother and father had not reconciled and remarried, that lift of my shoulders, quick and easy though it is, would be beyond me. But given that they did, I can afford to be generous about the beautiful, charming, and oh-so-casually destructive force that was Hana Watanabe.

Or in any event I can pretend to be generous about her, at least in the presence of her daughter.

"People fall out of love," I say, raising my voice so she can hear me as she cracks out the ice cubes she has taken from the freezer. "Happens all the time. And then, go figure, divorce rates are high."

Try as I might, I cannot help but sound a little bitter myself. "Rei, I really don't need an ice pack."

She has placed the ice in a plastic bag and wrapped a dish towel around it. "Shut up," she says calmly, holding it to my head. "Let me feel useful, for once."

"You danced to entertain me while I was making the bread," I say, taking the ice pack from her and pressing it back onto my head. Despite what I said, the numbing of the pain that it brings is welcome. "That was very useful."

Rei walks around to the other side of the counter and sits back down. "Ha ha," she says, almost absentmindedly.

Then, suddenly, she shivers.

"Are you cold?" I ask, sliding off the stool. "It was because you were holding the ice pack, wasn't it? I can shut the windows—"

"No, don't. I'm not cold in the least. What was that expression your mom liked to use? Someone just walked over my grave." Her smile is only a little forced. "Maybe it was Orson."

"Orson wouldn't do that," I say. When it comes to distracting Rei, there is nothing more surefire than cats. "He was such a sweet-tempered cat. He was born with this tiny defect in his hind paws—a misplaced toe, so that his nail stuck out. He used to click when he walked, as if he were wearing high heels. He was like this big old cuddly tom in drag."

"I wish I could have met him," she says. Once again, it is clear that her mind is elsewhere. She hesitates and then adds, slowly, "Claudia, there's something I should tell you too."

I want to say that what we have here is a regular soap opera, with dark family secrets exposed every minute, but she is swaying in her seat, and something tells me that this is not the time.

Rei carefully places the palms of her hands on the edge of the countertop, bracing herself. "I know you think my mother fell in love with someone else and that's why she left your dad. I know that that's what Henry thought, and that that's what she let him think, even though she refused to actually say there was another man." Rei seems to be speaking quickly, even for her, so much so that it is almost hard for me to follow, and I wonder for a moment how much damage that bump on my head has caused. "But that's not what happened. There never was anyone for Hana but Henry."

"So why did she leave him then?"

We stare at each other. Rei's eyes drop first. "It's—it's a long and complicated story. Maybe I could tell you some other time."

Like the bell that marks the end of a round of fighting, the timer goes off with a ding. It is time for us to head back into our corners, to be hosed down and pep-talked by our trainers. I slide off my stool, pick up a pot holder and, opening the oven, slide the bread out. It is cool enough in my apartment that the gust of heat that I am met with is not unpleasant: mild as the month has been, winter is undeniably on its way. The smell of bread, warm, fragrant, and almost filling in itself, is everywhere.

After placing the bread on the cooling rack, I turn back to face her. "Those seventeen years when I didn't see you—I thought throughout that entire time it was your mom's doing." My voice sounds oddly robotic. "I thought your mother decided you shouldn't talk to me; I thought she must have insisted on it."

"Why would she do that?" Rei is frowning, puzzled and, for a split second, a little defensive about her mother, just as she used to be in the old days. Then she recovers and shakes her head. "She did lots of terrible things—some so terrible I can't even tell you, at least not yet—but she would never do *that*."

There is nothing to say. Still, she is watching me expectantly; clearly some kind of response is required here. "Oh."

"It was my decision entirely. My mother never asked—in fact she told me to call you—but I thought I owed that to her. And besides, Henry didn't need to have a constant reminder of my mom, which is what I would be. I knew he'd be kind and that he probably would even continue to be a father of some kind to me"—tapping her forehead with the heel of her hand, she rushes those words, and then slows down again—"but I figured that it'd be better for him not to see or hear about me."

Better for him. And what about me; what about you? Was it also better for us? I do not say these words aloud, yet Rei nods again, seeming to hear them anyway.

"I was miserable about it," she says flatly. "And outraged at the sheer absurdity of it all. We were brought together and told we were sisters because of a marriage, because two people related to us had a yen for each other and then had a ceremony in a church and were given a piece of official-looking paper. And then they stopped having a yen for each other and so, suddenly, we weren't sisters anymore. As if that could just be taken away. It was absurd and I knew it, but I bought into it anyway. The lines were drawn, and I thought I had to be loyal to my mother, when it was clear all along that you and Henry were my real family. My mother"—she all but spits out the words—"she's just an accident of birth, of biology."

Once again we fall silent. If I listen hard, perhaps I will be able to hear the clicking of Orson's high heels as he comes down the hall again, or even the low and infinitely more masculine-sounding rumble of his purr. And then I think I almost hear it—click click, a brisk and elegant sound. No, it's just the bathroom faucet, dripping again; Orson will not come out today.

It is almost twilight, which used to be Rei's favorite time of the day—who knows what she prefers now? The light is fading fast from the room. In another couple of minutes, when it is too dark to see her face, I will turn on the lights and shut the windows, leaving one or two open a crack so that the soft evening air can still steal its way inside. In another thirty, I will make tea and bring out the butter and the jars of honey and jam and creamy peanut butter, and she and I will sit down to eat the bread together. The topics we discuss will be easy ones—what is going on with her work, perhaps, or with mine—and when the conversation lags, we will pretend that we are being quiet because we are listening for the clicking sound that a dead cat's deformed nails make against the polished wooden beams of my apartment's floors.

"Let me ask you this," I say. "Just one last question." I know she can see that I am trembling, but I no longer have the energy to hide the signs of my anger. "What made you change your mind? Why did you decide to come back to me?"

She looks down at her left hand, spreading it open and then cupping it, holding it away from my view as she has done throughout these days together.

Then she glances up at me, and with a rueful, perhaps apologetic smile that I can just barely make out in the half-light of the room, she shrugs. Did I really think that lifting the shoulders was an easy motion? Never again. Bony to the point of fragility though her shoulders are, the way she moves makes them seem impossibly heavy, and she looks exhausted afterward, as if the motion has cost her much.

"You get sick like this, and loyalties change," she says, almost under her breath.

She is dead wrong here, of course. Her loyalties have not changed all that much; otherwise, she would have explained why her mother left my father. Whatever Hana did to her, Rei still cannot bring herself to break her trust.

Yet at this point, at least, there is little that I can do. For whatever reason, she has no one else to turn to; she has been ill and she needs me, and she is not ready or perhaps even able to talk.

I stand up and, feeling my way through the dark, move toward the open windows.

IT IS LATER IN THE EVENING, not long after Rei has left, that the phone call comes.

"Hello?"

"Claw?" Then, as if sensing how I flinched at her use of my child-hood nickname, she corrects herself. "Claudia? Is that you?"

I try but I find I cannot make a sound.

"It's Hana," she says, with her usual gift for the obvious.

Chapter Twenty-One

Hana
California, 1999

SHE TAKES A FEW MOMENTS TO RESPOND. "HANA?" SHE
says at last, and Hana can hear the breathy quality of
her surprise clearly through the thousands of miles of
telephone wire that separate them.

"I've been thinking a lot about you lately," Claudia
continues slowly. "How have you been?"

What had she been expecting? Claudia's no longer
a nine-year-old, hostile to her daddy's new girlfriend;
nor is she even a teenager, resigned but every bit as
hostile still to his new wife. She always had been a loving, fiercely loyal child, but those very qualities had,
Hana knows, conspired against a good relationship
with her stepmother: not only did she feel compelled
to hate Hana because of her devotion to her mother,
there was the fact that Hana had confused and divided
her loyalties between her parents.

Still, no matter how mature Claudia's become, no

matter how loving she's always been, she can't have forgotten that Hana stole her father from her mother and then, after eight apparently happy years, left him.

Which is to say that there's no reason whatsoever for Claudia's friendliness.

Whatever the source of her warmth, though, perhaps it opens the way for idle chatter. Such as, for starters: what's happened to Henry, is he happy, is he still gardening, and how's his bad back?

But there are far more pressing matters at hand. "Fine," says Hana. "I've been fine, thank you for asking." Although she tries to swallow, her mouth is too dry. "I'm looking for Rei."

A hesitation, and then: "But she's not looking for you."

So here it was. It's hopeless, of course. Despite all of the arguments she's amassed and prepared, Hana is tempted to thank her now and hang up, and so save herself the attenuated anguish of more disappointment. After all, while Kei had been invariably kind and soothing when Hana called to voice her worries about Rei, for months she would not issue more than vague reassurances about Rei's general health. She had, she told her mother, made a promise to Rei, and that was all there was to it. Until yesterday, when Hana, distraught with fear, had demanded yet again, *Who's taking care of Rei? Is she all by herself?*

She's with Claudia, Kei had said, the words lumbering out of her mouth. Hana could hear how she was already regretting them even as she spoke. *Claudia's taking care of her.*

And that was all Kei would say; that was all the help she would proffer. So why should a woman who was, once long ago, Hana's stepdaughter step in, when even her firstborn wouldn't? Especially when it means a betrayal of sorts of Rei, whom Claudia has always protected as if she were her daughter rather than a sister of the most tenuous kind?

Still, Hana can think of nowhere else to turn. She has no choice but to attempt to convince her. "I know, but—"

"I'll help you," says Claudia, interrupting. "I'll help you find Rei."

Chapter Twenty-Two

Claudia
Boston, 1999

"CAN YOU LOVEBIRDS SPARE A CIGARETTE?" WHEEDLES A man standing at the corner. Vikrum roots around in his pocket for change and hands him a couple of quarters; we bid him good night and walk another four blocks, discussing the upcoming elections all the way. But as we step into the dark warmth of the restaurant, I find myself recalling the panhandler's words.

"It's odd that that man called us lovebirds, isn't it?" I say, after we have taken our seats. "When we weren't holding hands, or even walking close. How could he tell?"

Vikrum leans forward. "What you and I have," he says, "is so warm and so bright that it's obvious to everyone. Everyone within a mile of us knows that we're in love."

I reach out and cup his face, smooth and warm, with my hands. He turns his head and lightly kisses the inside of each of my wrists in turn.

"A pair of lovebirds," I say. "That's us."

"Speaking of pairs," he says, "how's your *other* other half? You haven't mentioned Rei for a while."

"Good." Removing my hands from his face, I busy myself with the unfolding of my napkin. "Rei's good."

"Let's all get together," he says, in one of his bursts of enthusiasm. "Maybe we could go for a drive, the three of us, out to an orchard. Pick apples, pet goats, go for a hayride."

I move my head in a gesture that's more of a neck stretch than a nod. When was the last time we had the luxury of a whole day together? Then, too, Rei's telling silence on the subject of Vikrum weighs on my mind; then there's the welfare of two small children to consider.

"Someday," I say, echoing him. "Maybe," I add in a low voice.

I had thought I spoke too quietly to be heard over the music, but I must have miscalculated. He looks, as Rei would say, as if his crest (such a phallic image—do women even have crests, and if not, does that mean we do not get disappointed to the same extent that men do? Perhaps because our expectations are so much lower?) has fallen.

As always, when Vikrum's shoulders slump and his eyes look down at the floor or just gaze, unfocused, straight ahead, I can feel it physically, as a tightening in my chest. Despite all that I resolved in Rei's presence, I cannot help myself. Keeping him happy, as much as it is in my power to do so (and yes, it's heady, so much is it in my power to do so), is almost a reflex with me now.

"It's just that Rei does travel a lot," I say.

The explanation is weak, and comes too late besides. Vikrum nods, pulls out another smile.

He and I sit at our favorite table in our favorite meeting place, an Afghanistani restaurant named Akhbar's; our favorite waiter, an unfailingly well-dressed old man named Omar, hovers nearby.

Sopping wet and laughing, Vikrum and I first came running into Akhbar's more than a year ago, when a summer storm caught us by surprise. Ever since, we have waged a personal and (given that the restaurant world in Boston, as everywhere else in the late nineties, is governed by an unforgiving Darwinian code) almost certainly doomed campaign to keep the place in business.

The food is at best mediocre; the lighting, dim to the point of watch-out-don't fall-over-that-table darkness; the cleanliness of the silverware, definitely suspect. I love the restaurant anyway. Although Rei would no doubt cite my affection for Akhbar's as yet another example of how I champion the underdog, it has dips that are edible, ceiling fans that move lazily above our heads, and waiters who recognize us—so what if, as Vikrum always teasingly reminds me, that is only because they hardly get any other customers, and almost certainly no one who comes back more than once.

His teasing about the waiters aside, Vikrum may like Akhbar's even more than I do. It is always the first restaurant he suggests we go to; whenever I say we should try someplace else (this is, after all, a city filled with underdog restaurants), he coaxes, sometimes even getting on his knees and sticking out his tongue to do his best imitation, which is very fine indeed, of a dog begging, until I have to laugh and agree.

When I ask, he says he likes it because it is tucked away in a corner of a pretty street, not far from my apartment, because he enjoys calling it Akhbar's Bar (not only does the name allow him to practice his *Bahston* accent, the restaurant doesn't have a liquor license), and because he can make fun of the music they play in the background, cheesy pop songs from the seventies. Music that I think he may secretly love—I often catch him singing the same tunes afterward.

If it sometimes occurs to me that he might also like this place because he never has to worry about bumping into any of his wife's friends here, or a colleague from work—well, that's an unworthy thought, which I always manage to stifle more or less quickly. Besides, when I hear Vikrum belting out Diana Ross tunes in the shower after we make love, it is clear to me, too, that Barless Akhbar's plays the best music, bar none, in the city.

STILL OVERCOME WITH REMORSE at having canceled both of our dates last week, Vikrum has promised me a surprise for tonight. Although I told him a dozen times not to bother, after we have finished eating he unveils it, using a scarf rather than a veil, a red one that he drapes over my water glass. He mumbles some words and waves a hand; when he pulls the scarf away the water has been turned into wine. It is a neat trick, which I appreciate equally for its Biblical reference and for the fact that I prefer wine to water, but when I clap my hands with delight, he shakes his head at me, staving off the applause.

"Just warming up," he says. He has prepared entertainment. A rare and wonderful treat indeed—new magic tricks that he wants me to see.

Omar and a couple of the other waiters have been hovering by the kitchen door; drawn by the show, they have been edging closer and are now steps away from the table. I beckon them with a wave of the hand. "Come watch with me."

Omar beams. He goes to the kitchen, pokes his head through the door, and whistles. When he comes back to our table it is with reinforcements. Our table is surrounded by waiters and what might be delivery boys—maybe six of them, all told.

It's okay, Vikrum loves a good audience. Soon he's even turning to ask Omar if he'll help out. When Omar, blushing and grinning with pleasure, nods, Vikrum stands and leads him so that he faces us.

"Pretend you're about to get your picture taken," Vikrum tells him. "Pose for us all."

Omar—I would never have taken him for such a ham—strikes a

matador's pose, his waiter's napkin thrown over his shoulders like a cape, his noble profile turned toward us, his hands on his hips and his chest thrust out, *olé!*

"That's perfect," says Vikrum, "absolutely perfect. Now hold that, please." He waves the magic scarf in front of Omar, and when he pulls it away there is a single rose, dewy and blood-red, between Omar's grinning teeth.

Laughter and applause from the other waiters. With a puzzled look on his face, Omar reaches out to grab the rose.

"Be careful," I say, laughing as well, "aren't there thorns on that rose?"

Vikrum clucks his tongue. "It's true," he says. "You've got to watch out for those." Gently he takes the flower from Omar's mouth and then makes a big production of pricking his own fingers with it. "Man, are those sharp!" he says, shaking out his hand. He waves the scarf over it (hey presto), and holds it out for my inspection. The thorns are gone from the stalk.

"To our brave matador," says Vikrum, presenting the rose to Omar with a flourish, while the small crowd cheers. "For risking the drawing of blood for our viewing pleasure."

Next, Vikrum brings out a jar. Within it is an earthworm, lazily writhing and coiling on maybe a quarter inch of soil.

"This trick requires no magic words or gestures," he tells us solemnly. He covers the jar with his scarf. "In fact it is beyond my own modest powers to accomplish it. What we require is the participation of a beautiful young lady."

I roll my eyes at him, but I am the only woman in the room; when he holds it out to me I take the jar.

"If you would be so kind," he says, "please kiss the top of the jar five times."

Five times rather than the more traditional three. Vikrum has tailored the trick for me. He keeps his hand on my shoulder as I bend my head for the kisses.

"As you all will now see," he says, "as we all should in fact always remember—with the love of a good woman, anything is possible."

When he pulls away the scarf from the jar, there is a collective gasp. In the place of a blind worm there now sits a monarch butterfly on a branch, a proud glow of gold in the dimly lit room, slowly opening and shutting its wings.

"My God," I say.

"It's for you," he says. "You can keep it as a pet in the jar."

I am about to speak but he beats me to it.

"But knowing you, of course, you'll release it in the arboretum first thing tomorrow."

I nod happily, my head bobbing up and down to express not just my assent to his statement but also an affirmation of a question that has been troubling me, almost unbeknownst to myself. These past two years have not been a mistake.

When I first met Vikrum, I was overwhelmed by a feeling of relief. It was as if I had been missing him my whole life, as if I had been searching and pining for him all along, but had not known it.

No matter how long I live, I will never love anyone more.

"And now," he says, "for the final act."

An audience member gives an audible sigh. At some point someone must have gone and whistled to the kitchen staff as well, for several men in aprons have now joined the wait staff gathered around our table. Who would have guessed that so many people work in a restaurant visited by so few? I make a mental note: we need to leave a big tip indeed.

Vikrum places a plate before me, and over the plate the magic scarf. Holding up the center of the scarf with one hand to make a tent out of it, he mutters some words, which sound suspiciously like the lyrics of the song "Hey, Jude" said extremely fast, and waves his other hand in the air. He pulls the scarf away, and there on the plate rests a square box, large enough to fit a medium-size pumpkin, gift-wrapped in lemon-yellow paper and a dark blue bow.

Murmurs of appreciation from the audience.

"For me?" I say, drawing in my breath.

"But of course," he says, bowing.

"Oh, you really shouldn't have..."

I undo the ribbon and tear off the paper; the box is also yellow. Primed by the rose and the butterfly to a high state of expectation, the waiters and the kitchen staff are craning their necks to see what lies inside. A laugh rises up around us when I lift out another box, this one orange, from the interior.

I look over at Vikrum, and he smiles and nods.

"I seem to remember a girl once telling me," he says, bending his head down to whisper in my ear, "that anticipation is all too often the best part."

A couple of the waiters clap when I kiss him.

Inside the orange box is a red one, and inside the red, a purple. I am bouncing a little in my seat from the excitement; the crowd around us is whispering among themselves, making guesses, placing bets. Vikrum sits back, his face in the shadows, and watches me.

The fifth and tiniest box is smaller than the smallest baby's fist, a plain and simple white. Inside it is an object I roll out onto my hand: a slim circle of gold, which has attached to it something that picks up what little light there is in the room and sends it back to us, magnified and refracted, so that I seem to be holding a minute star in my palm.

The waiters and kitchen staff fall abruptly and completely silent. Bewildered, I look up at them; as if at some hidden command they are beginning to disperse, many of them on tiptoe. While it is too dark to tell for sure, most of them seem to be averting their eyes from mine—did Omar just give me a wink?—but without exception they appear to have smiles on their lips. In just a few seconds Vikrum and I are alone in the room. When did the seventies pop

music stop? How could a restaurant in Boston, even an extraordinarily unpopular one, be so still?

Vikrum has been watching me intently. "What's the matter?" he
says at last.

His voice is soft, but it still makes me jump.

"Wh—" My throat feels oddly strangled. I clear it and try again.
"What is this?"

"Don't you know?" he asks, tenderly.

"No."

With a smile he takes the circle of gold from me. Then he places
the ring—for that is what it is, the word comes to me as he is
passing it back to me—on the third finger of my left hand. It's an
exact fit.

"Does that help?" he asks, teasing; he is even laughing a little.
But his hands, which never waver, which are steady and sure even
as they throw knives at scantily clad beauties and pull shiny coins
out of the tiny ears of babes, are trembling as they hold on to mine.

Speechless, I stare at him.

"Claudia," he says, and now his voice is trembling too. "My love,
do you really not know what this is? This is a proposal—I'm asking
you to be mine, forever."

And then, suddenly, my voice is back. It does not tremble either.
"Vikrum," I say, "what are you doing? Did you forget about
Lakshmi?" There, I have done it. I have broken our unspoken rule
and spoken that unbroken word, the name of his raven-haired,
fragile-boned, wine-loving wife. As soon as I say it, I know why we
have had that rule: the very act of saying her name makes me want
to cry for what I have done to her. It makes me remember the day I
caught my mother weeping into her notebook, the equations she
had slaved over for months blurring into streaks of blue, and how
much I had hated Hana then.

"Are you asking me to move to Utah with you, to become your

second wife?" I ask. "Because I've got to tell you—I don't really believe in bigamy, and I definitely don't want to practice it."

"No, you've got it all wrong," he says, shaking his head. He sounds calm but his eyes are enormous and dark. "It's a real proposal. It's a promise for the future, when the kids are grown. It's how I feel about you. I want us to be together for the rest of our lives—"

He has gone crazy, that is clear. I am trying to control my breathing, but I cannot seem to manage it; every gulp of air rasps. "But we can't be together forever," I say. "We're barely together now; you already have a wife."

Looking up to face Vikrum, I speak through clenched teeth. "Don't you know how hopeless this situation is? What were you thinking? How could you put me through this farce of a proposal? Didn't you realize it would just point out to me all that I may never have?"

"Do you think I don't realize that?" he cries out. Nothing about him is calm anymore; with his trembling hands, he tugs at his hair. "Do you think I haven't been tormented by the thought of all that I've been depriving you of? Every day I think about how much you want to have children. Every day I think about how you should be with a man who can be with you, who can love you, twenty-four hours a day.

"This was a stupid idea." With a wave of the hand he dismisses the butterfly and the boxes lying in disarray on the table—an idea that took God knows how many hours of careful thought and planning. "But I was desperate. I thought I was losing you. I *knew* I was losing you, I could feel you slipping through my fingers." Those magician's fingers, so adept at hiding objects in a twinkle and making us believe they are lost for good, until they just as quickly reappear.

"And I couldn't bear it," he concludes in a whisper.

For a few long moments we look at each other across the

expanse of the table. "Well, I can't bear this," I say, whispering back. I push my chair back and, swaying just a little, come to my feet.

"Wait! I'll end the marriage now," he says, pleading. "Tonight, if you like. Just don't walk away from me. Don't walk away from us."

I stop and look at him, hard. He is breathing quickly and his eyes look red and more than a little wild, but he gazes back at me steadily. My first reaction is to lash out at him again for making promises that he cannot or at least will not keep. Yet as I look at him, my anger ebbs away, as it should. He may be speaking out of desperation, but he means it; if I say the word, he will leave Lakshmi and his children before the day is over.

"You can't do that," I say. Sure, Vikrum complains about the dense network of his extended family and the obligations they impose on him. Yet his identity is deeply bound up in his grandmothers and parents and the whole doting brood of uncles and aunts and cousins. He cannot violate what they stand for, for the simple reason that he stands for the same. "You know you don't really want to do that." At least not now, at least not yet. "Think of the children."

Vikrum drops his gaze and lowers his chin—a gesture acknowledging the truth of what I said, or is that the bow of defeat?

"Please don't go," he says.

"I have to." So my voice is shaking after all.

I take the ring off, but before I give it up I pause. What am I doing? He is the only man I have ever truly loved. But a far more insistent question is also asserting itself: what *have* I been doing for these past two years? I let go of the ring, trying to drop it back into the small box in which I found it, but my eyes are blurring too much and I miss. With a thud and a clatter it drops onto the table and rolls to a stop.

Vikrum reaches out a hand and places it on my wrist; it is without much difficulty that I shake it off. I dump out money from my wallet, bills and coins scattering everywhere. It covers far more than my half of what the meal comes to, yet I know Vikrum, he will leave the extra for the tip. I want to kiss him one last time—five last times—good-bye, to cup that dear, round face once again in my hands and hold it, to drink it in with my eyes so I will have it imprinted forever in my memory. Yet I cannot risk such a dangerous act. Besides, it's already there, it will always be there.

Stuffing the wallet back into my jacket pocket, I gather up the butterfly in the jar and walk out of the restaurant.

THANK GOD for the small mercies. Outside, it's raining; everyone who sees me running through the streets will blame my haste on my lack of an umbrella, and the wet on my cheeks on the turbulence of the skies.

The show is over, and it is clear to everyone now that what had seemed like magic was only smoke and mirrors.

Chapter Twenty-Three

Rosie
England, 1999

TEETH HAVE MEMORY. YEARS AFTER THE INTRICATE APPA-
ratus of braces (made of metal and cement, no less, the
most unyielding substances of man's devising) has been
removed, front teeth grow resolutely back into their familiar overbite; canines move stealthily but steadily
until they once again occupy their old cozy niche in
front of their dear neighbor the incisor. Rosie learned
that from a magazine she picked up somewhere; since
she hasn't flipped through anything but books on number theory, various editions of the *Journal of the American
Mathematical Society,* and the occasional George Eliot
novel in either her home or office for some years now,
she probably read it while sitting in a doctor's office of
some kind. Not a dentist's office, though. What the article led you to conclude was that whatever thousands
of dollars spent on Junior's orthodontics would have
been better applied toward a new hi-fi system.

Not too good for the dental industry if *that* got out.

From what Rosie remembered—which, somewhat unexpectedly, was rather a lot, even now, even though she was almost in her seventh decade—she thought the article was suggesting that teeth were stubborn, that they were old and set in their crooked ways and intransigent about adapting to any reforms. Although she took what she and her dental hygienist thought was unusually good care of her teeth (as if it weren't enough that she actually had a dental hygienist, there was the fact that to work out a problem, she never just stared into space; she flossed), she knew nothing of dentistry. Still, she would respectfully submit that perhaps the esteemed writer of the article got it a little wrong.

If teeth do backslide, if they, over time, slip back into the well-worn grooves of their past, into their old offending stances, then maybe it was less a question of stubbornness than of nostalgia. Maybe they wanted to resume what they thought of as their rightful place in life, the only one they had known for so many years. It was only natural; in fact, it was to be expected. For some time now, Rosie has been of the opinion, arrived at through observation as well as personal experience, that the siren call of the familiar is surprisingly difficult and, for some, perhaps even impossible to resist. Would Odysseus, lashed with thick sailor's rope to a mast, have been able to break free if it were Penelope who sang? To confuse classical and Christian references: why but for the lure of the familiar did Lot's wife turn around to cast a final glance at her burning town, at the house where her children were born?

Rosie could imagine how many people—the writer of the article, say—would sneer if they heard her go on in this vein. *It's teeth you're talking about, for chrissake. Aren't you getting a little carried away, comparing enamel and bone to mythic figures from the* Odyssey *and the Bible?*

Well, yes, perhaps (she'd say civilly; it was beneath her dignity to respond in any other way). But it does seem as if we can learn how our minds and hearts tick by observing how the other parts of us work. Anyway, it wasn't she who came up with the idea that teeth are stubborn.

So you can put that sneer in your pipe, Mr. Article Writer, and smoke it.

Because as with teeth, so with the body. It remembers its old place, and it will long for it; it will sneak back into it even if it seems wrong and at first feels all wrong, even if ten years have passed. Rosie knew that because her husband came back to her after ten years apart, and because she took him in when he did. Call it what you will, nostalgia or habit or maybe even a lack of imagination, but her body acted upon it; overriding her own initial resentment and even hatred of Henry, it leaned toward him, longing to take up its place once again by his side.

It's an unpalatable notion, the thought that change isn't really possible, that despite what the heart wants and the mind knows, two bodies will grow back together like teeth, and if you're trying to decide what to do about your married lover, it's one that will break your heart. Rosie was not sure that she could bear to watch her daughter's heart break, let alone be responsible for delivering the blow that shattered it, when just thinking about what Claudia has been going through makes her shake as if with cold or age.

But if Claudia had turned to her instead of to Henry, if she had asked her what she should do about Vikrum, that's what Rosie would have said.

THE WORST OF IT WAS (she whispered to herself, often enough that it was becoming a refrain), she only had herself to blame.

Claudia was her father's daughter. Claudia thought so and Henry thought so. And, once upon a time not so long ago—though not now, though certainly not now—Rosie had, with resignation rather than sorrow, God forgive her, thought so too. She was not sure how it had happened that her only daughter, the child she had wanted so badly, had slipped away from her.

But there it was, and she only had herself to blame. This last visit, to take just one particularly damning example. From the moment they had seen Claudia at the train station, standing by her sensibly small suitcase as she scanned the parked cars, looking for them, she and Henry had known that their recent worries about their daughter were justified. They'd had an inkling when she decided to fly out here so suddenly, calling them just five days ago to say that she'd be arriving for a long weekend, but they'd made themselves suppress their own doubts. How nice, they'd said to each other, how lovely that Thanksgiving fell in November and that Claudia had decided, for once, to brave the holiday crowds at the airport, and her own fear of planes too, to keep them company on this most un-English of all holidays.

STANDING BY THE PARKED CARS, she didn't look much different from the last time they had seen her, four months ago: a woman with long, dirty-blond hair that could badly do with a haircut (Rosie couldn't help noticing that, concerned though she was with what was going on inside Claudia's head rather than with what was growing over it), dressed in a blaze of bright colors. Who looked, in her mother's view at least, young, really more like a girl than a woman—it was only out of respect for Claudia's views about proper feminist terminology that Rosie came up with that term first in her mind.

That girl looked tired, sure, and perhaps even red-eyed, but she had just taken an overnight airline journey, the nickname of which alludes to that phenomenon, so it was not the shadows on her face that tipped her parents off about her troubled state of mind. She stood with her shoulders hunched forward, but because her posture had been like that for years now, maybe ever since she had had that growth spurt as an adolescent, it was not her stance that made them freeze for a fraction of a moment.

So how was it that they had known instantaneously that that girl, *their* girl, was unhappy? Rosie suspected that it was some kind of parental sixth sense that clued Henry and her in, just as it was some type of long-term marriage sixth sense that made it unnecessary for them to signal their thoughts to each other as they sat, side by side, in the car, in that split second before they both, as one, shook off that paralysis born of fear and launched into action, calling out the window to their daughter and getting out to hug her and help her load her luggage into what the English call the boot. And maybe Rosie, like her husband, did possess and would always possess an intuitive knowledge of the girl they had raised.

The idea that Rosie was not completely devoid of the apparatus necessary for proper parenting was so comforting to her that for a few treasured moments of peace, she did not try to think beyond it. But she was, by training, used to following a thought to its logical conclusion; moreover, she was, by temperament, a person who preferred to look unpleasant facts in the eye. So it was not long before she was squaring up to the hard truth behind the notion that was providing her with comfort.

If she was right in her supposition, if she was in fact equipped with the same instinctive understanding of their daughter that Henry had, then her failure to act—her failure to ask questions, to listen, to give advice and, most of all, to provide consolation, to sit with her daughter and hold her, as her arms ached to do—was that much more acute.

HENRY BRUSHED BY HER as she stood at the stove. It would not take Rosie long to realize that that was one of the things she would always remember about that morning: how her husband had brushed by her—the lightest touch, an almost imperceptible tickle, but a brush nevertheless—as he passed.

She was frying eggs. Claudia had said she was not hungry, but Rosie knew that she must be or, at the very least, that she would be; it's a long journey from America, and Claudia had confessed that she was not able to eat the breakfast they served on the plane. Busy over the stove, Rosie did not hear Henry approach—while her hearing is, admittedly, not what it once was, it is also true that for as long as they have been married, no matter how cold the floor is, Henry has padded about noiselessly in socks. She did not even know he was in the house; she thought he was outside, calling for the cats, so that when she felt his body warmth and the rough sleeve of his sweater—his favorite one, a dark red and all-too-worn cardigan that Claudia gave him some years ago—against her own bare arm as he moved across the tiny kitchen at his usual deliberate pace, she turned around in surprise.

She turned in time to see Henry come up behind Claudia, slowly place his left hand on her right shoulder and then, with even more care, his right hand on her left. He has large hands; as Rosie knows from experience, they are heavy. Claudia, who had, as always, seated herself on the most rickety of their three kitchen chairs, looked up at her father, craning her neck very far back to meet his eyes, and smiled.

Watching from the stove, Rosie wondered if she had ever seen her daughter look so exhausted.

"You're taller than ever, Daddy," Claudia said, making a visible effort. "You may even have grown an inch or two. What's Mom been feeding you lately?"

Once Rosie's husband loved to talk (just as Rosie loved to listen); since his illness and the subsequent slurring of his speech, he has become a man of few words and usually eloquent gestures. But his voice is the same as it has been throughout his life, gentle and rumbling.

"Y'all right, Little Claw?"

When she saw Claudia's eyes begin to blink fast, Rosie dropped the spatula she had been holding onto the floor. She reflexively stooped to pick it up before rushing the two steps over to her husband and her child.

Claudia's face was buried in Henry's stomach and she was crying in the gigantic, heaving sobs of her childhood. With his large hands, Henry held and stroked the back of her head; in his low, slow, and infinitely soothing drawl, he murmured incomprehensible words, as to an infant.

Not until the eggs began to smoke did Rosie realize that she was still holding the spatula. One of her hands was pressing against Claudia's shoulder in the exact spot where Henry's hand rested a good two minutes ago; the other held aloft the greasy utensil. She was standing close to but a little apart from the closed circle—yes, it was definitely closed, as all true circles are—that Henry and Claudia made.

Rosie reached out an arm and, without removing her hand from her daughter's shoulder, placed the spatula on the counter and turned the stove off (so there were in fact advantages to a small kitchen, just as the realtor promised). She passed the back of her free hand across her eyes.

A minute later, she had quietly taken her hand off her daughter's shoulder and was walking back to the stove. About to pick up the pan, she turned around to glance one more time at her family instead. Should she still be standing beside them; was she being remiss? One long moment, then two. Then she was turning around and throwing the scorched batch of eggs into the garbage, removing three new eggs out of the carton to start another.

Eventually (Rosie told herself sternly, making sure to keep her eyes fixed on the pan) both Claudia and Henry would need to eat,

even though for now she continued to cry, he to stroke her head
and to murmur his calming words.

SHE WAS PRETTY SURE that it was then, during those minutes she
stood at the stove frying up a second batch of eggs, that she gave
up on what she perhaps in another time would have considered
one of the rights of motherhood. Claudia did not confide in her
during the three days that she stayed with them, even though they
went on long walks, just mother and daughter, even though they
clung hard to each other on the day that she left, and the reason for
that was both simple and obvious: by failing to step forward to
help her daughter, Rosie had lost the right to her confidence. So
when, the day after Claudia's departure, Henry sat Rosie down and
told her that Claudia was in love with a man who happened to be
already married, a man who had two children and who did not in-
tend to leave them or his wife for at least another dozen years, she
humbly accepted the news of her daughter's predicament and the
fact that it came to her secondhand as punishment to which she
was due.

The worst part of her punishment was that she, who did not deserve to be confided in, could not by the same token help through
counsel. It was not for her to advise her daughter that just as teeth,
those strangely shaped bits of enamel and bone, yearn for the positions they have always known and eventually go back to them, so
too do lovers, no matter how ardent, return to their wives. She
could not tell Claudia that she wanted her, too, to know what it
was like to stand side by side with someone, a pair of crooked
teeth; she could not describe to her the sweetness of living with
someone for so long that you no longer had to rely on the spoken
word to signal your thoughts to each other. She could not say how
glad she was every day—every hour, every minute—that she and
Henry were standing at their rightful posts as they entered the last

stage of their lives, and that such a happiness was what she wished above all for her daughter.

Because, after all, Henry's sleeve had touched Rosie's arm as she stood frying eggs at the stove. She had been standing closer to Claudia than he was, but inattentive to her suffering; she had been in her husband's way when he, slowed in his walk as well as his speech by his illness, shuffled forward to offer their daughter aid.

Chapter Twenty-Four

New Jersey, 1974–82

"THE VERY LAST TIME WE LEFT JAPAN," REI WOULD BEGIN,
her voice barely above a whisper, so that Claudia had
to strain to hear, "I carried a dragonfly with me on the
plane to America." By the time Rei first told this story
to her stepsister, more than two years had passed since
she had been in the country where her parents were
born and raised, and she had begun to forget Japanese.
But there were some words that came to her if she
thought hard enough, others that suddenly floated up
to her, unbidden, like the memory of a dream that she
had had the night before, and others still that she remembered and that, she felt strangely certain, she
would always remember. The word for dragonfly fell
in that last category. *Tombo.* Sounding, to Claudia's
American ear at least, like *tomboy,* which was the term
that Rei's relatives in Japan applied to Rei (not without
affection and more than one tear, for she was young

yet, as well as recently bereaved, and would with proper training doubtlessly soon grow out of those unfortunate American ways) when they saw the way she chased after dragonflies, climbing trees, scrambling over rocks, and wading through streams in order to get to them, from morning until night.

The dragonflies that Rei spent her days chasing were in Karuizawa, where her grandparents had a summer home and where she and her family came to stay for two weeks every summer. While it was always a great relief to escape to the cool green mountains and the silver streams of Karuizawa after the heat and the humidity of Tokyo, when she returned to Japan after having lived in America, she could see that her grandmother was not un-justified in her continual lament that the region she had been visiting since she was herself a little girl was becoming spoiled. In the evenings, the pathway by the neighboring lake was thronged with people, and the air by the road leading in from Tokyo smelled of the city, of smoke and, faintly, of garbage. Even on clear nights, Rei could not see the stars as she had in Massachusetts.

Still, there were the dragonflies, which went a long way toward making up for the fact that the fields were not as large and empty as they were in America. Some were striped gold and black like a bumblebee, their bodies fat as Rei's middle finger; some were scarlet, lean and long; a number were a deep yellow that was offset by the black of their wings. There were the *kagero*, which, her mother said, reading to her from her old reliable Japanese–English dictionary, meant *a shimmer of hot air*, so thin and light that Rei was not surprised to also learn that they lived only for a day. The *kagero* were easily identifiable because of their transparency, and also because when they perched, they did not hold their wings out but, rather, folded together like hands in prayer. They were the only ones she refused to catch, even for a few seconds, for surely a moment or two of captivity for one of them would be the equivalent, for her, of years away from sunlight. In their variety, size, and number, the dragonflies in Japan were not like any that she had ever seen in America, not even close.

Eight hundred eyes. That's how many dragonflies have, at least in Japan, or so Rei had heard. Eight hundred, which is to say a whopping four hundred tucked away within each of the two eye-like orbs that anchor the front of its body. Thanks to this legion of optical organs, the dragonfly can see what's going on behind it as well as to the left and the right and in front. Looking at one closely, Rei thought she could see its eyes, a multitude of tiny dots that floated in the orbs. Was it possible that eight hundred was the actual number and not an approximation? Once she did try to count them but, worried about the strain on her own ("I only have two," she would say, sighing, years later to her stepsister; "I couldn't exactly afford to wear them out"), she gave up after reaching sixteen.

That they had what seemed to be an excess of eyes did not render the dragonflies immune to visual trickery—indeed, quite the contrary. With her arm, Rei would draw a large circle in the air in front of her intended prey, over and over, gradually coming closer and shrinking the circle until she was drawing a small one with her finger, right in front of all eight hundred of its eyes. Her mother had taught her this trick years ago, and it never failed. Its wits dulled by dizziness, the dragonfly would sit there, pliantly waiting for Rei to pick it up with her hand.

She never kept the dragonflies for longer than a minute. She was interested only in examining them closely; she wished to admire, from a privileged vantage point, the brilliance of their colors, the intricacy of their patterns, and the dizzying multitude of their eyes. Most of all, perhaps, she wanted to throw them up in the air and watch them lift up, shining wings whirring, and bound away.

For just as Claudia had a need to take wounded animals of all kinds home with her to nurse them, Rei had an obsession, active only during the eighteen months she and her suddenly incomplete family returned to live in Japan, with letting captive ones of all types (including the ones that she herself had captured) go free. She took her white mouse, Taro, who had been born and raised in captivity, out to her favorite field in Karuizawa and watched him wander off, zigzagging to sniff at the occasional clump of plants, standing on his hind legs every so often to lift his nose into the air, until she could no longer see him. She could not bear to wait until summer to let her pair of parakeets go, so she threw them up into the dusty air of Tokyo and saw them, startled, beat their wings hard until they found themselves borne aloft and then shakily fly away. She pointed them westward, toward Karuizawa, which was the direction that they flew; four months later, when she found herself in that region of rolling fields once again, she looked for them tirelessly but fruitlessly, in all the trees and bushes.

She lived in a tiny apartment in concrete-lined, perpetually overcrowded Tokyo. Her sister yelled at her throughout the day and cried herself to sleep every night, and her memory of her father was already fading. Her mother, who had once been so energetic and cheerful, no longer seemed to have the energy to talk. Hana sat listlessly at home, occasionally patting her belly in the unconscious gesture that she still had not managed to lay aside, although months had passed since the miscarriage that had followed swiftly on the heels of her husband's accident.

But just because Rei could not fly away, it didn't mean that no one else could.

THE DECISION TO TAKE A DRAGONFLY back to America with her was a spontaneous one, which seemed appropriate given that the decision for them to go back at all was too: Hana had arrived at it suddenly, after seventeen months of living in Japan, with a certainty that appeared to bring with it a measure of her old vitality. It was fortunate that at least some of her energy had returned, since Hana's plan to move her daughters and herself back to the States was not easy to execute. Her mother was horrified; her sister and brother, shocked.

Their reactions made sense, as Hana herself was willing to admit. She and Seiji had gone to America because his job had temporarily required him to be there. Now that he was gone, there was, as Hana's mother pointed out repeatedly and incisively, no good reason for Hana to leave Japan, and every reason for her to stay. She had Seiji's life insurance, but that would not be enough for her and her daughters to live on forever. She needed the help of the extended family, as well as, perhaps, a job. And what, after all, would she do out there; why should she consider going back? Sure, she had a handful of friends in America; of course her children missed its wide-open spaces as well as its freewheeling schools. But Hana had friends in Japan too. Children forget quickly. In no time at all, her daughters would not be able to remember America; why, already their understanding of English was slipping.

Hana had no answers to any of the questions put to her, and no defense to mount to any of her mother's arguments. Yet she was adamant. If she had not lost her unborn baby, who was, she had known, going to be a boy, someone who could carry on Seiji's family's name and shoulder the responsibilities that came with it—if, perhaps, her beloved aunt Sachiko had not died a few years ago, quietly slipping away in her sleep—then maybe, just maybe, she would have considered staying. But given what had happened (given all that had happened, in less time than it takes to complete the verse of a song; would she ever be able to get over how the life she'd loved, how all of their lives, could change in a flash?), she would not live in a country that she had never liked. She would use her American-born daughters' passports to get herself a new green card, and she would move them all back to the country where she and her husband had lived, and they would stay there for the rest of their lives.

So no matter how much she argued and how persuasive the

arguments that she amassed were, Hana's mother was unable to make any headway.

Rei, by contrast, met little resistance in her plan to take a dragonfly back with her to America. She had caught it in Tokyo, in the small garden that abutted their apartment complex, the evening before they were to leave for the long trip back to America. She seldom saw dragonflies in the city, where the exhaust fumes could choke you and the smog was so thick and the buildings so high that sunlight seldom penetrated below.

The dragonfly that she caught that evening was a small one, in a pleasing but not particularly bright shade of blue-green. In her first violation of her self-imposed rule of not keeping the dragonflies confined for more than a minute, she took it home with her and placed it into a small bamboo insect cage, never used, that her mother had bought for her long ago. After lining the cage with an assortment of leaves from the garden, she rested it on the very top of their towering pile of suitcases.

CUSTOMS, NEWARK AIRPORT. September 1972.

"Kei, you can put that bag on the cart too."

Rei looks up. Her mother looks exhausted, with her hair running away in every direction and with what look like tiny pillows under her eyes. Flying has always made her violently sick, and this trip was no exception. But now there is a smile flitting across her face.

"Not long now. We're almost there," she says. Placing a hand on Rei's shoulder, she beats out a light, excited rhythm with her fingers. Rat-tat-tat rat-tat-tat. "The *tombo's* okay?"

Her hand clenched tight around the handle of the cage, Rei nods.

If her mother feels skeptical about the dragonfly's chances, if she is thinking back to what happened when, twelve years ago to the month now, she made her first trip to America with a *daikon* stashed in her bag, she does not let on. In later years, Rei will not be able to recall what she and Kei and her mother talked about to while away the long minutes spent standing in line—at passport control, the women's room, baggage claim, and then the women's room again—as they waited to reenter the country. Still, she will be able to tell her stepsister with certainty that one subject that did not come up was the damage inflicted on American vegetation by the Japanese beetle (with its metallic sheen and the way it changed color in a flash from green to brown to gold and then back again, as beautiful, although in a very different way, as the architectural dragonfly; you could stick a pin through it, Rei always thought, and it would not look amiss on your hat or breast). Yet another perfectly serviceable conversational topic that goes unaddressed is the fact that many years ago, that beetle had, somehow—stashed away in an unsuspecting traveler's cargo, perhaps, or riding in style in a carton of fresh fruit—also made the long voyage across the Pacific that they had just completed.

The line ahead of them sways and moves; Hana leans over the cart to give it a push, and the Watanabe family takes another step forward.

IT WILL BE ANOTHER TWO HOURS before they reach their old family friend's house in New Jersey, where they will stay for a week before moving into a new house of their own: while both Kei and Rei want to return to Boston, Hana has promised that this new town will be a better place, a fresh start, for all of them. They'll all be tired and spent, but it's the late afternoon of a cool, windless fall day, and Rei will not see much point to waiting until the morning. Accompanied by her mother, she'll step out into their friend's large yard (seemingly as large as any of the fields in Karuizawa, and graced by two old willow trees, the leaves of which make a curtain, long and thick enough to hide a young girl), and she'll open the door to the small cage in which the dragonfly has lived for the past two days.

It'll take some coaxing and some tapping on the cage to make the dragonfly realize that it's now free to go.

FINALLY IT'S THEIR TURN. The customs official who takes the passports from Hana and looks them over is a woman. She is young, with soft brown hair, and her uniform is a little large on her, which makes her look even younger and more girlish (or so Hana thinks) than she actually is.

"What have you got there?" the customs official asks Rei, gesturing toward her cage. She has already looked over their documents and their bags and listened carefully to the stammered comments Hana gave in response to her questions.

"It's a dragonfly." The words come easily to Rei. Listening, Hana knows that it was ridiculous of her to worry that her children had lost their English—if only her own was so good! In her fatigue, which borders on nervous exhaustion, as well as her profound relief at getting them all there, she finds herself singing a song in her head that she had made up out of the rhythm she had beat out on her younger daughter's shoulder: *It's going to be fine it's going to be fine.*

"I caught it in Tokyo," Rei continues proudly.

"A dragonfly? May I see?"

With a grave nod, Rei passes the cage over to the woman in the uniform.

SHE'LL STILL BE FEELING the thrill, almost like a small shock, that she gets as she sets an animal free, when the crow appears. It will all happen very fast, the bird flying in a straight line toward the dragonfly, its beak opening and then shutting in a split second. Many, many years later, when Rei tells this story to her stepsister for the hundredth time, the unfolding of this scene will serve as a sort of wry punchline—"as if it wasn't bad enough that my father had died and we had hardly any money and my mom didn't have a job, that damn crow had to swoop down out of nowhere and swallow my dragonfly...."—but when she witnesses the quick death of the insect she had kept in a cage beside her for the voyage over from Japan, she'll look up at her mother, mutely, and she will not feel like laughing.

For a few seconds her mother will also be silent, gazing up at the spot where the dragonfly had vanished. Then, suddenly, she will move, crouching down beside her daughter so that they are eye level.

"Listen to me," she'll say, her hands holding Rei's shoulders firmly. "Listen. It was a good thing that you did. That moment of freedom—here, where the air's so fresh, and the trees and grass are so green—was worth more to your dragonfly than a whole lifetime in Tokyo. You have to trust me on that."

And Rei will nod slowly.

Later that evening, she'll cry herself to sleep, her face muffled in her pillow so that neither Kei nor her mother will hear. Later still, the next day or perhaps the one after that, she'll think over what her mother had said while standing at the foot of the willow tree and she will come to believe it, just as she always, eventually, comes to believe what her mother says.

"THAT'S A BEAUTIFUL DRAGONFLY," says the customs official, passing the cage back to Rei. "Go ahead, and welcome back to America. And you'll take care of that dragonfly, won't you?"

"Thank you," says Rei, her good manners bringing another smile to her mother's face (*it's going to be fine it's going to be...*). "I will."

Chapter Twenty-Five

Rei

Boston, 1999

HER KNOCK IS DISAPPOINTINGLY FEEBLE, NO MORE THAN a faint scratching at the door—so faint that it would do dishonor to any one of my cats, even little Heidi. After I run over to open the door I'm grateful for the advance warning that her knock gave me: Claudia still looks broken, her eyes blank, her mouth straining to come up for a smile. When she drops her bags onto the floor and we hug, she holds on to me, tight, for a second longer than usual, and I don't think it's just because she's glad to see me again.

I had hoped for more from the three days that she spent in England with her parents, but maybe she's still tired from the journey. She's never liked to fly any more than my mother has, and of course it's almost nine now, which means that it must be late indeed by her clock.

When I first saw her after Vikrum proposed to her,

Claudia was so quiet she seemed almost catatonic. She didn't cry and barely even spoke. It took me hours just to find out what had happened.

"Welcome back," I say. "Come on in."

Claudia stoops and begins to rummage through one of her bags. "Mom wanted me to give you this," she says, pulling out a box of chocolates and a tin of Fortnum & Mason tea and handing them to me. "She also sends her love. As does Dad, of course. They asked a lot of questions about you—they said they're really looking forward to seeing you when they come visit in the spring."

"They did? They are?" I say, taking the chocolates and the tea and feeling myself redden with pleasure. Claudia turns away to fuss with her bag, pretending that she didn't notice the rise of color in my cheeks, but it's all too obvious she did. I don't care, though. My days of trying to make it seem as if I couldn't care less about her mom—the days when I practiced a misplaced, unappreciated loyalty to my own—are long past.

"Thanks for letting me stay here again," she says, walking through the door. "Hey, little guy, it's good to see you." She bends down and strokes Worm, who's winding himself around her ankles; he arches his back and lets out a raspy purr.

"What else are family for?"

She just gives me another tired smile, but it's a phrase that I love to say, to her. I should savor it, after all. God knows, it's one that I won't get to use very often to anyone else.

For the past two and a half weeks, Claudia has been camping out most nights on a futon here, set up kitty-corner to my own narrow bed. She has explained that she can't bear to be in her apartment now, haunted as it is by the ghost of a cat and an empty bed. If her aversion to staying in her own spacious, well-organized, and homey living space has anything to do with the fact that Vikrum has been leaving her dozens of pleading messages every day, she doesn't say, and I don't ask. Our nights together follow an easy routine. We order in pizza or Chinese food, curl up with the cats, play a game of Scrabble or a round of gin rummy, and then turn in. Once or twice we've stayed awake in bed, talking for hours; usually, though, she seems to prefer just to be quiet. While I sometimes worry I'm not saying the right things to her—how wise she's always been, through all these years, whenever I've been sad or upset—I try just to let her be.

My apartment is tiny, a studio and not a large one at that, but it's at the very top of my building, with a view of treetops and far-off church towers, and it's filled with light. Claudia calls it my aerie. *Aerie*—I said to her, the first time she used the word—it has such an airily wonderful sound. Especially, for me at least, when it's applied to my own living space.

I've been here almost two months already, a thought that makes my mind spin if I dwell on it (it's bad enough to think that I've been that long in Boston, a town I was not sure I could even visit; what's worse is that that thought inevitably and unavoidably leads to the next, the fact that it's been six months, a record to end all records, since I've talked with my mother). Yet the small space of the apartment is still filled with unpacked boxes, creating so many nooks and crannies that even the cats haven't found them all.

It embarrassed me at first, having Claudia here when the apartment was like this, but she's spent so much time over here in the past three weeks, I've almost stopped noticing. And, predictably, she's made a point of emphasizing to me that she doesn't mind. She's made fun of me for how I've arranged the boxes and suitcases to maximize the light and the space and to create intimate corners in which to sit; she's said that even the way I pile up my stuff is art and that I should start up a business for interior decorating built around the aesthetic utilization of cardboard and plastic cartons. I *shouldn't* settle in more, she's insisted, only three-quarters joking: the apartment's perfect as it is. But despite these so-typically-

Claudia words of kindness, of course there's no way she would ever have let even a week, let alone two months, go without unpacking.

Still, at least her suitcases fit right in. I slide them into a corner and then we sit, almost hidden from ourselves by all the unpacked boxes, two travelers who still haven't quite made it home.

"DON'T YOU WANT TO sleep yet? You must be exhausted."

Claudia shakes her head.

"Not to mention jet-lagged—"

"Jet rag," she says, so suddenly that I start a little; I must have been dozing off. "Do you remember how Dad used to love saying that? He got us all saying it. Your mom took it well, I remember. She was always a good sport."

"Sure," I say, stretching and yawning. "I remember."

Shoving her hands deep in the pockets of her pants, Claudia hunches herself over. "You didn't think he was good for me, did you? Vikrum, I mean, not Dad, of course."

The lamp next to me is flickering. I turn to make sure the bulb is secured and remind myself to get a new light. "Hell, no," I say, as I have in some variation the past ten times she's asked me.

Claudia is beginning to rock. Her eyes look swollen—when was the last time she slept?

"That said," I continue, "if he's what makes you happy, then why not?"

She looks up, startled. "But there are his wife and kids . . ."

"His wife and kids aren't the ones suffering," I remind her. "And you love him so much. He must be worth it, because otherwise you wouldn't love him so. And also," I add, knowing suddenly that I'm right; Claudia is too true herself to fall so deeply in love with a man who is any less, "because otherwise there would be no justice in this world."

"He is worth it," she says. "Or at least he's definitely worthy of me, anyway. I always thought the question was whether I deserved him."

"You just have to make a decision, one way or another," I say, hesitating. I'm not used to offering advice to my capable stepsister—indeed, it's been a long time, too long, since I've been in the position to give help to anyone rather than to receive it—and I have to feel my way. "Either be with him and be happy, accept that he has another life, a set of obligations that he's going to honor no matter how much he loves you, or resign yourself to being without him. Feeling guilty about his wife and children shouldn't play a part in what you decide, although I'm not sure if you, in particular, can help it."

Claudia tugs at the ends of her hair. "I wish that it was only about feeling guilty." She speaks so low, her words seem little more than a series of sighs. "I'm scared too. It might never work out, after all. Maybe even after his kids leave home, he still won't leave his wife. I might never have a life in which I can fall asleep with him at night and know that he'll be lying beside me in the morning. I might never be able to go away with him on long weekends; I might never be able"—this last phrase a whisper—"to have children with him."

It is only with considerable effort that I manage not to cry out at the thought of all that she is being asked to give up. "You have to decide," I say, the steadiness of my voice a surprise, "if what he's offering is enough for you."

"It's not enough," she says simply. "You know that, and I do too. But at the same time, it's more happiness than I ever dreamed was possible."

Claudia turns and looks out the window. It's so dark out that there's nothing to see but our reflections on the glass, yet she gazes with rapt attention. When we first met, her eyes were bluer than they are now, and I thought them beautiful but also strange and cold.

It is difficult for me now to believe that I could ever have thought such a thing about my stepsister, even when I was a child.

"You know all those stories about my mother and her aunt Sachiko, the ones we grew up on..." I begin. The window forgotten, her attention is now directed solely at me. "I always thought that if those stories taught us anything, it's how quickly our lives, lives that we love and count on, can change." Are the shadows in the room playing tricks on my eyes, or did her gaze just flicker to light on my hand? "Nothing is really certain. Which means that we can step cautiously, watching the skies with dread, or we can stride forth with confidence and live out our lives the way we want to."

A small sound, not a word in either English or Japanese, escapes from Claudia's lips. Then she nods, shivering a little, even though the room is warm.

"Is there anything I can do for you, anything I can get?" I say. "A blanket, a pillow, any kind of special food? I could still make a run to the store—"

"No." Leaping from the arm of her chair onto the floor, Mr. B stretches himself out on the rug, showing off his stomach for the world to see. Claudia watches him absentmindedly, then leans over and gives him a pat. "But thanks. I do appreciate this. After all that you've been through yourself—"

"After all that I've been through, it feels good to take care of someone else for a change."

Silence. The lamp flickers again and then goes out. My eyes droop; my mind fills with almost unbearably bright images of dragonflies and the blue of the sky through an airplane window.

"You know, there might be one thing you could do, though."

"What's that?" I say, sitting up and rubbing my eyes. The room is almost completely dark. I shake myself, stand up, and walk to the kitchen, a mere three steps, and pour myself a Coke. "Do you want some too?"

"No, I'm good," she says. "Well, good except for the fact that Vikrum used to tell me stories too sometimes."

"And?" I ask, almost tempted to smile, guessing what's coming.

"Aa-nd," she says, stretching out the word, "stories are like comfort food to me. Like bubble baths or clothes shopping or chocolates are for some people. Stories are what cheer me up the most."

"Okay," I say, going to the living-room area and sitting down again, caffeine fix in hand. "Fine. If that's what it takes to cheer you up, I'll do it. What is it you want to hear about?"

"You know, don't you? What I always wanted to hear about when we were young. Same old, same old." She looks at me expectantly, waiting. "You really don't know? I want to hear about your mom. More specifically, about you and your mom. What happened, why you aren't talking, and how it is you came to live here, in Boston, where you always swore you'd never want to live."

"I was worried that that's what you'd want to hear about," I say, but she has me in a bind. With her in this state, I can't deny her anything that she wants, let alone needs. "Well, it's fair enough." It's more than fair, if I'm really now expecting Claudia to take the place of the family that I did have. But not fun, and certainly not easy.

She waits.

"Do you know that when I first told my mom about the cancer," I say, opening my hand up and then closing it tight, "I just assumed that she'd take it well? I always thought of her as a pillar of strength during a crisis."

Claudia doesn't say anything and I have my head down, thinking for a moment, so I can't see the expression on her face. But it doesn't matter; I don't need to see her or hear from her at this moment. I know that she's nodding; I know that she, too, is thinking about how my mother's hands darted out, lightning quick, never mind that she was slow and dreamy with pregnancy, to cover the eyes of her daughters during an accident within a stone's throw of the Canadian border.

Chapter Twenty-Six

Rei
Boston, 1999

FOR ME, UNLIKE, SAY, FOR YOU, WHAT CAME AS A REVELA-tion was not our parents falling in love but their being in it (I say slowly, a little tentative, rusty after all these years; does it seem strange to Claudia that I'm detour-ing so quickly in my story? If so, she doesn't show it, shifting her body weight and seeming to relax more deeply in her chair, settling herself for the ride). Which is to say that my mother's and your father's marriage was much more astonishing in its fourth, sixth, and then eighth year than it ever was at the start.

Sure, their initial passion was startling. Maybe my mother wasn't so old when she met your dad, a youth-ful forty-one to his forty-four, but you and I were only nine at the time, after all. You remember, don't you, how we thought of her, how she might as well have been in her dotage? So it was weird and cringe-inducing to see her blushing and giggling like a girl; it was even worse that the chances of walking into her and Henry necking like teenagers were so high that all of us daughters had to clomp around the house like construction workers, in the vain hope that they would have enough time to untangle themselves from each other before we entered the room.

Still, it was the way they acted after a few years of humdrum marriage—a few years of paying taxes and balancing the checkbook and getting the kids off to school and squabbling over the wet towels in the bathroom and going to sleep and waking up together, day in and day out—that was the real revelation. They stopped cooing and, mercifully, speaking in baby talk to each other and took up inaudibly murmuring instead; it seemed they no longer had to finish or even fully articulate sentences around each other to be understood. They held hands wherever they went; she ran to meet him at the door when he came home from work; after dinner they dozed off together, side by side on the couch, the day's papers spread out unread on their laps.

A prosaic existence, maybe, for a girl who could have been an empress, but I always thought of my mother's life as poetry.

THE FIRST TIME I SAW IT, I compared it to a spreading stain. It was just a freckle at first, a small, irregularly shaped mark, light brown, just to the left of the dead center of my left palm. I had had it in that guise for years, one more variable in the dense pattern of lines on my palm, and I thought of it as an inkblot that had somehow failed to wash out of my skin. But when, one year, it began to grow and change, I (tracking its transformation over the months with bemusement) began to think instead of tea soaking into sheets, brown slowly encroaching on white. Except that that comparison didn't hold either, since the mark wasn't just brown anymore. A colorful swirl about a half inch in diameter, it looked like a black-

and-blue bruise except that it was darker, with actual black in it as well as brown.

Over time I began to wonder if it was in fact a bruise, even though I had of course been observing how it spread. But while the mark bore a resemblance to the splotches of purplish blue that blossomed usually on my shins, it seemed curious that I couldn't remember hurting my hand, and even more curious that when I pressed on the spot, I felt no pain. Had I forgotten how I had slipped on the ice and slammed my hand on a rock as I hit the ground? Had it slipped my mind that I had pinched the flesh of my palm on a clothespin as I hung my delicates to dry? I couldn't decide which was more incredible: that I so lacked coordination or that I was suffering from such a lapse in memory; at times like this I found it hard to believe that I was only in my thirties.

Sometimes I tried to see the stain as an abstract pattern rather than a strange growth on myself. While this was a feat that eluded me almost entirely, the couple of times I came close to succeeding I could see that that mark was in fact almost aesthetic, reminiscent of a few of my mother's paintings. I even wondered if I should show my hand to her. After all, it was seldom that she could feel superior about the range of her English vocabulary around her daughters; she'd have a field day showing off her knowledge of the precise name for each of those different colors.

It wasn't until my routine gynecological checkup, the one that I schedule every other year, that I had the first inkling that something might be really wrong. Sitting upright, my legs no longer spread, I was about to reach for my clothes when the doctor asked me if I had any last questions. "There is one thing," I said, looking down at my hand. "I have this odd mark on my palm that keeps growing."

The doctor was an older woman, gray-haired, heavyset, and reassuringly sedate. "What?" she said, her voice pitched so high that I knew immediately to be scared.

For the next year, I would be told again and again how lucky I was that my gynecologist had diagnosed my symptoms and had immediately referred me to a specialist: the type of skin cancer that I had, one that primarily afflicts young Asians and African-Americans, is rare enough that usually only dermatologists know what it is. If she hadn't known about it, I probably would have died.

As I'd learn, acral lentiguous melanoma, to give it its official name, strikes randomly. One doesn't contract it because of smoking, which isn't something I've ever taken up, or because of staying out in the sun too long, which I sometimes still do. As doctor after doctor told me, it was simply bad luck.

I'd meet a lot of doctors in the next year. But before I did, I had to call my mother and give her the news.

"I FELT GRATEFUL THAT my mother is so good in a crisis," I say. "It was a bad time, and I really needed her. It was just after I broke up with Max, and I didn't really have anyone to turn to."

Claudia twitches, then sits up.

"It's okay," I say quickly. "It wasn't as bad as you'd think. I joined a support group, and Kei, who was pregnant for the first time and much nicer as a result, helped out a lot. It was almost kind of funny—she kept bursting into tears, she said it was because of the hormones. Totally unlike her, of course, and it actually made me laugh, it happened so often. We grew closer then, for the first time.

"You really shouldn't worry about it. What I went through was a different process than chemo. Interferon, it was called. I only felt a bit nauseous, and only sometimes."

Claudia takes in a breath, preparatory to what I'm not exactly sure—a scolding or an outburst of affection or, perhaps, both at once.

"Don't be mad because I didn't call you then," I say, breaking in once again, and pleading now. "I thought about it, believe me. But you know that it was hard enough to contact you when I did, after so much time had passed. I just couldn't come to you after a decade and a half apart and make you nurse me through a potentially fatal illness. I know you would have, and gladly"—I add, tilting my head and smiling as reassuringly as I can—"but I couldn't ask you to do that."

Clearly not even close to being mollified, she reluctantly settles back into her chair.

"Still, after I got through the worst of it, all I could think about was getting in touch with you. After all that happened with my mother, after all that happened with this hand of mine"—I look down at my palm, although there is nothing more to see—"well, I knew I had to see you again. I know I'm not the first to say it, but a brush with death really does change your attitude toward life. The conclusion that I came to is that you need to be with the people you love, as much as you possibly can."

I look my stepsister in the eye. "Not to belabor the point, but I do think that's something you might want to consider as you decide what to do about Vikrum."

I USED TO LOVE getting sick when I was young (I say, continuing with my storytelling; the words are coming easier now, and the rhythm of it too). No matter how badly my throat hurt, no matter how high my fever, it was worth it to stay at home with my mother, to feel her cool hand on my forehead, to open my mouth for her, ahhhh, so she could peer in and say whether my tonsils were red and swollen. They always were, according to her, which made me wonder sometimes if my mother liked my getting sick—those days I stayed home from school, playing cards with her and eating ice cream as she sat by the bed—as much as I did.

There's no doubt that what happened would have been easier to take if I hadn't assumed, as I'd done throughout my life, that I would have her to lean on.

I took the shuttle from Los Angeles to go to her house to deliver the news. After some time in Paris, a few years in New Mexico and another handful in New York, she's gone to northern California to live.

She has changed over the years, although it's difficult for me to see it. I haven't spoken much about my mother to you, I know (I say, interrupting my own narrative, about to apologize, but Claudia shakes her head to forestall me). She's loomed so monumental in both of our imaginations, hasn't she? A towering presence. Well, at sixty-six, she's gotten smaller. She was always short, but she swears with some conviction that she's been shrinking in the past few years. She's also finally given up dressing in all those gorgeous colors she always loved, and while her hair's longer now, she always wears it coiled in a bun: a style that, paired with her cheekbones, may not be unflattering—it gives her a kind of austere loveliness, if you will—but is definitely forbidding.

But when you're with her, it's hard to remember those changes. She's still the same Hana she was, a tiny woman who has such presence that she seems both tall and strong, an artist who busily and tirelessly produces picture after picture, her hands and parts of her face seemingly always splattered with paint. Last I spoke to her, she was talking with a rather well-known local gallery about a good-size retrospective of her work. She baby-sits whenever she can persuade Kei to come visit. My mother is still a woman with energy to spare.

So, call me arrogant or spoiled or presumptuous, but I simply assumed that I could lean on her, as I have in every crisis throughout my life.

I TOLD HER DURING A LULL in our conversation. I had brought her sushi that I'd picked up from my favorite store in L.A., as well as some little cakes. We were sitting in her large, light-filled kitchen and talking about what paintings I've been restoring, about the latest forgotten, neglected work I've rescued from oblivion and brought back to something close to its original glory. She seemed in her usual good spirits.

Then I told her. Casually—perhaps, in retrospect, too casually. I gave her a quick rundown of the facts, and I stated them plainly. I have a form of skin cancer; it showed up on my palm. I'm lucky, I said; it's treatable, and we caught it early; I've already had a number of the treatments and the doctors are pleased, so I should be fine.

There was a pause when I finished. She had a slight smile on her lips and she wasn't even looking at me, her eyes fixed on the wall to her left. I wondered for a second if I had just hallucinated that I'd told her; I thought I'd been dreading telling her for so long that I had simply, wishfully, imagined that I already had.

But then I noticed that her eyes weren't in alignment, as if one had come loose and wanted to strike out on its own, to see wondrous things that its mate had never dreamed of. And then she began to scream.

For a few moments, I sat frozen. Clearly I've inherited little of my mother's ability in a crisis. My mother, so neat and self-contained, so quiet and well-behaved, screaming. I was terrified. What saved me was that I could almost understand what she was saying. She screamed mostly in sounds that had nothing to do with language, but mixed in with the noise, like a thread of music, was a Japanese word. *Anata*, the formal form of *you*, often used by a woman to her husband.

She was calling upon her Japanese husband—her first one, my dead father—for help. An unexpected move but not an act, I told myself, of complete insanity.

I passed her a box of tissues, because she had also begun to cry. I held her, keeping my arm stiff because the bones of her shoulders were so fragile that I feared they might shiver and crack. Yet I was furious at her.

It was selfish of me, I know. But she wasn't helping, and my Lord, did I need help then.

"YOUR CANCER," she said. "It's my fault." I had made her a cup of tea and she was sipping it; although she wasn't composed yet, she was, at least, no longer hysterical.

"How could it be your fault?" I said, wistful still—where were the soothing clucks of the tongue and the cool hand on my forehead?—but forcing myself to be cheerful. "That's the silliest thing I ever heard."

"The doctors warned me that if I had children, it was possibility that they get cancer and God knows what else."

"What are you talking about?"

"I hoped I no tell you." She dragged out her words so, it was evident that she'd erred in her choice of tense. As if realizing that her English was going, she slowed down and almost visibly took hold of herself, and then she began talking in Japanese, as she hadn't to me since I was young. She maybe even didn't realize at first that she was doing so, but I was able to follow all that she said, so I just let her. It seemed to make sense, somehow, that she would only be able to tell this particular story in her native tongue. Come to think of it, there was a peculiar but fitting irony, too, in the fact that I had to ask her my questions in English—the story that she was telling was so far beyond anything I could imagine or understand.

"You know how I was visiting my grandparents' house in Hiroshima in August of 1945?" she asked. "When my aunt Sachiko was exposed to the radiation of the bomb?"

I nodded.

"Well, I was exposed too. Not a bad case"—she added quickly—"even milder than Sachiko's. Just some nausea and vomiting. My family hushed it up, so that my life wouldn't be ruined. It wasn't so hard to do, because we lived in Nagoya, a long way from Hiroshima. But there were rumors. When I got tuberculosis, people wondered.... The doctors didn't think that the tuberculosis had anything to do with it, but they knew so little."

I didn't know what to say or, rather, where to begin. But then, suddenly, I thought of Kei—vain, pretty, weight- and fashion-conscious Kei. Who would have guessed that she would be so proud of how large her stomach would get during the pregnancies; who would have known that she'd be so fascinated by the changes that took place in her body, that she'd be so happy, even, to experience morning sickness? "Does Kei know? Wouldn't her children be at risk?"

My mother shook her head. Her face, tear-streaked and red as a child's, looked older than it had for a long time. "I didn't tell Kei. The risks for a child of hers were so small, and after Naomi turned out okay, I didn't think I needed to worry her when—"

"How could you not have told us?" I said. I wanted to hit her right in the middle of her face; I wanted to smash in that upturned nose and crush those delicate bones. "It's our past too. Who else knew? Did—"

She shook her head again, more slowly. "Your father didn't know."

"You married him and didn't tell him?" I asked.

"I couldn't tell him," she said, the words coming fast now, almost tumbling out, propelled by what I identified as a sense of relief. "You don't know what it was like. Those who survived the bomb were polluted, outcasts. His family wouldn't have allowed us to get married. And then, when we moved to America and started having children, it just seemed easier to forget." She explained that that was the real reason she couldn't even consider a proposal from the prince. She knew (as her mother must also have known, although she did her considerable best to suppress that knowledge) that the prince's family would have turned up the truth, the background checks on the women considered for his betrothal were so thorough, there was no way that her exposure to the bomb would not come to light.

"So what are you saying?" I asked, placing each word with care, lining them up one by one as if they were to be the foundation of an edifice that would stand. "Are you telling me that you married *Oto-san* because he was a way for you to keep your precious secret safe?"

At that, she drew herself up, her back stiff and proud. But her gaze still skittered uneasily from mine, and when she spoke, she was barely audible. "It was another reason to marry him."

"So everything you told us was a lie. So you never loved him after all."

For the first time that afternoon, she looked at me with disapproval, a mother putting her daughter in her place. "I did," she said with a hint of her usual tartness. Then, more softly: "Of course I did; you know I did."

"Is that it?" I asked. "Is there anything else you're not telling me?"

She hesitated. "Just one more thing. It's about Henry. It's about why we split up."

I shut my eyes, opened them. I wanted to cover my ears. But it was clear that having begun, she couldn't stop talking; her story needed to be told. "Go ahead."

"What happened was that he was rummaging through some boxes in the attic, and he came across an old medical file of mine, from my childhood. It was written in both Japanese and English— enough English for him to figure out that I had been exposed."

"And that made you decide to leave him? Because I know Henry didn't feel you were contaminated."

"We had been together for more than seven years by then. He couldn't believe I hadn't told him, and he couldn't forgive me for not trusting him. Can you blame him?"

"But you left him."

"I did."

"And you never told him why you were leaving?"

"I didn't," she said. She spoke clearly, her eyes meeting mine and her chin jutting forward with defiance. "He thought I met someone else, and I let him think that. There wasn't any reason to tell him, since there wasn't anything left to discuss."

That was all I needed to hear. I pushed my chair back, stood up, turned around, and walked out the door. I could hear her calling out my name but I didn't turn around to look back at her. If I had, I knew what I would see: a tiny, shrunken woman. I'd done it. I was finally immune to her peculiar charm—the combination of kindness and steel underlying an impression of helplessness that had made men fall for her, that had made them feel as if they were large and strong enough to accomplish anything: fight demons, stride around the world in a day to fetch her a rare lily, build a tower for her so high that it brushed against the sky and leap over it too.

SOMEWHERE BEHIND CLAUDIA there's a rustle and the rattle of a box shifting its contents. She blinks, then turns her head. I feel like telling her that it's her apartment that's haunted, not mine, but I keep my mouth shut, for how can I be sure?

"I haven't spoken to my mother since," I tell her, wrapping it up. "I moved out here as soon as I could, which is to say a couple of months, and I didn't leave a forwarding address. I was all set to tell Kei, but in the end I didn't. She was absorbed both in her baby and in the preparations for the new child—I'd never seen her so happy, and I thought, how could I bear to worry her?"

The story's over, and there's nothing more to say. Or, at least, there shouldn't be anything more to say, except that I, my mother's daughter after all, having finally begun, can't seem to stop.

"Do you know that way back when, she lied to Kei and me and said that Henry had fallen out of love with her because he was finally fed up with her inability to speak English? It seemed unlikely to us, since he always seemed to adore her so much. But then again, that last year together, they did seem to be growing apart, so we didn't know what to believe. So we supported her in the decision, and I made up my mind that I shouldn't see you anymore—for all those reasons I told you earlier, but also because I knew it would hurt her if I did continue to see you and Henry. She did love him terribly."

Claudia's head is cradled in her arms. "Jesus," she says.

"What I can't forgive her for is the way she left Henry. Loving him the way she did, she left him anyway, without giving him a single chance to present his side. How could she have done that, given who he was, given how happy they were together—how happy we all were together?" There it is. What is for me, perhaps, the heart of the matter, much as it shames me to admit it: the fact that she had deprived me of a father and a family that I had loved, for no good reason at all.

Claudia looks up. "You think she was wrong in imagining that my dad had a change of heart, right? Because I do."

I nod. "Of course your dad still loved her. You know how crazy he was about her; you know how true he is, how loyal. He was, I often think, one of the best men I've ever known. No, she left him because she was too proud. She couldn't bear that he thought her tainted; she couldn't stand that he no longer thought her pure and perfect.

"That pride was the real pollutant in her. And it ended up contaminating our family too, and finally destroying it."

"That's not too good," Claudia admits. From her, a major indictment.

What I do not tell Claudia is my belief that this flaw in my mother infects her work as well. It's the reason she's only achieved local success, despite all her hard work and undeniable talent: Her paintings are well-constructed and visually appealing, but they lack the devil-may-care swagger and boldness that characterize great works of art. With my mother, everything has to be refined and delicate and, inevitably, false.

But Claudia doesn't need to hear a critique of my mother's artwork. Like her father, she's always loved my mother's dramatically colored pictures and still keeps a number of them on her walls.

She should see something in my mother to admire, even if I don't.

"SHE WAS WRONG, actually," I say. Claudia has made us tea, soothing and honeyed, from a recipe of her own devising, and I cup it close to my face. "I spoke to a number of doctors, and all of them said that the fact that my mother was exposed to fallout from the bomb had no bearing on my getting melanoma."

"Your mother—" says Claudia. "Well, she called me. Just about three weeks ago."

My mother. For a second I allow myself to miss her; it's a taste like raw salt, sharp, powerful, and parching, which leaves my tongue numb. Then I shrug. "Ah," I say lightly, "I should have known." Then, in spite of myself: "How does she sound?"

"Worried. Frantic," she says. "Like a mother."

"Really?" I say, forcing a laugh. "Because she never did seem like much of a mother, really, did she? She was always so obsessed with her artwork. When she was young, she never thought about having children, you know. It was different with your mom"—how Rosie used to hover over Claudia! stroking her hair whenever Claudia gave her the chance—"she had her career, but I always thought that the proudest accomplishment in her life was you."

"Hana's made some bad mistakes. But you should see her," Claudia says, with the same gentle authority that she used to bring to bear—and, no doubt, will bring to bear again soon—when she told me to fasten the top button of my coat in the winter.

"Why? Just because she's my mother and—"

"No, that's not why. Because it's time. Because you miss her, maybe even more than I miss Vikrum, and that's saying a lot. And because—" she says. She stops and looks at me hard, and then she gives me a small, nervous smile. "As of yesterday, she's here in Boston, staying in my apartment."

Chapter Twenty-Seven

Claudia
Boston, 1999

AT FIRST I CAN HEAR NOTHING BUT THE FAMILIAR static—a problem with their telephone rather than with the thousands of miles of ocean that lie between us. Given that my parents are scholars in the fields of science and math, it might seem safe to assume that they would have electric appliances that would be, if not state of the art, at least functional. But that assumption would be wrong.

"Mom?"

"Claudia, honey, is that you?" she says. "Sweetheart, do you want me to call you back?"

My mother has always disliked using the phone. To make up for her own discomfort, she tends to sprinkle endearments into the conversation with an overly liberal hand. "No," I say, doing an even poorer than usual job of suppressing the irritation in my voice, "you know it's cheaper to call from here."

"Okay," she says. Chastened, perhaps, she is quiet for a beat. "How are you doing? How have you been?"

"Fine," I say. "Better, thanks for asking." I have called, as usual, to speak to Dad, but it is so seldom that my mother will attempt to chat on the phone that I cannot pass up the opportunity. "And you?"

"I've been thinking about you and that man—"

"Vikrum," I say. If I had not guessed before that she disliked the idea of him, I would have known now, from her tone as well as the term that she applied to him. Still, even though her dislike of him is hardly unexpected or, even, unwarranted, even though I am no longer with him, her refusal to use his name is a mark of disrespect that I cannot quite let pass. "His name is Vikrum."

"Vikrum." She stops and clears her throat. "Sorry, of course it is. What I want to say about him, about Vikrum, is that it's hard, I know, but—"

The rest of her words are lost in a perhaps propitious spate of static; all I can make out is something about teeth having memory.

Could there be a reasonable explanation for bringing up dental matters in a discussion of my married lover? My mother is getting older. Although I do not want to believe it, I cannot ignore the signs; the leaps that her mathematician's mind has always been prone to have grown increasingly steep. I picture her sitting in her study, where she always makes her calls. It is a small room, untidy, of course, and crammed with books and papers, but the view, of lush green hills and trees older than a century, extends for miles. When she leaves the window open, which is almost always the case, the air that blows in is cool and fresh, its smell a combination of flowers, grass, wood smoke and, faintly and not unpleasantly, farm animals. Except when her cats begin to meow or caterwaul, which is about as often as one would expect from three feisty felines, the only sounds my mother can hear are church bells, the rustle of leaves when a breeze sweeps through the trees, the calls of birds, and the occasional tinkling of a cowbell or two.

Almost a year has passed since I last tried to lure them back to America. While it's a tough sell, maybe it is time for me to try again. "You know, you guys might want to get a new phone," I tell my mother. "What if something happened to one of you? You live in such a remote area, and—"

The static seems to work both ways, though, and my little lecture is lost. "Hello?" she says. The line is suddenly clear, and her voice, pitched loud and deep, is deafening. This is the woman, after all, who has never needed a microphone while lecturing. "Claudia, can you hear me?"

"I'm here."

"Let me try this again: I want to talk to you about Vikrum." She pauses and then she adds, in a far less confident tone: "That is, if that's okay."

Absorbed as she is and has been in her work, she has always been there, eager to proffer help. When did I begin to realize that my mother needed to be taken care of too? Before she and Dad began to grow old, yes, but it is probably giving myself too much credit to think that I knew even before the force of nature that was Hana swept in to turn our lives upside down. "I'd like to hear what you have to say about him," I say.

She takes her time choosing her words, and begins with a point that I do not expect. "When I went back to your father," she says, "after we were apart for more than nine years, I couldn't be sure at first if we could make it work. He was still in love with Hana then. And I thought that maybe he always would be."

My mother is a riveting lecturer, able to make the manipulation and analysis of numbers not only lucid but engaging. Narrative, though, is another skill altogether, and I have to try hard not to think about the rising phone bill.

"I had stopped trusting him, of course," she continues. "I was furious with him, and horribly hurt. I'd maybe even stopped loving him, or at least I convinced myself that I had. But I went back to him anyway." This last sentence uttered with due emphasis.

A few moments of silence follow: the story is clearly over. "I don't understand what you're getting at," I say. "Sorry. It's an interesting anecdote and all, but you're going to have to spell out its relevance for me."

"My point is that the years we'd spent together as a married couple mattered," she explains. "We'd grown together over the decades. I couldn't not take him back. I would have spent the rest of my life missing him, and—"

"So what are you telling me?" I say, breaking in. "That Vikrum is never going to leave his wife and that I did the right thing because I would never be able to have him? Is that supposed to make me feel better? Because if so, it's not working."

"Oh, darling," she says. "You do miss him so, don't you."

She is silent, as usual, as I cry. Given how much she communicates via physical contact, it is not surprising that my mother hates talking on the phone; no wonder she feels a need to rely on pet names when she does so. It occurs to me now that I could do with her hand stroking my hair back, and the weight and warmth of her arm around my shoulders.

"I did a poor job of explaining what I meant," she says at last. "You know, at first I thought that that was the lesson my experience had taught me—that married people grow together like teeth, and that it's difficult and usually impossible to separate them. At first I thought that your being with Vikrum made no sense, but I've been doing a lot of thinking since you left, and I've come to another conclusion." Another pause.

"Which is?"

"I loved your dad," she says. "It didn't matter what he'd done. It didn't even matter that maybe he would have left me all over again. I loved him, so I had to take him back. I didn't really have a choice."

These days, when my mother is in her study, her cat Newton usually sits with or on her. In his youth, Newton's ability to leap and soar led us to conclude that he had been misnamed, but in his old age he seems to have succumbed to the force that clobbered his namesake on the head with an apple one day: once prone, he tends to stay put. He is, in other words, the perfect companion for my mother. She might be beyond industrious when it comes to her work, and she attended to her and Dad's move to England with a productive mix of energy and calm. But when it comes to love, the force of gravity seems to exert its pull more inexorably on my mother than on the rest of the world.

"You have to follow your heart," she says. I can almost hear her shrug. Then she echoes a phrase that Rei had used to me. "Nothing's certain, of course; an element of risk is inevitable. But I've always tried to follow my heart anyway. And even if your dad were to leave me all over again, I think, or at least hope, that that's how I'd continue to live."

The past eight years that my mother has been in England, coupled with her discomfort over the phone, have taken their toll on our relationship. Not, of course, that we were all that close before. I have always thought that we began to grow apart about the time that Dad left her and she found her life coming apart in her hands—the distance between us the unfortunate but perhaps unavoidable consequence of my desire to be as different from her as possible. Our physical resemblance notwithstanding, I seem to prefer to think of myself as my father's daughter—or, for that matter, my stepmother's daughter—rather than hers.

"That's all very well for you," I say, "but in our case, there are other people involved. What about Vikrum's children?" A girl, age six and going on sixteen, except when she laughs; a boy who gives out gifts when he shakes hands. "Not to mention his wife."

"The kids have him every night, don't they? He's taking care of them and, it sounds like, her as well. You, on the other hand, seemed to be taking care of him, and he of you," she says. "So I could ask you just as easily: what about him; what about *you?*"

Chapter Twenty-Eight

Claudia
Boston, 1999

THE SIDEWALK IS CROWDED; IT IS THE MIDDLE OF A SATurday afternoon and Newbury Street is filled with shoppers and late lunchers. Two months ago, when I walked down this sidewalk to meet Rei for the first time in seventeen years, I felt as if I were flying. Even at her slowest, Rei walks much faster than I do, but as we head toward that same café now, we progress at a pace that no one could call swift.

Harboring the enemy is not a light offense, and Rei has not forgiven me yet. But she is close—perhaps, even, as close as I am to forgiving her for her absence during the past seventeen years. We have passed through the tears (mutual) and the yelling (her) and the begging (me) to what I sincerely hope is the last punitive phase, a silence that straddles the rather wide ford between grudging and companionable.

Contrary to what Rei first thought, I have yet to see

Hana. I made the arrangements, over the phone, to leave the key to my apartment with my neighbor for her, but I have yet to have a face-to-face encounter with the woman my father once loved.

Rei slows her pace, but we are already going so slowly that all we can do is come to a halt. Even though we are ten, maybe fifteen minutes late already, I stop too.

Our hair, worn to the exact same unfashionable length, blows about in the wind and threatens to fly into our eyes. We stand, two women in our thirties, silent and grim-faced and dead still in the middle of a busy block.

THIS IS WHAT I MISS about Vikrum: his feet, large and floppy and flat, the nails on them ridiculously perfect. His smell, a fresh and clean fragrance—was that Lakshmi's detergent?—mixed with the dust of chalkboards and books and the scent of his flesh. The way he listened to me, wide-eyed and earnest as the children in my classroom were—if I were lucky and I had chosen my book well—once a week on storytelling day. His enthusiasm, boyish and wild, its pull so strong it could tow me along in its wake.

That even after two years of what seemed constant conversation, I still could not guess what he would say next.

"I CAN'T BELIEVE I LET YOU bully me into this," Rei mutters, her teeth clenched. "Because you're heartbroken, and can't stop thinking about *him*"—the look she throws me belying the flippancy of her words—"I've been letting you off easy. But I want you to know I still can't believe it."

Am I transparent, every thought exposed for plucking by the glance? "If you've been letting me off easy, then I'm just going to pray you never keep me on hard. And you couldn't not see her. After all, she took a plane out here, and you know how she is about flying. Not to mention the fact that she came to *Boston* for you," I say, mimicking the exaggerated emphasis of Rei's words.

I take her lack of disagreement with my argument as a small battle won.

As if at a hidden signal, we begin to walk, brisk now, the edges of our skirts slapping like a baby's hands against our ankles, our arms swinging by our sides.

WE SEE HER, as I spied Rei more than two months ago, through the window of the café. She is facing into the room, the door directly in the line of her vision. All we can see is the back of her head (her hair worn, as Rei said, in an austere bun; it is largely black still, but woven through with silver), and the edge of her chair cuts off all but the top part of that, yet so saturated is she with the mysterious element of charisma that I feel as if I cannot look away.

In a few moments, when I have regained enough of my equilibrium to form a coherent sentence, I will explain to Rei that I cannot go inside because I cannot take my eyes off the back of Hana's head. Accustomed to people having that reaction to her mother, Rei will nod with understanding and enter the café by herself.

If only.

Rei's tugging on my shirtsleeve now (watching us today, would anyone be able to guess which one of us had set up this meeting, and who had refused to attend and cried?), and if I told her I was incapable of leaving the view from this side of the window, she would let out a dry bark of laughter and remind me that I *promised*.

We step through the door. As it swings shut behind us, I notice that Rei is vibrating; I believe it is from trepidation until I realize that it is the quiver of the needle of a compass in the moment before it snaps to point north. Do compass needles, like daughters, sometimes rage at the fact that they are never allowed to chart a course wholly on their own; do they yearn, once in a while, to point due west or, for the hell of it, south-southeast?

I know Rei wants to bound across the café again, just as she did when she first saw me. Her eagerness to do so is like a hum, infectious and palpable. Yet she walks quietly beside me, every measured step an effort of will.

Seen from the front, Hana is still beautiful—her bone structure is such that she has gotten more striking, if that is possible, with age. But the set of her head is not as proudly regal as it once was, and as we approach her, I am startled at how small she is. Perhaps Rei's right and she has shrunk over the years, or is it only that I have gotten taller and that Hana's choke hold on me has lessened over time?

For a moment they appraise each other, mother and daughter.

Hana's lips are stretched in a smile. "Reiko," she says, or at least she tries to, but then her lips twist out of that overstretched smile and, suddenly, she begins to cry.

"Oh, Mo-om," says Rei, lengthening the word into two syllables in the manner of American daughters everywhere.

As they move to hug each other, their heads collide so farcically, it might as well have been choreographed.

The three of us are tucked away in a corner of the café, and Hana is crying almost completely silently.

Still, people are turning, concerned looks on their faces, to look at the small, weeping woman and the girl who holds her tightly: Hana has always had charisma to spare.

She is the woman who has dominated my imagination since I was a child, the stories about her, as extravagantly colored as her paintings, the backdrop against which my own life of grays and light blues has been played.

* * *

"ARE YOU OKAY?" she asks Rei, rubbing the sides of my stepsister's arms with vigor, as if she needed warming.

"I'm fine," Rei asserts, only a little shaky. "And cancer-free, if that's what you're asking."

Dropping her hands to her sides, Hana gives Rei a hungry, searching look. I cannot tell if she is disappointed by the barely perceptible tinge of coolness in Rei's voice; she may have guessed before that winning her daughter back would be neither easy nor quick. Does she recognize that the damage done by a betrayal is a measure of the act in question, but also and perhaps even more of the nature and depth of the relationship that has been violated?

Of course she does. Hana may have been overly proud, but she never was stupid.

Now she turns, her arms outstretched, to me. Her shoulders are so narrow, I might be holding one of my students, except that they expect to be hugged hard, and Hana I embrace as if she were a flower in more than name.

"I'm very lucky," she says, reaching up to pat me on the shoulder. "I see two long-lost daughters today."

"Rucky," she says, and "rong-rost." How my father used to love her accent.

We pull up chairs and sit around the table. There is still a guarded look in Rei's eyes, but what she was dreading most about this encounter was the first few moments: I am officially free to go. Hana is here for another five days still; there is time for us to catch up later. Yet just as I am about to utter an excuse, she turns to me.

"How is your father?" she asks.

These words sound stiff, and for a second I think that she is only asking out of politeness. Then I look up and see how closely she is watching me, the shine of her eyes, which she attempts with limited success to veil, as she awaits my response.

She loved him. How could I ever have doubted it?

As if that were not enough, nipping at the heels of that revelation comes a pesky pug of a thought: what a waste. Because true love is rare. Because he loved her too—so much more (much as it tears me up to admit it) than he ever loved my mother, peaceable and content though they are now.

So to answer my own question, perhaps I doubted that Hana loved my father because the idea that she did, and left him anyway, was too sad to contemplate.

"Dad's good, thanks," I say automatically. True love is rare: a sentiment so trite it could not even be the title to an eighties pop song, and yet here it is making me catch my breath. "He's—" There is no point in worrying Hana with a report of his stroke, and hurting her with an account of his remarriage is not even a question. "He's retired," I conclude lamely. "He keeps himself busy with gardening."

"Oh," she says. Then, as if realizing more needs to be said, she adds in a fainter voice, "I'm glad."

Not so long ago, my reflexes were fine. I am about to ask Hana about her work, her house in California—anything—when Rei sits up. "Claudia's teaching at an elementary school," she says to Hana. "She's the best-loved teacher in all the land."

Rei is still hurt by what Hana did, of course ("What scares me is the possibility that years might pass," she had told me, chewing on a nail, "before I can really forgive her"), and yet here she is diving in to save her.

They are going to be fine on their own.

Hana looks at Rei and then at me. Finally she smiles. "I'm sure she is."

"Her students bring her apples every day," says Rei. "So many of them that if she ate them all, there wouldn't be any doctors living in the greater Boston area." Hana looks at her questioningly. "There's a saying," Rei explains. "An apple a day keeps the doctor away. Never mind, it's not all that funny."

Did she take care of her mother when she was younger too? I do not remember it myself, but I probably did not notice: if you hate someone and at the same time feel an overwhelming fascination with them, it's hard to be attentive to the possibility that they may be in need of care.

Rei must have wanted to shield Hana from me; perhaps she even tried. I owe a raft of apologies all around.

Rei is now talking about the students—college level, she says, not the apple-bearing kind—that she sometimes teaches at the museum, while Hana nods and listens. I look at one and then the other, searching for a familial resemblance and finding none. Rei's face is long and pointed at the end, Hana's, a smooth oval. Their bodies: Rei's seemingly made up entirely of endearingly gawky limbs; perhaps because of her dancer's posture, it is Hana's torso, compact and graceful, that you notice most—after, of course, her face. Even the black of their hair is not the same. The parts of Hana's that are not silver are so dark as to be almost blue, while Rei's is streaked faintly and naturally with brown.

Then, too, there is the matter of their personalities. To take just one pertinent example, look at how differently they approach love: Rei so impulsively affectionate, Hana cautious to the point that she was, at least once, self-destructive.

Does Dad regret the years that he spent with Hana? If he had known how his marriage with her would end, would he have chosen not to buy a monkey wrench that he did not need on a snowy afternoon in March; would he have stayed at home with his first wife and biological daughter instead? If I asked him, he would probably try to save Mom's and my feelings. So it is a good thing that these are questions that I do not need to put to him. I know that his answer, his real answer, to both would be no.

You take what you can get, he would say, for as long as you can.

At the next break in the conversation, I seize my opportunity.

"Excuse me," I say, pushing my chair back. "I just realized I have an important phone call to make."

Rei cocks an eyebrow at me. "The proper phrase," she says, drawling out the words, "is 'I just *remembered* I have an important, etc.' If you're trying to make a tactful exit, then you might as well get your excuse right. Unless, of course"—here she unleashes one of her grins, and I know that she has guessed what I am about to do—"you really mean that you just realized you have to call someone."

I throw her a small smile back, and stand.

"I'll see you soon," I say to Hana.

She thanks me and hands me my house key. This morning, she moved out of my apartment into a hotel in Cambridge, within a half mile of Rei's place. Today, for the first time in weeks, I will go home to my own apartment. The three of us make plans to have dinner tomorrow, and then we go through another round of embraces.

There may be little to mark Hana and Rei as mother and daughter, yet when they hug me, they each whisper in my ear.

"Let me know how it goes with him," says Rei. "If you need me, call me and I'll be there."

Hana's whisper is so quiet, I could almost have just imagined it. "Thank you for bringing her back to me."

At the door, I turn back to look at them. They sit close but do not talk, looking away from each other in a way that makes it clear that what they are experiencing is not just a lull in the conversation. But then, as I continue to watch, Hana turns to Rei and begins to speak.

Will it really be years before Rei truly forgives her mother? Perhaps. Surely what counts, what is cause for celebration, is that they are already halfway there.

* * *

I SEE HIM SITTING ON MY STOOP from halfway down the block. His head is buried in a book, but when my downstairs neighbor, coming home from a run, takes the steps in two bounds, he looks up quickly. It is as he is bending his head down to his book again that I catch his eye.

I lower myself down next to him, a decorous six inches between us, and sit gazing straight ahead of me: I do not dare look at him directly. He turns and stares at me but then, as we continue to sit, he catches on and follows my lead.

"How long have you been here?"

"Today," he says, looking down at his watch, "about half an hour."

"You were here yesterday too?"

"Yesterday, and the past five days before that. Maybe two hours each day. At first I came in the morning or the evening, so that I'd catch you on your way to and from school, but when that didn't work, I began trying to come at different times of the day. It sounds creepy, I know," he says. Out of the corner of my eye, I see him shrug. "But I was desperate to see you."

Chances were that on one of those days, Hana walked by him as he sat here. Perhaps the ends of her skirt brushed against his arm. After seeing him there for the third time that day, maybe she even nodded a hello at him.

"It's not fair to you," says Vikrum. "I keep thinking that if I were a better and stronger person, I'd be able to walk away, never bother you again. But I can't. I miss you too much."

"It's not not fair," I say, speaking too fast. "What I mean is—" Then I make the mistake of turning to look at him.

He looks terrible. Gaunt and pale, with darkness under his eyes. I have always loved his laugh wrinkles, but here, in the bright afternoon light, I can see each of the lines edging his mouth and those running parallel across his forehead. While he usually looks younger than thirty-two, anyone seeing him now would think he is far older. It is all over for me; all I can do now is lean into him and cry.

TOMORROW, WHEN I SPEAK to Rei, this is what I will say to her.

How hard it is, and how terrifying, to come to the realization that not all is perfect in your fairy tale. That whereas the damsels in the stories, in their eternal and often passive pursuit of the happily-ever-after, benefit from the intervention of fairy godmothers, of wishing wells and talking mirrors and helpful dwarves (and not just two dwarves, or four, or even six, but seven), we are on our own.

That while I finally concluded that my fairy tale, flawed though it is, is worth holding on to for as long as I can bear it, her mother decided differently, and that that is no less valid a choice.

I DISENTANGLE MYSELF from Vikrum's kisses, take his hand, and pull him to his feet.

"Come inside," I say.

"Are you sure?" he asks, suddenly uncertain. "You deserve so much more than what I've given you, than what I can give you—"

"You're what I want. Even like this. I'm sure of that now. Come inside."

So he does.

Chapter Twenty-Nine 🌸

Hana
Boston, 1999

UNBIDDEN BUT NOT, FOR ONCE, UNWELCOME, A MEMORY
of her second husband comes to Hana as she sits waiting for her daughter and stepdaughter in a Boston café.
One afternoon, coming by his office to pick him up for
lunch, she was a few minutes early, and not wanting to
disturb him in case he was hard at work, she quietly
poked her head in through the half-open door. He was
sitting on a stool, in front of him a container filled with
earth that was the warm, rich color of burnt sienna. As
she watched, he picked up a handful of soil and let it
run through his fingers. Then he scooped up another
handful, held and examined it, cupped, in his palm.
She was about to call out to him when he lifted up the
soil to his nose and smelled it, and then, taking a pinch
of it, placed it on his tongue.

She was in her late forties at the time, a mother to
two teenage girls and stepmother to a third (so old

they seemed, and at the same time so young, to an almost wrenching extent), and she was standing in the dusty, echoing hallway of the geology department of the most prestigious small college in the area. Given this context (she reasoned), perhaps it wasn't so surprising that she felt not only disconcerted but also ashamed that she was aroused—the way his tongue felt on her! and of course his hands too—by the sight of her husband of six years smelling and tasting a handful of dirt.

Hana crept back out into the hallway and sat herself down on the corner of the bench (earmarked for students, and therefore narrow and hard) placed outside his door.

A few minutes later, Henry was in front of her, folding almost in half to reach down and kiss her, standing back up and tying the scarf she'd bought him their first Christmas together loosely around his neck. It was a cold day, the winds gusting hard, but he didn't even own a winter coat, and he always just laughed, as at a joke, when she suggested that they get him one.

"How did it taste?" she said, with a nod back at the lab.

He looked puzzled for a moment, and then his brows lifted. "You saw me do that?" he asked, amused. "I was checking to see if it was silt. It was."

Hana stood, and they began walking down the hall. "You can tell by tasting?"

He shrugged. "When you've been around soil for as long and as much as I have, you can."

So modest was he usually about his work, and reticent too, she thought for a moment that he was referring to his gardening. But then he went on dryly: "It's hard to believe, I know—the scientist at work." Looking down at her, he brightened. "Actually, it's one of the real perks of being a geologist. You develop a taste for it, after a while. And that's not to mention all the minerals contained within one mouthful of the stuff."

Hana smiled up at her husband. His arm was slung around her

shoulder, outside it was cold but so bright that the sky was a brilliant blue, and she felt like making a joke back at him. Something about how now she knew why he ate her cooking with a gusto that, if it were feigned—as she, who had few delusions about her own culinary skills, always thought it had to be—then it was well-feigned enough to have her children, at least, fooled: if he spent his days eating dirt, then it was no wonder he could put on a happy face over a dinner of food meant for people, even if the meal in question was rubbery hot dogs with a side of overboiled cabbage.

But the joke was too complicated, and she remained silent.

Henry joked with their children often. While it was tacitly understood that Hana would not participate in these jokes, which almost always involved wordplay, while she usually busied herself in the kitchen or with her reading at those times, she did enjoy them when she understood them; she had, on occasion, even essayed puns herself, though never yet with Henry.

The children usually groaned at Henry's jokes, but he never cared, laughing out loud at them himself. It gave Hana particular pleasure to hear him laugh. For such a soft-spoken man, his laughter was surprisingly loud. It came from the stomach and made him shake all over, which seemed odd to her because, of course, he was by all rights far too elongated to have anything to shake.

They were nearing the exit of the building. She could hear the winds howling beyond the doors.

"Are you going to be warm enough? Here," he said, "let me button up the top of your coat for you."

As her daughters used to with her when they were younger, she lifted her head up, submitting to his ministrations. When he finished, every one of her buttons buttoned and her scarf tucked tightly around her neck, he tilted her chin up and kissed her. She thought she could taste the loam in his mouth, a hint of something dark and rich, or did his tongue always taste like that?

The kiss lasted a long time, a clear reminder that he was her husband rather than her parent. When they drew apart—a move necessary for her mind to function with any sort of clarity—Hana realized that Henry had, somehow, managed to pick up on the lust that had required her to sit down, hard, just minutes earlier.

"What does it taste like?" she asked, a little breathless, stalling for time so she could lean into him a few seconds longer. "The soil, I mean. Is it really any good?"

"Hmm," he said. Despite all the layers she was wearing, they were holding each other so close she could feel the hum of that sound vibrating through her. He began rubbing his hands in circles on her back. "How does one describe a taste? That sample was a little salty, and rich too. And I could feel the texture of it, the grit of it, on my teeth."

"Do you think I should make it tonight for dinner?"

It wasn't really funny at all, of course, nor was it witty in the least, and it didn't involve an iota of wordplay. There was a short pause after she made her joke, as Henry tried to absorb what she said.

Then Hana had the pleasure of hearing her husband's laugh boom out, echoing through the hallway, so loud that it temporarily drowned out the shriek of the wind.

HENRY, AT THE AGE OF FIFTY-TWO (an age that seemed so old to them that they used to marvel together, half-seriously, at the fact that he'd attained it), once said that when he looked back on his life now, he saw a pattern. It was as if all the thousands of different pieces fit together. "Seamlessly, even," he told Hana in his slow drawl, drumming a long index finger on her arm for emphasis. He said that he had thought, while he was living it, that the course of his life had been wholly random—determined by a series of accidents and encounters, some more lucky than others, and by decisions arrived at under pressure and in great haste, made out of need and whim and a what-the-hell bravado rather than by dint of careful reasoning and thought. But as he looked back now, it was clear to him that there had been an outside force guiding his fate.

A greater plan, maybe even a master one, he'd called it too, but Hana, perhaps predictably, had preferred the idea of a pattern: a visual concept and, as such, one that she knew she could grasp.

At the time she hadn't paid much attention, dismissing these ideas as a consequence of a new hobby of his, churchgoing (a practice that his daughter hadn't liked any more than she had, but for different reasons: Claudia had scolded her dad for loosening his already tenuous hold on his Jewish roots. For Hana, it was quite simply the boredom of the church services that had been hard to take, since she knew that, protest though he might, he'd wanted her presence beside him, and so she had felt obliged to accompany him on every fourth Sunday or so). Hana had given his ideas about a pattern no serious thought as a viable theory. But now, as she, at the definitively advanced age of sixty-six, waits with a mounting sense of excitement for Rei and Claudia to arrive, she thinks again about what Henry had said and wonders if it isn't true.

That she is thinking about Henry, and that she has been doing so with some frequency for the past two days, comes as a surprise to her. She would have guessed that while in Boston, she would be thinking of her first husband, and not of her second. Melodramatically, perhaps, she had thought that this city would be so crowded with memories of the life that she and Seiji had led that she would not be able to move; her mind would get stuck, trapped and immobile as her body used to be in the Tokyo subway cars during rush hour.

Instead, Boston has turned out to be just another town. She remembers it unexpectedly well—she still has a sense of the streets, even though in the past twenty years much of what stands on them has changed, and she always knows where the Charles is in relation to where she is, as surely as she knows up and down. But it doesn't make her remember anything startling or painful about

Seiji. Indeed, this small, innocuous city seems to have the curious effect of making her think not about him (a development that makes her feel melancholy and even a touch guilty, so faraway does her first husband seem; when did he turn into a memory that elicits a tender warmth rather than a pang?) but about the man who took his place.

There is one way, of course, in which it makes perfect sense that she's thinking of her second husband. After all, any minute now—they're six minutes late already, so really any second—his daughter will walk through that door.

His daughter, accompanied by Rei.

Hana cranes her neck, even though there's nothing obstructing her view of the door and the street lying beyond it. She feels for the handle of her teacup without taking her eyes off the door; she lifts the cup to her mouth and pours the one or two remaining drops down her throat.

THE FIRST TIME Henry told her about Claudia, Hana had thought about her unborn child. Her third, who would have been (she knew it, just as she knew that Kei was going to be a thumb-sucker and that Rei would be a giddy child, hopelessly in love with motion) a boy. She had lost him soon after Seiji's accident, along with so much blood that she wondered, with a sense of calm that bordered on hope, if she, too, was going to die. Neither that calm nor, mercifully, that feeling approaching hope had lasted for long, yet though she had cried for her third child, a part of her was never sure whether she had been mourning him, or Seiji, or the life that they all would have had. So when she heard about Claudia—and she heard about Claudia within minutes of meeting Henry, by which point she was already hoping, she was already determined, that their fates would be entwined—Hana thought of it as another chance. At last she would have a third child.

What Hana hadn't counted on was, of course, Claudia herself. Almost immediately Claudia made it clear that she was more than content with her own parents and didn't need another. The best that Hana could do was to approach her as a friend, and not a very close one at that; their relationship, to her own continuous disappointment, was never more than barely civil.

Eventually Hana came to believe that it was only what she deserved. She already had a third child. Insufficiently mourned for, and one whom she had not had a chance to hold or even name, but a third child regardless. It had been terrible of her to think that she could so easily replace her son; it served her right that Henry's daughter wanted nothing to do with her.

Yet that didn't mean she couldn't think of Claudia, secretly, as her fourth child.

Four children. A large number for a woman who never imagined having any as a child herself. Hana can still remember what it felt like to want a life without children, and at times she could even still imagine herself leading it—an existence in which the forms and colors of her paintings, so vivid and consuming, fill all. The thought of such a life puts her in mind of her childhood ambition, ridiculously unattainable but oh! so well worth pursuing: to bring as much beauty into the world as she took out of it.

Hana knows that Rei, with her university degrees and her background in theory, does not think highly of her old-fashioned views on art. Rei believes that Hana had the potential to be a great artist, with paintings hanging in museums, but that she was undone by her relentless pursuit of beauty. What she does not understand— what Hana will, perhaps, explain to her in time—is that Hana never harbored any ambitions for museum exhibits. She would be more than content if, after her death, her paintings went from garage sale to garage sale, canvases splashed with color and light that passed from one set of hands to the next.

Contemplating this fate for her paintings makes her solemn. She has so many more paintings to create, and there are but a few years that remain to her.

If she had been childless, how much more would she have painted? Hana would be wistful, except that she remembers too clearly a day thirty-eight years ago, when she took Kei out for one of her first walks. Pushing her in a baby carriage up a small hill, Hana began to sob. A doctor today might call it postpartum depression, but she knows that what she was feeling then was a sense of loss, as keen as she had ever felt, because she and her baby were no longer one, because she had to push her in a contraption with wheels that kept them two meters apart rather than carry her inside her.

And then, too, there was the day on which Rei was born. Why had fears about giving birth to a child with deformities only surfaced during her second pregnancy? She'd known, none better, that it was a risk, albeit a small one indeed, for someone exposed to the atomic bomb to have a child, but she'd been blithely impervious to worry when she was pregnant with Kei. Maybe she had become nervous about her second pregnancy because having another child, when the first one was so pretty and healthy, when she and Seiji woke up every day, it seemed, with grins on their faces and songs on their lips, seemed to be tempting fate.

Perhaps she had been taking a chance, but once again she'd been lucky. On the day that Rei was born, she'd sobbed again, but with joy this time, counting (in Japanese, as she would count, she knew then, for the rest of her life, even if she never set foot in her native country again) the dear, pudgy five fingers on each hand, the unbelievably small toes on each foot, the perfectly formed nails, again and again: *Ichi ni san shi go. Ichi ni san shi go.*

A life without her children is one that she can imagine; it's just not one that she could bear.

* * *

RISKING A GLANCE AWAY from the door, she takes a quick peek at her watch. Thirteen minutes past the hour. Hana takes in a long, slow breath of coffee-scented air in an effort to hold on to her calm.

"You want to know what the really amazing thing is?" Henry had asked, when telling her about the pattern in his life. "When I see that a pattern exists, I no longer see anything to regret."

Thinking about it now, she has to agree: that is an amazing concept indeed. When she has looked back on her life, which isn't often, Hana has usually thought of it as one filled, regrettably enough, with regret. She should have told Seiji to be careful as he stepped out of the car to retrieve a fallen suitcase; she should have made sure that it was fastened more tightly to the top of the car in the first place. She should have told Henry when they first met about her exposure to the bomb; she should have told Kei and Rei when they were young.

She should have held on harder and longer to Henry.

Today, though, perhaps for the first time, she's thinking that there's another way to look at the unfurling of her life. For so long, what she has focused on is the tenuousness of one's existence, its terrifying inconstancy. The way in which your life can change in an instant: as you're stepping outside to let your hair dry, or as you, with one hand on your swelling belly, tilt a mirror toward you.

Yet as Hana looks back, here in this Boston café, on the past sixty-six years, the moments she remembers are other ones— smaller, perhaps, and less dramatic, poor material for stories that get passed around like towels (here Hana smiles; she always smiles when recalling how Rei used to hold Claudia spellbound with stories of herself and her family), but no less monumental when it comes to tallying up the sum of a life. Seiji shyly holding out a *daikon* to her in a crowded airport; Henry placing a pinch of soil on his tongue; the miracle of five fingers on each hand, *ichi ni san shi go.*

If life is a pattern, then those are the threads that glow the brightest.

HANA RISES SO SUDDENLY to her feet that she has to steady herself with the table.

Her daughters are here.

Chapter Thirty

Claudia
Boston, 1999

NEITHER OF US CAN STOP GRINNING, EVEN AS WE KISS. We hold on to each other tightly, lying together as close as we possibly can, for the joy of it—we both know that the threat of loss is gone.

My body feels as if it is glowing. And who knows, it might actually be: there is magic in Vikrum's lips.

"Do you believe that bodies have the capacity to remember?" he asks, when we finally stop to breathe.

"It's funny that you ask me that. My mother was just saying the other day that teeth have memory. And muscles do too, don't they? It's not through our minds, at any rate, that we remember how to ride a bike and throw a baseball and drive shift."

He nods. "These past three weeks, I've been waking up to find my body contorted into a very certain position. Every morning it's the same. My mind really hasn't been functioning so well lately. Otherwise it probably wouldn't have taken me so long to figure out that I was waking up wrapped around a space that fit the exact proportions of your body."

Sometime soon, perhaps, I will call my mother to let her know that Vikrum and I have grown together like teeth.

"Which made me think," he continues, "that we should be buried together. Not just in caskets side by side, but in the same box. That way, my body can be curled around yours until the end of the world. Or until we turn into commingled dust, whichever comes first."

"How . . . romantic," I say, laughing. "Oh, wait. Did I mean to say how macabre?"

"The former," he says promptly. "That's all you meant to say. Because there's nothing macabre or the least bit scary about the thought of dying, as long as we're together."

His hands pass over my face, casting spells wherever they land, and then he places his lips against mine. Is Vikrum correct in his belief that bodies possess the ability to remember? I pray that he is, because if so, I will use my muscles, flesh, skin, bones, and teeth as well as my mind to store for eternity these memories: the wild tenderness of these kisses; the exact pressure and texture of his fingers on my face; this moment of happiness, shimmering and pure.

I cannot afford to let these memories fade. One day, perhaps, they will be all that I have of him.

"Would you like to meet Rei?" I say at last. "Maybe over lunch or dinner?"

He props himself on his elbow to peer into my eyes. "Do you really have to ask?"

"No, I guess not," I say with a smile. "You know, her mother's here too. She'll be staying for a few days more. I don't know if you're interested, but—"

"You mean I could meet Hana as well?"

"If you want to."

"I do," he says. "It's funny—over these last few days, I've been thinking a lot about what you told me about her. All those rules that she broke, the way that she chose the life she wanted to lead and then proceeded to live it. Her example could probably teach me a thing or two, don't you think?"

His gaze is so bright and eager, I have to drop my own. "I don't know," I say. "But Rei's stories about her have sure had an influence on me."

"So how soon can we all get together?"

"Tomorrow, maybe," I say, savoring the knowledge that Vikrum and I have time ahead of us like a luxurious unfurling of the body. "Or the day after that..." My voice is trailing off. When did I last sleep a full night? "...or the day after that."

I BLINK, STRETCHING, and then yawn.

"Hush," says Vikrum, his voice a rumble in my ear. "Go back to sleep. I'll be here when you wake up."

It is on the tip of my tongue to tell him that the sleep I am heading into is a deep one, and that he should not be making promises he may not be able to keep. But I keep my mouth shut. Even if he has to go before I wake, it's all right.

I burrow into the warmth of his arms and shut my eyes.

After all, no matter what happens, I have Rei by my side.

Acknowledgments

My mother, Hiroko Sherwin, a novelist in her own right, brought her talent and her knowledge of Japan to bear on this novel. James Sherwin read numerous drafts and gave me trenchant feedback.

That this book was finished at all is because of my editor, Danielle Perez, whose belief in it was as steady as her revision suggestions were astute.

My agent, Sandy Dijkstra, was always on hand to dispense advice and warm encouragement. Sandra Zane, whose critical eye is always illuminating and often brilliant, stepped in at a crucial juncture to whip this book into shape.

Fellowships from the MacDowell Colony, the Ucross Foundation, and the Radcliffe Institute provided me with the quiet needed to make this novel grow.

The companionship and counsel of the following people shaped this novel: Jerry Berard, Francesca Bewer, Andrea Cohen, Ioanna Christoforaki, Shannon Jamieson, Claire Sauvageot, Ali Sherwin, Scott Swanay, and Eve Zimmerman.

I would also like to thank Greg Curci for his patience, Suzy Becker for her help, Mahmoud Hamadani for the title, and in particular Kyoko Mori and her cats for long conversations.

Finally, I owe a special debt to my stepsister, Miranda Sherwin. In that my relationship with her has taught me how family transcends bonds of blood, her influence has been as profound on this novel as it has been on my life.

About the Author

Mako Yoshikawa has studied at Columbia University and at Oxford. She has been a Vera M. Schuyler Fellow of Creative Writing at the Bunting Institute at Harvard University and is a doctoral candidate in English literature at the University of Michigan. She is also the author of the novel *One Hundred and One Ways*. Yoshikawa lives in Cambridge, Massachusetts.